T0152311

NOT GUILTY

What Reviewers Say About
Brit Ryder/Kris Bryant's Work

Shameless—*Writing as Brit Ryder*

The story is full of twists and turns, none of which I was expecting and it made me want to devour this book even more. The sex scenes were phenomenal and to be honest, my mind was blown.

If this book doesn't tick off at least one of your fantasies, you'll definitely be adding one on. I can only hope this is not the last we see of Brit Ryder and her erotic stories because as soon as I was finished I was craving more. 5 Stars of Sexiness!

Lucky

"The characters—both main and secondary, including the furry ones—are wonderful (I loved coming across Piper and Shaylie from Falling), there's just the right amount of angst and the sexy scenes are really hot. It's Kris Bryant, you guys, no surprise there."—*Jude in the Stars*

"This book has everything you need for a sweet romance. The main characters are beautiful and easy to fall in love with, even with their little quirks and flaws. The settings (Vail and Denver, Colorado) are perfect for the story, and the romance itself is satisfying, with just enough angst to make the book interesting. …This is the perfect novel to read on a warm, lazy summer day, and I recommend it to all romance lovers."—*Rainbow Reflections*

Tinsel

"This story was the perfect length for this cute romance. What made this especially endearing were the relationships Jess has with her best friend, Mo, and her mother. You cannot go wrong by purchasing this cute little nugget. A really sweet romance with a cat playing cupid."—*Bookvark*

Against All Odds—(*co-authored with Maggie Cummings and M. Ullrich*)

"I started reading the book trying to dissect the writing and ended up forgetting all about the fact that three people were involved in writing it because the story just grabbed me by the ears and dragged me along for the ride. …[A] really great romantic suspense that manages both parts of the equation perfectly. This is a book you won't be able to put down."—*C-Spot Reviews*

Temptation

"This book has a great first line. I was hooked from the start. There was so much to like about this story, though. The interactions. The tension. The jealousy. I liked how Cassie falls for Brooke's son before she ever falls for Brooke. I love a good forbidden love story."—*Bookvark*

"This book is an emotional roller coaster that you're going to get swept away in. Let it happen…just bring the tissues and the vino and enjoy the ride."—*Les Rêveur*

"People who have read Ms. Bryant's erotica novella *Shameless* under the pseudonym of Brit Ryder know that this author can write intimacy well. This is more a romance than erotica but the sex scenes are as varied and hot…"—*LezReviewBooks*

Falling

"This is a story you don't want to pass on. A fabulous read that you will have a hard time putting down. Maybe don't read it as you board your plane though. This is an easy 5 stars!"—*Romantic Reader Blog*

"Bryant delivers a story that is equal parts touching, compassionate, and uplifting."—*Lesbian Review*

"This was a nice, romantic read. There is enough romantic tension to keep the plot moving, and I enjoyed the supporting characters' and their romance as much as the main plot."—*Kissing Backwards*

Listen

"[A] sweet romance with a touch of angst and lots of music."
—*C-Spot Reviews*

"If you suffer from anxiety, know someone who suffers from anxiety, or want an insight to how it may impact on someone's daily life, I urge you to pick this book up. In fact, I urge all readers who enjoy a good lesbian romance to grab a copy."—*Love Bytes Reviews*

"Ms. Bryant describes this soundscape with some exquisite metaphors, it's true what they say that music is everywhere. The whole book is beautifully written and makes the reader's heart to go out with people suffering from anxiety or any sort of mental health issue."—*Lez Review Books*

"I was absolutely captivated by this book from start to finish. The two leads were adorable and I really connected with them and rooted for them. …This is one of the best books I've read recently—I cannot praise it enough!"—Melina Bickard, Librarian, Waterloo Library (UK)

"The main character's anxiety issues were well written and the romance is sweet and leaves you with a warm feeling at the end. Highly recommended reading."—Kat Adams, Bookseller (QBD Books, Australia)

Forget Me Not

"Told in the first person, from Grace's point of view, we are privy to Grace's inner musings and her vulnerabilities. ...Bryant crafts clever wording to infuse Grace with a sharp-witted personality, which clearly covers her insecurities. ...This story is filled with loving familial interactions, caring friends, romantic interludes and tantalizing sex scenes. The dialogue, both among the characters and within Grace's head, is refreshing, original, and sometimes comical. *Forget Me Not* is a fresh perspective on a romantic theme, and an entertaining read."—*Lambda Literary Review*

"[I]t just hits the right note all the way. ...[A] very good read if you are looking for a sweet romance."—*Lez Review Books*

Whirlwind Romance

"Ms. Bryant's descriptions were written with such passion and colorful detail that you could feel the tension and the excitement along with the characters..."—*Inked Rainbow Reviews*

Taste

"*Taste* is a student/teacher romance set in a culinary school. If the premise makes you wonder whether this book will make you want to eat something tasty, the answer is: yes."—*Lesbian Review*

Jolt—*Lambda Literary Award Finalist*

"[*Jolt*] is a magnificent love story. Two women hurt by their previous lovers and each in their own way trying to make sense out of life and times. When they meet at a gay and lesbian friendly summer camp, they both feel as if lightening has struck. This is so beautifully involving, I have already reread it twice. Amazing!" —*Rainbow Book Reviews*

Touch

"The sexual chemistry in this book is off the hook. Kris Bryant writes my favorite sex scenes in lesbian romantic fiction." —*Les Rêveur*

Breakthrough

"Looking for a fun and funny light read with hella cute animal antics, and a smoking hot butch ranger? Look no further. …In this well written, first-person narrative, Kris Bryant's characters are well developed, and their push/pull romance hits all the right beats, making it a delightful read just in time for beach reading."—*Writing While Distracted*

"Kris Bryant has written several enjoyable contemporary romances, and *Breakthrough* is no exception. It's interesting and clearly well-researched, giving us information about Alaska and issues like poaching and conservation in a way that's engaging and never comes across as an info dump. She also delivers her best character work to date, going deeper with Kennedy and Brynn than we've seen in previous stories. If you're a fan of Kris Bryant, you won't want to miss this book, and if you're a fan of romance in general, you'll want to pick it up, too."—*Lambda Literary Review*

Against All Odds

"This story tugged at my heartstrings and it hit all the right notes for me because these wonderful authors allowed me to peep into the hearts and minds of the characters. The vivid descriptions of Peyton, Tory and the perpetrator's personalities allowed me to have a deeper understanding of what makes them tick and I was able to form a clear picture of them in my mind."—*Lesbian Review*

"*Against All Odds* is equal parts thriller and romance, the balance between action and love, fast and slow pace makes this novel a very entertaining read."—*Lez Review Books*

Visit us at www.boldstrokesbooks.com

By the Author

Writing as Brit Ryder:

Shameless

Not Guilty

Writing as Kris Bryant:

Jolt

Whirlwind Romance

Just Say Yes: The Proposal

Taste

Forget-Me-Not

Touch

Breakthrough

Against All Odds
(with Maggie Cummings and M. Ullrich)

Listen

Falling

Tinsel

Temptation

Lucky

Home

Scent

NOT GUILTY

by

Brit Ryder

2021

NOT GUILTY

© 2021 BY BRIT RYDER. ALL RIGHTS RESERVED.

ISBN 13: 978-1-63555-896-8

THIS TRADE PAPERBACK ORIGINAL IS PUBLISHED BY
BOLD STROKES BOOKS, INC.
P.O. BOX 249
VALLEY FALLS, NY 12185

FIRST EDITION: JUNE 2021

THIS IS A WORK OF FICTION. NAMES, CHARACTERS, PLACES, AND
INCIDENTS ARE THE PRODUCT OF THE AUTHOR'S IMAGINATION OR
ARE USED FICTITIOUSLY. ANY RESEMBLANCE TO ACTUAL PERSONS,
LIVING OR DEAD, BUSINESS ESTABLISHMENTS, EVENTS, OR LOCALES
IS ENTIRELY COINCIDENTAL.

THIS BOOK, OR PARTS THEREOF, MAY NOT BE REPRODUCED IN ANY
FORM WITHOUT PERMISSION.

CREDITS
EDITORS: ASHLEY TILLMAN AND SHELLEY THRASHER
PRODUCTION DESIGN: SUSAN RAMUNDO
COVER DESIGN: DEB B.

Acknowledgments

Because of the positive reception of *Shameless*, I decided to write a full-length erotica romance with these characters. It was more difficult than I thought, especially since I'm used to pouring my heart out on the pages. I can't tell you how many times I had to take the emotions out of the scene. Writing sex is fun, but writing it without an emotional entanglement is a challenge.

Thank you, Rad, Sandy, and the team at Bold Strokes Books. I love the freedoms I have and the encouragement that comes with signing the contract. Ashley is not only my content editor, my save-my-ass-you-can't-write-that warrior, but she's my friend and has my best interests at heart. Shelley will work around the clock to get copy edits back, and I'm always like—it's 4 a.m. Go to bed already. We still have three weeks. She's my comma and hyphen warrior. Without her, my books would have none.

My support group is incredible. I used a beta reader on this one because I wanted to get a real reaction. Wynnde was honest and her suggestions made this a better book. Karen and Rach were my cheerleaders during the editing stage, and their excitement for the book gave me the confidence that this could be readable and enjoyable.

I want to thank KB Draper for just being awesome and having writing dates across rooms, on Zoom, and on the back deck during the pandemic. Just being there helps me so much. I love you dearly, and I can't wait until we can drink coffee at the Roasterie or Opera House again and write in four-hour blocks. Or, you know, text, scroll through social media, write 500 words, and repeat.

Thank you to Paula, Melissa, Georgia, HS, Elle, Nikki for checking in and your virtual hugs. We've all had a rough year and your love and support helped me in ways you will never know. Shout-out to my new BFF Morgan. You're awesome. Stay that way.

I know we aren't supposed to say covers are important, but they are to me. Deb did this cover in record time. She found something that was sexy, powerful, and captured Claire perfectly. Thank you for reading my mind and giving me the space to write my stories. Fiona Riley has pushed me to stay on a writing schedule. For every 1,000 words she writes, I write 100. They all add up though. Thank you for your late night texts and making me write when I really just wanted to binge-watch a ridiculous show. I love you, stay perfect.

This is the first book where I can thank my patrons from my Patreon page for supporting my efforts to supply wet food and necessary supplies to older shelter animals. It's amazing how far your pledges go!

And, as always, thank you to my readers for reading my books and promoting them on social media and to your friends. It's the highest compliment and I'm forever grateful.

CHAPTER ONE

By the second seminar, I'm toast. A month ago, I spent five days in Vegas with my best friend to blow off steam, but it feels like a distant memory. My life now is five days a week of classes, seminars, lectures, and a ton of homework on the weekends. We're focusing today on how to run a successful trial and organize dockets. It's helpful, but I'm anxious for mock trials to start next week. I'll be handed my own courtroom with my first case on day one. My dream, the one I had since college, is right in front of me.

"Hey, Ruth Junior. Are you keeping up?" Kevin McIntosh is another newly appointed judge who was handed the position because he was born into a Kansas City family whose name is synonymous with politics and the law. It was pure nepotism, but I resist teasing him because I want to give him a chance. He's smart and competent. One day I might need him for something.

I lean over and whisper, "Piece of cake. Need to copy my notes?"

He smirks. He isn't cocky, but confident. He was born and bred for this life. His grandfather, father, and mother were all lawyers. Now his parents own a number of profitable businesses, including a construction company, an engineering company, and one that manufactures airplane parts.

A lot of people think I got my seat too quickly and didn't put my time in, but winning a ninety-million-dollar case against a massive pharmaceutical corporation catapulted me to the top of the list. Kevin was the first to introduce himself, and although we aren't technically friends, we know the value of a positive relationship in this business. We talk several times a week during breaks. We don't have a lot in common other than our thirst for success and justice. He has a wife and two small boys. How he has time to study is a mystery.

"I can't wait for next week," Kevin says.

"Shh. Pay attention." He's checked out of today's lecture. It's not exciting, but no way am I throwing away any learning opportunity. In a few weeks, I'll be reviewing cases for my district. My term needs to be perfect so I can make a name for myself and stay in Kansas City for a long time. I'm going to be tough, but fair. At least that's what I'm envisioning. I check the time. Only fifteen minutes left of lecture and then about two hours' worth of upcoming cases to review.

Jenn sends me a picture of herself rolling her eyes.

I can't wait until you get your robes. Then maybe I'll have my friend again.

It's terrible. I miss everything. You, good food, my bed instead of the couch. I'll call you after class.

Great. I have news.

That piques my interest. I finish jotting notes and quickly pack up when we are dismissed. I live only fifteen minutes from the courthouse, but I'm three weeks away from owning a two-bedroom loft down in the garment district. Worst timing ever, but I can't stop my life. There was a mix-up in the paperwork. I was supposed to close and move into my new place last month, but everything got pushed back, and now all my life changes are happening at once. It's stressful but a great problem to have. I call Jenn as I'm hustling out to the parking lot.

"What's your good news?" I ask.

One of my colleagues approaches, and I politely point to the phone. He holds his hands up and walks away. I'm not in the mood for small talk with people I don't know.

"Oh, look. You have time for me," Jenn says.

"Sarcasm noted. And I'll always have time for you." I make obnoxious kissy noises on the phone until she laughs. "Come on. Tell me your news." I unlock my Audi and hiss at the heat that pours out when I open the door. "Hang on. Let me switch over to Bluetooth." I throw my briefcase into the backseat and climb inside. The SUV still smells new, even though I bought it three months ago. "Can you hear me?"

"You're good. Okay, so remember when I told you about Orlando?"

"Florida?" Did I agree to go to Florida for another weekend getaway and completely forget about it? And if I did, is it coming up? I really need to limit my alcohol intake when we get together.

"No. Orlando. The guy I met at that swanky restaurant in Malibu. The one who FaceTimed me in Vegas?"

"Oh, yeah. How are things with him?"

"We're going away this weekend. Like packed-bags-and-cabin-rented going away."

"Wow, that's fast." When she snorts, I cringe and quickly retract my words. "I mean, not that I'm one to talk, but I didn't think you were looking for anyone."

"I'm not. It just kind of happened. When was the last time I wanted a relationship?"

I choose not to drop Deanna's name. That whole ordeal where she broke Jenn's heart after cheating on her with Jenn's sister was better forgotten. Her sister broke up with Deanna shortly after stealing her away. Jenn said the holidays last year were unbearable. She and her sister never discussed it. "So, we're talking boyfriend material already? I mean, a weekend away is one thing, but the 'b' word is a whole different ballgame."

"That might be a premature thought. As much fun as Vegas was, I just need more. You have your new career to focus on, and you live so far away. I work too much and don't play enough. And most of my friends are settling down so they don't have time for me. I just want someone to spend time with."

"Just make sure you're doing it for you and not because everyone else is doing it," I say. Jenn is pan and dates the entire spectrum. Sometimes we're interested in the same women. The woman I hooked up with in Vegas was right up her alley. Had I been paying closer attention, I would have noticed that Jenn was ignoring a woman who was her type in favor of concentrating on her phone. She must really like Orlando. "He seemed pretty nice when he called."

"He's too nice. I'm still trying to figure out what's wrong with him," she says.

"Handsome, rich, dotes on you. Sounds horrible to me." I'm concerned because he does sound a little too perfect. "Maybe a weekend away is the best plan. You can find out if he has any flaws, and I can run a background check."

"You can do that?"

I laugh. "I never really thought of it, but I probably could. I know some cops, but I'm not sure I can get a favor this quickly. We could always hire somebody to check him out. We can't be too careful."

"Maybe we'll wait on that background check. It sounds kind of creepy, and we're better than that," she says.

"We're better than that right now, but you never know." I pull into my parking spot. "When do you leave?"

"Tomorrow. I'll drop a pin and text you his info, so if I disappear, you can find my body and know who did it."

I hear her text come through. "I hate when you talk like this."

"I hate that we even have to talk like this."

"Have fun, be safe, and call me when you get home Sunday night, or I'll send out a search party. I want to hear about everything. Yes, even the naughty parts," I say.

Jenn laughs. "Will do. Kill it tomorrow at lecture. I can't wait to see you in your robes."

"That won't be for a while, but I'm excited to take the bench. Go, get packed."

"Have fun studying," Jenn says.

"Have fun getting laid." I make another kiss sound and end the call. I pull up a trusted food-delivery service while taking the elevator up to my apartment and place an order, knowing full well I have at least two hours of reading and then another hour of reviewing my notes. I don't want to cook and don't have time to.

"How's life?"

My neighbor, Cassidy, a twenty-something party girl who doesn't seem to have a job is leaving her apartment dressed for a night on the town. She's wearing tall wedges and a small blue dress that hits mid-thigh. She's straightened her normally frizzy blond hair, and her makeup is thick. Clubbing is in her near future.

"Work's busy, but life's pretty good." I point to my briefcase as if she knows exactly what I do. "Looks like you're going to have some fun tonight."

"Well, Thursday is Friday eve, so I have to take advantage, right?"

She sounds like she doesn't have a care in the world. I loathe lazy trust-fund babies. I overheard her friends teasing her one night about her parents giving her a hefty allowance while she finds herself, but that was a few years ago. I guess she's still looking. I smile and wish her a good and safe night. I won't be seeing her once I move.

I open my door and kick off my heels. I love my shoe obsession, but today I'm tired, and the heels are pinching my toes. I prematurely packed a lot of my wardrobe, including sensible shoes. I'm stuck with suits, summer dresses, and a fuck ton of sexy heels. I throw my jacket on the back of the couch and head straight for the wine. After the info dump of the last ten hours, I need a quick break before I hit the books. Dinner will be here in less than ten minutes, according to my app. I slip into leggings and an oversized T-shirt and flop on the couch, pouting at the long night ahead.

Three hours later, I have notes scattered everywhere. I hope once I'm settled in my job and understand the process better, I won't stress every minute. I'm wound tight. I stand, stretch, and roll my neck for relief. I have no idea if I'm going to retain this information or if I've just wasted my entire night. I need release. The last person I hooked up with in town ended up getting engaged. That gives me a lazy idea. I open OkCupid and look through profiles of the women I'm attracted to, but most want the marriage, two point five kids, and a house with a fenced-in yard for Rover. That simply isn't me. I want sex. That's it. I pull up Tinder and browse available women. I spend a solid forty-five minutes swiping left. None of them are worth the risk of casual sex. I sigh and toss my phone onto the couch next to me. I'm going to be under a microscope until I retire.

I head to my bedroom and get ready for bed. Still too restless to sleep, I slip my hands under the sheet and start massaging my pussy. Even though I'm tired, my clit jumps at the friction, and I know I need to come. I reach into my nightstand for lube and liberally coat my pussy with the warming gel. My breath hitches the harder I press, but I don't want to come this soon. I like the buildup and the drop. I climb toward my orgasm twice but don't let myself come until I'm completely exhausted. When I do, I'm loud and my body jerks with each pulse. Although I wish I had somebody here doing this to me, my orgasm is both satisfying and relaxing and the perfect way to end my stagnant night.

Tomorrow I'm taking the bench for the first time. Today is a clean-up day with Judge Martinez, my mentor, but his cases were rescheduled due to a bad case of food poisoning, so I find myself with a rare afternoon off. I have to get out. I'm spending too much time inside immersed in the law. My anxiety is getting the best of me, and I need to expel this pent-up energy.

I have the afternoon off. Ideas?

Sex. I highly recommend afternoon sex.

I can always count on Jenn to give it to me straight. *Are you having sex right now? Tell me yes. One of us needs to be having it.*

No. I'm at work. What happened to your workaholic afternoon?

Judge M got sick. I need to get out. Suggestions?

My recommendation of sex stands. Get dolled up, go somewhere public, and find a hot top to take care of your needs.

She's right. I haven't gotten laid since Vegas. That feels like forever ago. Her idea has merit and would relax me before my big day.

I just googled events in KC. There's a great exhibit at the Nelson. Try that. And if that doesn't work, go to the other museum. The modern-art one. You're sure to find somebody who's up for a good time. Nobody goes to a museum to look at art.

I send her a laughing emoji. *I'll keep you posted.*

Jenn attended law school with me at UMKC. We spent a lot of time studying at the Nelson Atkins Museum of Art a few blocks from campus. Jenn tagged along because we didn't have to be quiet like we did at the library. Giant traveling exhibitions make their way to the Nelson during their coast-to-coast travels, and I enjoy seeing them when I have the time. Lately, that hasn't been my luck.

Even if I don't find anybody, I can still go appreciate the art on display. I look through my closet and find a dress that I've worn only a handful of times. It's scarlet and sexy as fuck. A bit much for an afternoon at the museum, but it's a special day. I slip it on and run my hands up and down the smooth sateen material. It shows off my breasts and flares out a bit at the waist, accentuating my curvy hips. I feel like a pinup girl. I style my hair with soft waves and pull up one side with a Victorian hair comb that my grandmother gave me when I was a little girl. I find my *Prohibited Rouge* lipstick, smooth it over my lips, and wipe a tiny bit from the corner of my mouth. I love lipstick. I dab my lips together until it's even and thicken my mascara. I slip on my red heels, grab a clutch, and head out.

Chapter Two

The greeter who stands by the front entrance gives me an appreciative look. Because I'm dressed for attention, I don't mind it. He wishes me a nice afternoon after I slip cash into the donation box.

The Nelson is impressive and beautifully designed. The tapping of my heels echoes in the foyer, and I smile at the sound. I enjoy wide open spaces for that reason. I make my way down the long hallway and wander into the room of Italian Baroque artwork. I sit on the bench and lose myself in a giant Caravaggio painting. I don't know how long I've been sitting here, but a person drifts into my peripheral vision, interrupting my concentration on *Saint John the Baptist in the Wilderness*.

"They say he killed a man."

I look up and see the most gorgeous butch standing in front of me. My irritation at the interruption fizzles once I look into eyes so beautifully gray they render me speechless. I can only smile. She looks at the painting. "It was a cop. So even hundreds of years ago when cops were probably more corrupt than they are now, it was still a really bad idea to kill one."

She's confident and borderline cocky. I lean back and look her up and down. I like what I see—tall, attractive, and very interested.

I wait to answer her until I see a flash of doubt that she's read me wrong cross her face. She hasn't. Delivery is key. I smirk and tilt my head. "I have a lot of cop friends."

"So do I," she says.

Game on. She rocks back on her heels and turns. "Any other favorites here?"

I nod at a Rubens on the other wall. She walks over to it and studies the information plaque, which gives me time to look at her. She is tanned and fit with an energy brimming off her that I'm drawn to.

"He's very sensual," she says.

I stand and purposely slow my step so that she takes the time to notice me. The clip of my heels echoes in the room. My approach is unmistakable. I don't stop until I'm in her personal space. She bites her bottom lip and stares at my mouth. I wonder if she likes my lipstick. I look at the painting. "He's known for adding color when others dared not to." She makes a noise as if agreeing with me. I lean closer and whisper, "I want to touch it."

She looks surprised at first and whispers back. "If the guard wasn't there, you could touch anything you wanted to."

Heat flashes across me as her warm breath brushes my cheek. I want to touch her. I want to put my hands on her broad shoulders and feel her strong arms around me. I touch her forearm instead. Her muscles instantly tighten under my fingers. I've never been this bold before.

"Maybe if you distract him, I could get away with it." I put my hands on my hips and lift an eyebrow, challenging her.

She looks at the guard and back at me. "What if the alarm goes off?"

"Then we run." It probably isn't a good idea for me to get into trouble the day before I take the bench, but our chemistry is off the chart, and doing something wrong feels right with her.

"In those?" She points at my red heels.

"You'd be surprised what I can do in these."

"Do tell."

"There isn't anything I can't do in my heels. Sometimes I wear them and nothing else." I don't know where my boldness is coming from. And how does this woman pick up my fuck-me vibe so quickly?

I look at the Rubens again. Touching something so beautiful that's hundreds of years old would be a dream come true. The stranger nods at me and walks to the guard. I watch them interact and realize she's distracting him. I look around and once the proverbial coast is clear, I reach out and quickly brush my fingertips across the corner of the painting. The texture is both rough and smooth. I wink at her and shiver at the look she gives me.

She returns to my side. "Was it worth it?" She smiles, and straight white teeth peek out from behind full lips.

I hold my dress out and curtsy. "Thank you." I lean in because she smells fresh and woodsy. Her dark hair sweeps across her forehead, and I have an urge to brush it back with my fingers. She looks at me with hunger, and I swallow hard at how intense her stare is.

"Let's go to the next room. They all can't have guards."

She motions for me to go ahead of her. I walk slowly and deliberately, knowing she's watching me. Although she's playful, she's tense. I feel her energy behind me. I swell with excitement at the possibilities. She passes me and directs me into a room.

"What's your favorite wing here in the museum? I'd love to see it with you." She slides her hands in her pockets, drawing my attention to her crotch. She's packing. The unmistakable outline of her strap-on is visible behind the zipper of her khakis. I feel weak in the knees knowing that I'm going to get fucked soon. I lick my lips and turn my gaze to meet hers.

"I like it all," I say.

"All of it?"

For a moment, she seems unsure. Her sexy smile is crooked, and her eyebrow is slightly hitched, as if she's waiting for my consent. I don't hesitate. "Every last inch." Her smile grows, and she bites back a small laugh.

"Well, then we have a lot more to see."

She follows me out of the room, only this time she's closer. I can feel her body heat. I lead her to the American colonial wing, where the rooms are dark, with roped-off displays. I bite my bottom lip and follow the makeshift wooden path that's there to add authenticity to the room. It leads to a cut-away of a typical American homestead log cabin featuring a table with two chairs, a fireplace with a large cauldron hanging over it, and a bed covered with animal pelts. Her mouth is inches from my ear as we take in the scene before us.

"Not a very comfortable bed," she whispers.

I bend down to pretend to read the information on the plaque and feel the full length of her dildo as my ass brushes her crotch. I don't move. Neither does she. I close my eyes and try hard not to push back into her, into her cock, so I stand instead. This seduction is a marathon, not a sprint. I feel her warm hand on the small of my back. "Life back then must have been...um...hard." I can't look at her. I'm too close to dropping to my knees to satisfy her, and this is a very public place. I move on to the next display. She touches me this time, running her fingers up and down my arm. I lean over to read the plaque, and she holds my waist and slowly pulls me against her. Her fingers are long and dig into my hips. I hear her moan softly, and my confidence grows. She keeps me flush against her when I stand.

"What does it say?" she asks.

I reach back and touch her thigh. Her breath hitches at my touch, and her muscles twitch under my fingers. I turn my head so our faces are close, but she doesn't kiss me. "The diet of the early American settler was rough." I silently beg her for a kiss, a touch, her hands on my body, but she's teasing me. Fine. Two can play this game.

"Let's go to the next one."

I break the connection, missing the heat of her body against mine. I turn and can't help but look at her crotch. I swallow hard. It's big, and I'm growing wet just thinking about her deep inside of me. She walks to me, her eyes never leaving mine, and stands behind me again. I lean into her this time as she snakes her arm around my waist as though I might flee. I'm not going anywhere. I grind against her, hard. She splays her fingers on my stomach just below my breasts.

"What does this one say?"

I feel her tongue tracing the outside of my ear. Her mouth is hot, wet, and I want it all over my body. I moan out of desire and frustration and rub up against her. "I have to bend over to read the plaque." She places her hands on my hips and unabashedly grinds into me. We both moan. Damn, she feels so good. I try to tell her what the plaque says, but I can't. We've crossed the line, and we either need to create space or find somewhere to fuck. She must be reading my mind.

"Perhaps we should find a more private place."

She releases me just as an attendant saunters into the room. We nod at her and slowly leave the colonial wing as if we were in there admiring the art when, in fact, I can't remember a single thing about it. She walks behind me, and I catch her looking at my ass and legs. I smirk at her and lead her into one of the Impressionist rooms. She stops at a Monet and smiles. I'm curious as to what she's thinking. I'm thinking about sex. Maybe she's not done looking at art.

"Is this your favorite?" I admire her strong jawline and the corded muscles of her forearms. I notice tiny beads of sweat at her temples even though it's cold in here. I can't wait to mold myself against her and feel her sweaty body against mine.

She seems embarrassed by my question. "If I said yes, that would make me like every other person." She slides her hands in her pockets again, and my eyes are immediately drawn back to her crotch. I almost lick my lips in anticipation.

"You smiled when we walked in here."

She stares at me. "I smiled because the view makes me happy."

Oh, she's good. My heart speeds up at the unguarded look of pure lust she shoots me. The energy inside me bubbles up. I have to expel it, so I walk into the next room. She follows, but instead of walking with me, she sits on a bench. Her eyes never leave me. The other patrons in the room nod at me as we cross paths and smile cordially at each other. Once they leisurely stroll into other rooms, and it's just me and her, I lean over her, putting one hand on her thigh and the other on the armrest. My cleavage is inches from her face, and her appreciation of it is obvious.

"It's too bad the contemporary art wing is under construction," I say.

She touches my neck and runs her fingers over my full bosom. Her touch is so light, but each finger delivers a delicious shock that races through my already charged body. When her finger brushes my bottom lip, I suck it into my mouth and twirl my tongue around it. My intent is obvious. I see the delight in her eyes and how her hips twitch with each suck on her finger. She moves my hand from her thigh and puts it on her cock. I feel how long and thick it is and want it inside of me.

"Shall we go make sure that it's still under construction?" She stands. I don't move. My hand is trapped between us, and I stroke her. She slips her hand into mine and leads me away. I'm done with the teasing. I want her inside me. I take charge and march us to a staircase that's closed to the public. She pulls me back to her.

"I need to taste you," she says. She touches my cheek softly, then crushes her mouth against mine.

She tastes warm and like spearmint. I don't even try for control. I'm ready for anything she wants. Her body vibrates against mine as though she's struggling to restrain herself. She's sexy and demanding, and I know I'll do anything to satisfy her. Her fingers slip under the straps of my dress, and I silently beg her to rip them down and free my breasts. My nipples ache from straining against the tight fabric.

I hear footsteps getting closer and pull away from her, panting hard. We freeze and stare at one another. She's disheveled and sexy as fuck. Two buttons are undone on her shirt, and I don't know if I unbuttoned it or she did. She unclips the *Do Not Enter* chain barrier, and we quickly but quietly descend the stairs. She's several steps behind me, obviously watching me.

There's a powder room down here that I've always thought would be the perfect place for a tête-à-tête. I find the bathroom and pull her inside. I'm relieved to find the couch, chaise, and wingback chairs weren't moved during the construction. "There are cameras down here, but not in this room." I know because this has always been my fantasy—public sex.

She cups my elbow and walks into me until my back is flush against the door. I almost swoon at her command over me, over us. I look at her expectantly. She rubs my lipstick off with the pad of her thumb so she can kiss me again. Before she can, I turn and place my hands above the door in a gesture of surrender. I gasp when she drops to her knees. Her fingertips press into my calves. I inhale deeply as her warm hands move higher. I whimper when she reaches the back of my thighs and automatically spread my legs.

My panties are soaked. I don't know why I wore any today. I hold my breath and moan when she rips them down. She holds my hand while I step out of them. I rest my forehead against the door and watch as she slips my panties into her pocket. I can only imagine why she wants them, and the thought of her touching herself while smelling me is hot. Her hands slip to the front of my thighs while she flicks her tongue over the back of them. Her hair lightly brushes my ass as she moves closer to my pussy. I push back because I want her tongue inside me or on my clit. She surprises me by spreading my cheeks apart and running her tongue up and down the sensitive strip. When she enters my pussy with two fingers, I moan and clutch the door the best I can. I'm tight at this angle, but I want more of her. She deepens her thrusts, and I gasp.

"Yes, oh yes." I don't recognize my own voice.

"Do you like this?" Her voice is a growl. I whimper. "Are you ready for my cock?"

"Yes."

She finger-fucks me a few times more before she pulls out. I turn and sag against the door. I watch as she licks me off her fingers, then touches my lips. I suck them into my mouth and moan as I taste sex. She takes my hand and leads me to the chaise lounge, where she sits and moves me to stand between her legs.

"You taste incredible," she says.

"What do you want?" I look at her flushed skin and swollen lips, and the only thing I can think about is her mouth all over my body. My heart speeds up at the lust I see in her eyes. Heat pools between my legs, and I squirm at my body's neediness.

"Turn around."

Excitement leaps in my chest. I lift my eyebrow at her and slowly turn. She unzips my dress and turns me to face her again. I'm afraid to touch her, as if this fantasy will vanish, and I'll be standing alone in this bathroom.

"Now take down your straps."

Her voice is low but commanding. She settles back on the lounge as if I'm going to give her a show. Truthfully, I'd do anything for her. I slowly lower the straps until my breasts are bared. A full smile settles on her lips, and I know she likes what she sees. I massage my breasts and pinch my nipples to relieve some of the ache. It's not enough. I groan in frustration and close my eyes, pretending she's touching me, but it's not the same.

"Open your eyes."

I watch as she leans toward me and sucks one of my erect nipples into her mouth. The shock of her hot mouth sends electricity through me with every pull of her lips. I rake my nails on the back of her neck and push her into me. I need more. She bites, and I hiss as pleasure and pain hit me at the same time. I move her mouth to my other breast.

"Again." It's the only word I can form. She sucks and bites even harder. I cry out as pain and pleasure collide throughout my body.

"Did I hurt you?"

I cup her chin and make her look at me. "Only in a good way. You have the perfect mouth. Beautiful shape, fantastic ability." I touch her mouth. It is a wonderful instrument, and I'm torn between wanting her lips on my pussy or kissing me. I'm shocked by how much I want her to kiss me, how much I want that connection. It's never been my thing.

"You haven't even experienced the best part yet." She's sure of herself. I am, too.

"I can't wait." I hear her breath catch when I reach for her zipper. I'm trying to go slow, but we both know that's not going to happen. She's already wearing a condom, but I've never liked the flavor of latex, so I peel it off and kneel between her legs. Her mouth is slightly open, and her eyes are almost closed, but I know she's watching me. I look at her before my tongue flicks over the tip of her shaft. Her eyes widen with appreciation, and I feel her shift her hips slightly. I lean my breasts on her thighs and work my mouth up and down the dildo. She smells like sex. "Will you please fuck me now?" I don't even care that I'm begging.

She pulls me into her arms but doesn't kiss me. She points to the chaise instead. "Lie down."

I lie down and spread my legs as far apart as my dress will allow me.

"I want to see your beautiful pussy. Pull your dress up," she says.

I do what she commands. I'm naked except for my dress, which is pushed down and pulled up to gather around my waist. She stares at me for a few moments before she adjusts herself between my legs. The head of the dildo glides up and down my wet slit before she presses into me. She is too gentle. I guide her inside and gasp at the thickness. Her body vibrates with what I imagine is anticipation as she waits for me to adjust to every inch. It's big, but I don't want her to stop. I arch my back as she pushes to the hilt, and I cry out. She holds me steady, carefully, and waits for me to relax.

"Are you okay?" It's sweet that she's worried about me. Her mouth moves down my neck as she waits for my answer.

I stroke her hair and start moving my hips in a circular motion. "You feel so good." She moans when I push into her. "So good." She picks up my cue and starts fucking me harder and faster. I feel myself letting go. I need more. She sucks the sensitive skin on my neck and bites down more the faster my hips buck against hers. I cry out with pleasure several times, and she stops. I look at her with confusion.

"You're going to have to be quiet. We don't want anybody catching us."

"I promise I'll be quiet." I'm lying. "Just don't stop." I grab her ass and tilt so she can move faster and harder. I push at her legs and she stops again. I groan with disappointment. My thighs are quivering—a sign that I'm close to orgasm. "Why did you stop?"

"Is this too hard? You're pushing against my thighs." She kisses me deeply, and I whimper with desire. She doesn't know that I like it rough.

"It's so you'll fuck me deeper." That does the trick. She pulls out of me, grabs my hips, and turns me so I'm on my stomach. I smile. She lifts my ass in the air and plunges into me. It's so perfect that I cry out. Tears form in the corners of my eyes, and I brace myself against the arms of the chaise. She pushes deep into me. I feel her sweat drip onto my ass as I push back. My knees rub back and forth against the textured fabric of the cushion. I know they'll be raw, but I don't care. I push myself up on my hands and throw my head back in pure ecstasy. "I'm going to come. Don't stop, don't stop." Our eyes lock in the mirror beside the chaise, and my stomach drops at the look she gives me. I watch her fuck me, and when my orgasm tumbles over me, I yell with abandon and sink onto the couch, gasping for breath. She strokes my back. I stretch out and wait for the aftershocks to roll over me. I have no words to describe what just happened. Amazing, incredible, stunning, unbelievable. I don't know what I did to deserve her, but she's perfect.

"Roll over."

I can't imagine moving right now, but something is so commanding about her that I oblige. She pulls me closer and hooks my knees over her shoulders so her face is inches from my pussy. I should be embarrassed by how wet I am, but I'm proud. She kisses a trail from the inside of my knee to my slit and latches on to my swollen clit with her warm mouth. I tense and focus on not coming immediately. I want this to last, but she can read my needs like nobody I've ever been with before.

She pushes my legs so my knees are up to my chest. I cross my arms under my knees to give her access to every part of me. She touches me everywhere. Her tongue is on me, her fingers inside, and I'm finding it hard to process the pleasure. I don't care who hears me. I don't even care if somebody walks in and watches us. My legs quiver and I tense up. I try to halt my impending orgasm, but I fail. I ride my second orgasm with her face pressed against my pussy. She doesn't stop, but after the third, I give out.

"I can't. I want to, but I can't." I don't recognize my own voice. My legs and arms are too heavy, and I drop them onto the couch. She slides up my sweaty body until we're face to face. She's so beautiful. I touch her flushed cheeks and run my thumb across her bottom lip. Her gray eyes are hooded with passion and her lips swollen, almost bruised. "Kiss me." I don't know why I want her to kiss me so much. She gives me what I want, and for a moment, I allow tenderness to slip inside. Today has been amazing and is still going strong.

"Do you know what I want?" she asks.

Just the question makes my stomach drop in anticipation. "I know what I want again. Are you sore?" I ask. She'd fucked me hard for a long time. Her stamina is amazing, but I'm worried she might be too sensitive.

"More important, are you sore?"

I answer by pressing against her. She smiles at me and readjusts her strap-on. It dawns on me that she hasn't orgasmed. Everything up to this point was for me. The next several minutes is for her. I lift my hips, and she teases me with the tip. I hook my legs around her waist and wait for her to penetrate me. The second she pushes through my tight opening, she moves fast and hard, so fast that I forget everything other than hanging on to her. I watch as she climbs higher, moves faster. When she's close, I pull my knees to my chest to allow her to move freely. She moans her appreciation and drills into me. I'm surprised when my orgasm explodes. She drops on top of me, panting heavily. I run my fingers through her short, sweaty hair and place a small kiss on her forehead.

"I'm squishing you," she says.

She tries to pull away, but I hold her in place because I need her warmth and a tender moment. "Stay. Just for ten more seconds." "You were very loud. I expect the guards to come busting in any moment."

She makes me laugh, even though the noise I make doesn't sound like myself. "Oh, I was loud? I believe you're the one who just howled." I release her, and she pulls me into her arms and adjusts my dress.

"Do you think we got away with this? Or do you think we're being videotaped and are somebody's entertainment tonight?"

I tamp down the panic that squeezes my chest at her questions. Tomorrow, I take the bench as an honorable judge, but today? I'm a woman who just had incredible sex. I walk to the mirror to adjust my dress and check my makeup. I smirk at her in our reflection. "We were definitely my entertainment." She winks and puffs out her chest at my compliment. She hands me my purse and adjusts her package and her clothes while I pull out a cigarette and matches. I light the cigarette and inhale deeply.

She quickly masks her surprise. "Share?"

I hand it to her. She takes a few drags and hands it back. We smoke in silence. I'm lost in the recent memories. She's quiet, too. I catch her staring at me several times. She looks like she wants to say something but remains quiet. It's probably for the best. We don't need to complicate this incredible afternoon with words or promises we won't keep. She runs her fingertips over the swell of my breasts.

"So soft. So lovely," she says.

The flutter in my stomach at her appreciative words makes me uncomfortable. I need to get away from her. I extinguish the cigarette under a stream of water and throw it away. "Shall we?" I don't wait for her. I open the door and walk out. She follows me but is a few steps behind. Before we reach the foyer, I feel her fingers gently grasp my elbow, and I stop.

She pulls me back against her body and rests her hands below my breasts. Her thumbs rub the bare skin of my cleavage.

"Thank you." Her words are almost a whisper against my ear. I turn in her embrace and look at her as though I'm seeing her for the first and last time. Her strong jawline and disheveled hair tug at something inside me, and I know I need to get away from her right now before I do something dumb like give her my name or phone number. "No, thank you." I run my fingers down her shirt and walk away. It's the perfect afternoon and exactly what I needed.

CHAPTER THREE

I need to tell you what happened to me today." I'd waited until nine my time to call Jenn in California, but it killed me.

"That's how you answer the phone?"

Jenn sounds tired. I slow down because she must have had one hell of an afternoon. She was fine at lunch when we texted. "I'm sorry. Hi, my love. How are you?"

Big sigh. "My day was total shit. I can't even tell you everything that went wrong."

I pause. Maybe now isn't the time to brag. "Do you want to talk about it?"

"No. I'd rather forget about it. Tell me about your day. Did you take my advice?"

I nod, even though she can't see me. "It was the best advice. I had the most amazingly unbelievable experience at the museum. Great call on your part."

"Details."

I hear the engine turn so I know she's in the privacy of her car. I can say anything I want. "I met someone."

"Like met met? Or like bumped into somebody that might be dateable?"

"Like met-and-fucked met," I say.

"Wow. Tell me more."

I launch into the story of how my mysterious lover approached me about art, and less than an hour later, we were downstairs fucking. "She literally took my breath away. Who goes to a museum to fuck? She does, that's who."

"See? I told you. I know things. And she was packing?"

"Oh, yeah. She was ready for sex."

"For you?" Jenn sounds confused.

"Well, somebody."

"That's fucking hot."

"I'm not going to lie. I'm still delightfully sore," I say. I crawl into bed in case I fall asleep on the phone.

"What did she look like?"

"She's about six feet tall, dark short hair, and get this, she has gray eyes. And she's very strong, even though she was on the thin side. Perfect skin. Total butch. And a great lover."

"I'm already in love. How big was she?"

"Delightfully satisfying. I can't believe she was able to keep it hidden in her pants." I take a moment to recall the first time I noticed it.

"Okay. Start at the beginning."

I leave nothing out. Everything this mysterious woman did to me, everything I did to her, and how we just went our separate ways when we were done.

"So, you didn't get her number or give her yours? Why the hell not?"

I think about that, and although regret pricks my mind for not giving her my phone number, I know it was the right thing to do. I'm too busy for a relationship, even a purely sexual one, and she's seemingly just like me. She didn't press me for information. "We both got what we wanted. Plus, it makes for a juicy memory. I mean, years from now we'll be sitting at a bar comparing stories, and this one will always be, hands down, my best one-night stand."

"And it wasn't even that. And that's what makes it so brilliant."

Lust isn't anything I'm ashamed or proud of. It's something inside of me that growls like hunger pangs, and it's something I need to feed. Today I ate well. My anxiety is under control, and I feel invincible. I'm ready for tomorrow. No distractions, only my full attention.

"Claire Bear, good for you. That makes me happy. And you're right. Best pickup ever."

"How's Ophelia, or Orville, or Othello?"

She laughs at my attempt to cheer her up. "He's doing well. It's weird. I look forward to spending time with him. It doesn't bother me when he calls or wants to hang out. He's a sweet guy. What's he doing with somebody like me?"

"You are beautiful, smart, powerful, fun, rich, and anybody would love to call you their girlfriend. I'm sorry you had such a shitty day, but I know it'll get better. You are Jennifer Fucking Matthews, lawyer extraordinaire. You kick ass and take names. You spit out criminals for a living."

"Well, technically evil empires, but keep going. This is exactly what I need." I hear a small smile in her voice.

"And you're beautiful, and Orlando Bloom is lucky to have you in his life."

A genuine laugh. "I wish it were Orlando Bloom. It's Orlando Thomas."

"Yeah, well, I don't think Bloom's wife is going to give him up without a fight."

"She can keep him. I kind of like mine," she says.

I hear her downshift the Porsche and know she's zipping in and out of traffic. "When was the last time you saw him?"

"This morning."

"Oh. Were you at his place or was he at yours?"

"I was at his place, and it's across town, so it took forever to go home and change. Then I was late to the morning meeting. Scratch that. I showed up ten minutes before it was over. And I just got off the phone with him. He suggested that I bring clothes over to his house for when this happens again."

And there it is. The truth. Jenn is upset that she's falling into another relationship.

"Look. He's a great guy, right? Don't fight it, sweetie. Let it happen. It sounds like maybe this is a good idea."

"But I'm not ready to settle down."

"You're not settling down. You're just dating, sticking with one person. You aren't getting married or moving in together. Just headed toward a monogamous relationship," I say. It's something she's good at but, for whatever reason, fights against. My lifestyle fits me. My lifestyle doesn't fit her. Maybe Vegas was a bad idea.

"How about I fly out there over Labor Day and meet Mr. Bloom?"

Another stress-relieving laugh. She's starting to shake off her bad mood. "Let me check with Big O and get back to you, but I could really use a friend."

"If my life wasn't in complete and total chaos, I'd fly out this weekend. Who moves during a new job?" I can't believe how shitty the timing is.

"But it's going to be fabulous, and soon you'll forget about the headache. Okay, thanks for cheering me up. Go to bed. Rock the black-robe look. Make the city a better place."

I end the call feeling a little stronger about tomorrow after talking about today. My day was surreal. I wanted to get out and have a flirty time, but in my wildest dreams I never thought I'd meet somebody who wanted the same thing—raw, lustful sex. I can't stop thinking about her. Not because I want something that isn't there, but because something's there that I don't want.

"How do I look?" I turn to one of my law clerks, April, for her approval or impromptu pep talk, whichever she can spare. I'm not her first judge, and she's been very helpful.

"Very professional."

She barely glances at me, busy with something on the computer. I stand in front of her desk until she gives me her full attention. Her fingers slow on the keyboard, and she looks at me again for longer than three seconds.

"You look very strict. I like the glasses. Lose most of the lipstick. This is court, not a bar."

I smile at her honesty. It's exactly what I need. "Thank you." I have seven minutes before the court introduces me. I'm wearing a sexy cream-colored suit under my robe because it makes me feel confident and powerful. My heels aren't sensible, but they lift my ass up. My hips and legs are sore from yesterday, but I have to dress for success. I refuse to be the judge who wears tennis shoes and elastic-waistband pants under my robes. I dab my lipstick off and straighten out my collar. Kevin's nickname jumps into my head because I do look like Ruth Bader Ginsburg, only fifty years younger.

"We're ready for you, Judge Weaver."

The bailiff nods and introduces me to the court. "All rise. This court is now in session. The Honorable Claire Weaver presiding."

I enter the courtroom with my head held high and focus strictly on getting to my chair without falling. First impressions are everything. Once I'm settled, I look out at my courtroom for the first time. I inherited Judge Tulver's docket and am excited that this arson case is my first.

"Thank you." I straighten out my papers. "What's on the docket?"

The bailiff announces the first case. I scan the crowd and stop when I see a pair of gray eyes I know entirely too well. I look away, but my body reacts, and I pray nobody notices. My mysterious woman from yesterday who fucked me hard and thoroughly is sitting in the middle of my courtroom, in uniform. Panic flutters up from my stomach and rests heavily against my heart, forcing it to beat faster. It occurs to me that she is involved in this case. She's wearing a fire investigator's uniform. I dig through my paperwork until I see the witness list. I hate that I don't know her name, but thankfully only two fire investigators are on the list. Carl Renfield and Emery Pearson. Emery. It's a great name and fits her.

"Will counsel please approach the bench?"

Both lawyers look confused but walk up to me. I cover the microphone so the court can't hear me. "I need to see you both in chambers." I bang the gavel and ask for a ten-minute recess. Even the bailiff looks confused. Everybody stands when I leave, and both lawyers follow me to my office.

"Thank you. Have a seat."

"Judge, what's going on?" The prosecuting attorney speaks first.

I don't know if I'm right on this. "I'm familiar with one of the witnesses."

"You've had this list for weeks now. Why are you bringing this up now?" The defense attorney smirks, knowing full well that I might have to recuse myself from this case.

"I didn't know her name until today. I recognize her in the courtroom. I had a chat with her during an art exhibit, but we didn't introduce ourselves."

The defense attorney reviews the list I hand him. "Emery Pearson?"

"Yes."

"Would you say you're friends?" he asks.

"More like acquaintances. I didn't even know she's a fire investigator." I'm sweating profusely and hope it's not visible to counsel.

"I don't have a problem then." The defense attorney shrugs at me. He knows it's my first case, and he's probably taking it easy on me because he's going to call in a favor in the future. Let the games begin.

"I don't either." The prosecutor hands me back the list.

"Then let's go have a trial," I say. Relief settles the tension between my shoulder blades, and I rub my neck on the way back to the courtroom. I take my seat and turn to counsel for opening statements. I can't look at Emery yet. I need to get my head back into the game and keep my throbbing libido under wraps. I can't jeopardize my career because my pussy's needy.

The prosecution begins with their statement, and while it's a compelling beginning, I'm not blown away, but I can't show any reaction. The defense attorney for Seamus Williams is very theatrical, and I find myself interested in what he has to say. It's going to be a tough case to defend, but he sounds positive and strong. It's not long before the prosecution calls their first witness, then their second. Emery Pearson is the fourth witness, right after her boss. She stands, and I ever so slightly hitch my eyebrow at her in recognition. She nods at me and takes the seat beside me, below me. I stare at her intently now that I know more about her. Yesterday was a stress reliever for both of us. Her voice is crisp and her answers direct. She commands attention. I stifle a shiver and tamp down the image of her buried deep inside me, her gray eyes roaming me appreciatively. I catch a whiff of her cologne and almost moan with delightful recognition. I mentally shake my head and concentrate on her answers. When she's done, I stop myself from watching her walk back to her seat.

I scribble notes because I don't want it to be obvious to counsel or her that she intrigues me. When I dismiss the court for lunch, I head straight for my office and shut the door. I tear off my robe and sit down to the meal April delivered. That's a nice perk, but my stomach lurches recalling my morning. I waver between pure excitement and pure dread at today's reveal. Of all the fucking luck. My first case. One afternoon delight almost blows my entire career. The fucked-up part is that I don't care. I want to be with her again. I poke at my lunch and tear off a piece of bread from my chicken-salad sandwich. I need something to calm the gurgling in my stomach so I pick up my phone and send Jenn a text.

I can't even begin to tell you the craziness of today.

OMG. What?

It's so unbelievable that even you won't believe me.

Jenn's face pops up on my phone with a FaceTime call. I dismiss the call. I can't risk being overhead. As soon as I hang up, I text her.

Sorry. I don't know who can hear me. My mysterious woman from yesterday is A WITNESS ON MY FIRST CASE

Shut. The. Fuck. Up.

I can't type fast enough. *I cleared it with counsel. But what are the chances?*

How did you clear it with them? Hey, I fucked a witness. Hope that's okay?

I drop several laughing emojis. *I left out the fucking part but told them we were acquaintances.*

I wish I had acquaintances like that. What's her name? I'll stalk her on social media.

Shit. Why hadn't I thought of that?

Emery Pearson. I jump on Instagram and fan myself at the hot photos she's posted of herself in uniform and working the job. There aren't many. Either social media isn't important to her, or she's got some serious privacy settings. I respect that. I have to be careful, too.

Wow. Seriously, wow. Look at her muscles. How tall is she again?

I smile at Jenn's line of questioning.

OMG look at her gray eyes! Are those contacts? That's amazing.

I had the same reaction only internally and in the heat of the moment.

Very sexy in uniform.

Jenn's texts are interrupting my perusal of Emery's Instagram. *Very sexy is putting it mildly.* She looks fabulous in her blues. Like swoon-worthy fabulous. My clit throbs at the thought of her fucking me wearing that uniform. Normally uniforms don't excite me, but now that I've seen how good she looks in it, my need to have her again rages inside me. A knock at the door startles me, and I drop my phone.

"Yes?" I grab a stack of papers and pretend that I'm reviewing them.

April sticks her head in. "You have ten minutes until you are needed back in court."

"Thank you." Shit, that was fast. Where did the time go? I text Jenn that I'll catch her tonight and take a few more bites of my sandwich. I need some nourishment to get through the rest of the afternoon. I have a feeling it's going to be an excruciatingly long one for all the wrong reasons.

CHAPTER FOUR

She is standing by a tree smoking a cigarette and drinking an orange soda. Her tie is loosened from her neck, and her uniform jacket is unbuttoned. It's hot outside. I watch her through a small slit in my curtains. She scrolls through her phone and, without warning, looks directly up at me. Our eyes lock and her message is clear. She's here for me. I can't let this opportunity pass. She made the first move. Again. It's my turn. I write my address and phone number on the back of my business card and quickly check my hair and makeup. I let my hair down and straighten my suit. I should stay and review my notes, but I need to see her. I grab my bag with all my drafts from today, briefly touch my robe hanging on the coatrack, and lock my door on the way out. April's already gone. Most of the staff leaves at five.

Outside, my breath catches in my throat, even though I've prepared myself to see and talk to her again. She's holding her glass soda bottle and studying the line of trash and recycle bins.

"Try the middle one," I say.

She pauses before she turns. Her eyes roam me up and down, and an appreciative, almost cocky smile perches on her red lips. "I was just leaving."

I reach for her cigarette and take a drag. The butt tastes faintly like artificial orange and mint from her lip balm. I take one last drag and crush the lit end on the side of one of the recycle bins. I refuse to buy cigarettes and really need to stop sneaking them. "I'm glad you waited." I smile up at her, remembering how she stood just as tall and confident between my legs only yesterday. I lean my weight on my other hip to find a spark of friction to ease my throbbing pussy. It doesn't help, and the way she looks at me only makes my body swell more. I close the gap between us, but not so much as to draw unwanted attention. I slip out my business card and slide it into the breast pocket of her sexy uniform. She shudders and closes her eyes. I turn and walk away, knowing she's watching me. I don't look back, and I don't search for her as I leave the parking lot. What did I just do? I have an hour and a half to get ready. That isn't enough time to shower, primp, and cook dinner. I call Tannin's and place an order for two mushroom risotto dinners with fresh bread and a salad to be delivered at exactly 7:05. Food is the last thing on my mind, but my caloric intake today is dismal, and I'm hopeful for a hell of a night. I need energy.

By the time I get into my apartment, I'm down to sixty-eight minutes. I know Emery will be prompt, if she shows up at all. Even if she's early, she won't ring until then. Fuck. Why are most of my clothes packed away? My options are power suits or yoga pants. I have to have something sexy somewhere. I almost weep with relief when I find my little black dress hidden behind my suits. It hits right above the knee and clings to me everywhere. I don't bother with a bra or panties. I have thirty minutes to perfect my look and will need every second. I blow out my hair the best I can. I don't look as polished as I did yesterday, but I still look good. There's a knock at the door, and my heart jumps.

She takes my breath away. The genuine smile, the hair that swoops across her forehead, and she's wearing that gorgeous uniform. I open the door wider but don't move. She has to touch me to get inside.

She hands me a crimson gift bag with red tissue paper. It's the exact color of my *Prohibited Rouge* lipstick. "This is for you. For later," she says.

I don't even care what's in it. I only care that she's here. I want to grab her by her thin navy tie and pull her inside. Without my heels, she towers over me, and that's sexy as fuck. "Are you coming in?"

I gasp when she lifts me up and walks into my kitchen. I wrap my legs around her waist. "We need to close the door," I whisper. She brushes her lips across mine. I grab her lapels and moan into her mouth at the delicious kiss. She sets me on the counter and pushes up my dress, so she's pressed against me. Her belt buckle rubs my clit, and I shiver with anticipation. Disappointment quickly replaces my joy when I notice she's not packing. I stop myself from frowning.

"Um. Excuse me? Does Claire Weaver live here?" a deep voice asks from the doorway.

We both freeze. Fuck. It's the delivery guy. I peek around Emery's shoulder. "I'm Claire."

A young man shifts from one foot to the other. He's red with embarrassment, and I wonder what he saw. Emery turns to block his view and walks toward him for the food.

"Thanks, buddy."

She slips him a tip even though I've already tipped him online and closes the door before he can see more of me than either of us want. I haven't moved. I want her to see me like this—wet and ready for her. Her shoulders visibly relax once the door is locked.

"That was close."

She walks back to me. I smirk and lean back on the counter. Her eyes flicker from my jutting breasts down to my exposed thighs. I spread my legs more for her enjoyment. She smiles and runs her hands over them, stopping right before her thumbs rub my sensitive lips. She isn't gentle, and I gasp with pleasure. I touch her face as though I haven't seen her in forever.

"Hi." I brush my hands over her lips.

She kisses them and kisses me. "Hi." She pulls back. "I'm Emery Pearson. It's so very nice to meet you."

"Trust me when I say the pleasure is all mine. I'm Claire Weaver." I drape my arms on her shoulders.

"The Honorable Claire Weaver."

I look down at my dress that hides nothing. My pussy is smooth, exposed, and ready. "Maybe not at this moment."

We both watch as she lightly touches my glistening slit. I run my fingers over the soft, short hair on the back of her neck, scraping my nails until I hit her scalp. She moans her appreciation.

"I've missed this," I say.

"You aren't sore?" Her voice is low with a hint of concern.

"Deliciously so. Don't worry about me. I can take it." I run my hands down the buttons of her jacket, enjoying the swell of her breasts. I lean in to smell her spicy cologne. "Are you hungry?"

She responds by bending down and running her tongue at the junction of where the warm folds of my pussy meet, and my clit pulses at her darting tongue. I jerk and spread my legs wantonly. It has only been a day, but I need her. My mysterious woman. "Emery."

She stops and looks at me. "Claire."

Her eyes are bright. I can tell she's happy to be here with me.

I don't realize I said her name out loud. "It's just nice to have a name with a…," I look into her eyes, "…with a face."

She kisses my thigh and holds her finger up for me to wait there. I don't plan to move. She puts the food in the refrigerator and washes her hands. I can't stop watching her. Everything seems so unbelievable.

"What do you want, Claire?"

She's back between my legs, but she waits for me to instruct her. "I want you to make me come."

"Mm. That's without a doubt." She pushes my knees up to my chest, and I lie back on the counter. I know she's going to make me forget about the discomfort of lying on the granite countertop and replace it with pleasurable pain. She presses her face into my folds and licks my pussy hard and fast. I pull at her shoulders and moan my approval. "This can't be comfortable for you." Without waiting for a reply, she picks me up and carries me to the couch. It's so fast I don't have time to react other than hold her shoulders.

"Where's your cock?" I reach for her belt and press my hand against her mound. Her hips jerk under my touch.

"This outfit is too tight to pack." She runs her finger over my pouting lips. "Don't be sad. You haven't opened your present." Excitement gathers in my chest as I fantasize about what's in the bag. How big is it? Will she wear it or just fuck me with it? "Is it present time?"

She shakes her head, and I pout. "Not yet."

She pushes up my dress, even though my pussy is already exposed. I feel sexier wearing it, so I leave it on. She runs her hands up and down my thighs and stares at me. My mouth falls open when I feel her thumbs slip inside me. I'm wet and ready. I feel completely unguarded. I watch her for as long as I can before passion overtakes me, and I succumb to the pleasure and close my eyes. My hips rise with each thrust. I've lost count of how many fingers she has inside me. At least two. Guttural sounds come from my open mouth as she thrusts fast and hard. I hook one leg over the back of my couch to anchor myself and meet each thrust even harder. She's so fast. Her moans echo mine. A flush spreads across me, and I know I'm going to come hard. I dig my heels down and raise my hips until the orgasm crashes into me. I'm shaking as she stretches my legs down and lies beside me on the couch. I'm not a cuddler, but this feels nice.

"Are you ready for your present?"

She's tense, and I know she wants to come, too. I nod, and she jumps up and disappears with the bag. Cold, I grab a blanket from the back of the couch and cover myself. The five minutes she's gone have given me time to relax, and the moment I hear her walking toward me, my pussy clenches with delight.

"I wanted to wear this here, but as you can see, the gift bag was the better idea."

She stands in front of me. Her cock strains the zipper of her uniform pants. She looks uncomfortable. I can't tell if it's because it's too big or she's just too swollen. I smile because she goes to such lengths to please me. I touch her crotch. It's bigger than the one she wore yesterday.

"Do you like it?"

I nod and run my fingers up and down the hard shaft. She steps back, unzips her pants, and pulls it through the zipper. It's thicker. I bite my bottom lip and imagine her pumping it in and out of me. She reaches in the bag and pulls out a small bottle of lube. Normally, I'd wave it off, but I think I'm going to need it. I watch her as she rubs her hand up and down the dildo. I reach back and grab the arm of the couch to steady myself. She kneels between my legs. The coolness of the lube makes me jump, but it'll warm quickly. She's slow and watches my reaction. The tight feeling as she pushes in is quickly replaced with a burst of ecstasy. She slowly moves inside me.

"Are you okay?"

I bite my bottom lip and stare into her eyes. "Oh, I'm more than okay."

She adjusts the base until she's comfortable and begins to move her hips. She's fully dressed, and while she's sexy in uniform, I want to see her skin. I've felt her muscles through her clothes, but today I want to see them slick with sweat and popping.

"Take off your jacket." I don't recognize my voice.

She presses herself deep inside me, and I arch my back. Fuck, she feels so good. She holds the position, and I watch as she slides off the jacket and places it over the back of the couch. I hold up my hand to stop her from moving.

"More?"

I nod. "I want to see your muscles. Show me."

She unbuttons her shirt and reveals a gorgeous six pack that I can barely reach. Her erect nipples strain against a white sports bra that presses her breasts tightly against her chest.

"Take the shirt off," I say.

She slips out of the shirt to reveal toned and tan arms. She leans over me, resting her hands on either side of my shoulders. I run my hands up her corded arms and link my fingers behind her neck.

"You're beautiful. Now will you please fuck me?"

She growls right before she kisses me and lowers her body so she's settled between my legs. She doesn't have to move a lot to please me. The dildo is thick and deep, and every little movement shoots sparks of pure pleasure.

"Since yesterday, I haven't stopped thinking about fucking you," she says.

She buries her face in my hair and starts pumping her hips against mine. I cry out and wrap my arms around her back, digging my fingernails into her skin. I'm marking her, and that only makes her fuck me harder. My teeth scrape her shoulder with every thrust. She's quiet when she comes and slows her hips as she works out her orgasm. She shakes and sinks into me to catch her breath.

"Wow," I say. Her sweaty forehead is hot against my shoulder. I place a small kiss on her temple. "I like my present."

Her chest vibrates as a deep laugh works its way out. She lifts her head. "I like it, too. I wasn't sure I was going to be able to control it."

She's still inside me. While not uncomfortable, her movements send sparks that aren't close enough together to jolt me into another orgasm, but I either need a break or another orgasm. I don't teeter on the edge very well. As if reading my mind, she slowly pulls out and pushes herself off me.

"We're not done here," she says.

She has marks on her shoulder. I imagine her back is covered with scratches. I don't feel bad. "We're not?"

I feel the tip teasing my pussy. She pushes into me and pulls all the way out. I groan with both delight and disappointment. She does it again. And again. I come on the fourth thrust and again on the seventh. My legs are numb, and I can barely catch my breath. "I can't. Oh, my God." She respectfully pulls out and lays her head on my stomach as we both allow ourselves to relax. I run my hands through her hair, needing contact that isn't sexual. Her hair is thick, and even though it contains product, I can run my fingers though it easily enough. She doesn't seem to care that I'm messing it up. "Are you hungry?"

She smiles, and tiny lines pop up at the corner of her eyes. "I could probably drink a gallon of water. And then maybe a glass of wine with dinner."

She pulls me up when she rises and respectfully tugs my dress back into place. I look at the stiff cock between us. She's right. It would never fit in her tight uniform. She grabs her shirt and excuses herself.

I clean up the best I can in the small half bath off the kitchen. I'm warming dinner when she returns. "I pulled two bottles of wine for you to choose from."

Her shirt is tucked into her pants, and her sleeves are rolled up to her elbows. Her mussed hair gives her a carefree look, and I wonder how old she is, but I don't ask. We are already getting too familiar. She's the first woman who has visited my apartment, and I've lived here three years.

"I've been dying to try this one." She holds out the La Crema Monterey Chardonnay bottle after she reads the label. I got it for my birthday from somebody at the office several months ago.

"Sounds like a good choice. I've been waiting for an opportunity to open it," I say. I bring the plates to the table, and she follows with two glasses of wine.

"It smells delicious."

"It's from Tannin's Wine Bar. They make the best risotto and have the best wine selection in town. Have you ever been?"

She waits for me to sit before taking her seat. She has manners, and I find that sexy, too. "I haven't, but if the foods tastes as good as it smells, I'll have to go."

We're quiet during the first few minutes of the meal, which gives me time to study her. Despite being in an unfamiliar apartment and knowing me only a little over twenty-four hours, she screams confidence.

"You have a nice place here. The Plaza has always been one of my favorite places to hit. Great restaurants, nice bars, quality shops."

I'm one street south of the shops. I stop myself from telling her I'm moving to the garment district, where it's quieter, bigger, and less crime ridden. "Where do you live?"

"I have a house just on the other side of the river," she says.

North Kansas City, where Emery lives, is charming and very family oriented. My new neighborhood has a hipper vibe and is geared more toward single people or people who don't have children. "That's not too far away." My new place is closer to hers.

"What's it like being a judge?"

I could tell her about my nerves and how the case she testified on is my first case, but I don't. I take a sip of wine before I answer. "It's very rewarding. It's nice to be in control most of the time."

She smiles at me and takes a sip of wine, too. "You're very young to be a judge."

I've heard that a thousand times already, but I'm not offended. "It's been a hard, fast climb." My double entendre gets me a raised eyebrow and a toast from across the table. "Tell me about why you got into firefighting. I'm assuming you worked your way up to investigator."

"I enrolled in my high school's fire-science program and fell in love with it. There's so much science to fighting fires, and nothing beats the high of beating one or figuring out how it started."

"Nothing beats the high?"

"I have the utmost respect for powerful things. Fire, science, women, the law." She gently moves her plate to the side and leans forward to give me all her attention. "They all give me a high for different reasons."

Her phone beeps and she checks the message that pops up. I watch her eyebrows jump and her lips press together tightly. Her news isn't welcome. I pour myself more wine. She waves off the invitation for more.

"What were your plans tonight? Before you invited me over." She gently swirls the small amount of wine in the bottom of her glass. She is graceful, gentle, but I know she's capable of the roughness I need.

"Take a nice hot bubble bath and go over notes from today."

She stands and walks over to me. "Come with me." I reach for her hand, excited for what she has in store for me. She pulls me into the bathroom and plugs the bathtub before turning on the water. "Do you like it hot?"

"I like everything hot."

Her gray eyes bore into mine. "Tell me if you want it hotter."

I reach in front of her and put my fingers under the stream. "This is good." The thought of a bubble bath with her wasn't in my head at all, but visions of us in my jacuzzi tub make my pussy clench with anticipation.

I add a few drops of a vanilla and brown sugar soak. The water bubbles up. I feel her fingers searching for the pull of my zipper. She finds it and draws it down. I step out of the dress as it pools to the floor. I'm naked and she's dressed. She helps me into the water, and chills pop out all over me as my skin adjusts to the heat. My nipples are painfully hard, and the goose bumps only increase my discomfort. I throw my hair up in a bun. The movement makes my breasts thrust out. She makes a noise that resembles a sigh and a growl. It takes me a few moments to slip down into the water. I smile as the small bubbles cover my thighs and rest just under my breasts.

"You're amazing," she says. She doesn't take off her clothes but crouches beside the tub.

I lean back as the water rises to my back. "Thank you." I find myself slightly embarrassed as she looks me over under the stark bathroom light. She notices my wince at the brightness and lights several candles on the side of the tub. She flips off the overhead lights, and I smile at the instant, sexy ambiance of the room with a low, flickering glow.

She dips her hand in the water and runs her fingertips over my breasts. My eyes flutter shut at her touch. I'm surprised that I respond even though I'm exhausted. Her fingers flutter between my legs, and my knees fall open as I greedily accept her attention. Through slitted eyes, I see that her rolled-up shirt sleeve is getting wet. She finds my loofah and lathers it with a jasmine soap she locates in the caddy by the tub. She smiles at the scent, so I know she likes it. I file that discovery away in case we have another night like this one. She carefully bathes me. It's nice. I close my eyes and enjoy the path her hand takes. She washes my entire body, slowly, sensually.

I open my eyes when I hear the water drip off the loofah as she drapes the loop over the faucet and close them again when I feel her hand between my legs. She finds my clit and rubs it softly. The water ripples against my body as her hand picks up speed. I push my knees against the tub and wait as my orgasm builds. I open my eyes and watch little specks of water splash on her white shirt and her mouth slightly open when I start moaning my approval. Even though I'm sore and my clit is raw, I still come for her. After every orgasm I want to be fucked, and this time is no different.

"Where's my present?"

A look of surprise replaces her unguarded lust, and she crawls over to the gift bag she's left in here for me. I take the dildo from the bag and slip it under the water. She leans back against the wall and watches me. One of her knees is bent. She drapes her forearm across it as though she's completely relaxed, but I can feel her tense energy from here. I moan when the shaft pushes through my tightness. She moans, too. My knees are still raw from yesterday, and the soap stings my skin, but the soft non-slip mat in the bottom gives me some cushion. I kneel and, once it's completely inside me, grab the sides of the tub as the pleasure washes over me. She pulls the other knee up and wraps her arms around both legs. I can tell she likes watching me, so I give her a show. I run my hands over my breasts and squeeze my nipples so hard that I gasp. Her entire body twitches, but she stays where she is. I rock my hips and, every so often, slide off my new toy. My moans grow louder every time I slide it back in.

"Touch yourself," I say.

She doesn't hesitate and slides her pants off. She spreads herself so I can watch.

"You stopped," she says.

I am frozen watching her. She licks her forefinger and brings it down to her clit. I watch as she flicks it quickly and efficiently. She wants to come. "Wait for me." My voice is raspy, but I can't find the energy to clear it. I want to taste her. I want to be the one to make her come, but I'm thirty seconds from another orgasm, and I'm selfish. I pull the cock from the bathtub and sit along the edge of the tub with my legs spread. There isn't much room, and bottles of expensive shampoos and soaps splash into the water, but I don't care.

"Yes." She's loud, so I know she's close.

"Stop."

Her hand stops and she leans forward to catch her breath. Her eyes drift down to watch as I rub the head up and down until I'm relaxed enough to push it inside. I moan and pull it out.

"Fuck." She breathes the word out, and it's sexy.

I put one leg up on the side of the tub and do it again. It's not comfortable at this angle, but seeing how Emery is so affected by watching me, I keep doing it. She touches herself again. I hold the shaft inside me and mirror her movements against my own clit until she comes. She is quiet but jerks several times and leans heavily against the wall, gasping for breath. A short laugh escapes her lips.

"Wow."

"Come here," I say.

She pulls up her pants with haste and walks the two steps over to me. She takes the dildo from my hand and motions for me to get back into the water. I slide down and keep my knees apart and wait.

"Just when I think you can't get any sexier," she says.

I guide the dildo between my legs, and she pushes it into me. The water splashes over the sides, but I don't care. I arch my back into her thrusts and am overwhelmed again with how wonderful this feels. I don't want to come. I want to be selfish and make her fuck me longer, but my body betrays me, and my orgasm crashes down. I don't realize she's holding me up until I feel her long fingers pressing into my shoulder, steadying me. I plant both feet on the tub floor, and she releases me once she knows I'm not going to slip under. The water sloshes from my trembling body. I'm so tired.

She straightens her clothes and blots the floor with a towel. She kneels again after the floor is dry and kisses me. "I have to go. Thank you for an incredible evening. Enjoy the bath."

I run my fingers over her smooth, flushed cheek. "Thank you for accepting my invitation."

"Thank you for being so God damn sexy, Claire. I'll lock the door on my way out."

Chapter Five

I ache all over. I check my phone for messages. It's almost eleven, but still early enough to call Jenn, who has called me three times and sent seven texts.

"Where have you been? I called you twice."

I don't correct her. "I was busy getting laid." I sound tired.

"Ooh, by the hot, tall, sexy butch?"

"Yep. She was waiting for me in the courthouse parking lot when I left tonight, so I invited her over for dinner."

"In front of everybody? Are you nuts?" She hisses her questions through her teeth as though people around can hear her.

I sigh. "Give me some credit. No. I slipped her my business card with my address on the back." I crawl under the covers and get comfortable. I won't last long, and I have an early start tomorrow. "I just wanted to say I'm sorry for not calling you earlier. I was busy."

"Was she just as good today as she was yesterday?"

I smile. "Oh, I didn't think she could top yesterday, but she did."

"Let me settle in. Top yesterday, and go," she says.

"She brought me a present."

"Flowers? Oh, please don't say flowers. I'm going to be disappointed if you say yes. Or, worse, chocolates."

"Come on. That's so last decade. Or last generation. Or whatever." I wave her off as though she can see me. "Let me start over. I asked her to come over for dinner and to keep her sexy fire-inspector uniform on."

"Oh, the sexy uniform we saw on Instagram?"

"The very same. It's her formal dress uniform. Anyway, her uniform pants were so tight that she couldn't pack, so she gifted me a giant dildo."

Jenn claps. "That's brilliant. And she used it a thousand different ways, right?"

"My couch and the bathtub." My voice is smug and proud.

"The tub? How is that even possible?"

"Well, that was more me alone with her watching, but eventually she took over," I say.

"I'm so jealous."

"You shouldn't be. You're having sex like ten times a week. Emery is my first since Vegas."

"I'm jealous because you're always so creative sexually. And you aren't afraid of anything. I mean sex with O is really awesome, but you know how I am. I get comfortable with somebody and get bored."

Jenn's not wrong, but I recognize a difference in her this time. She wants to settle down. She's slipped into a life she's happy with, and I think Orlando is going to do everything he can to make her happy. She's a real catch. Smart, attractive, career-driven, fun, and classy. "You won't get bored. You haven't sounded this happy in a long time. Okay. I need to get to bed. I'm sore and tired, and this case is draining me."

"Kill it. Good night, Claire Bear."

"On it. Good night." I plug my phone in to charge. I need to get to my office by seven thirty. My first case is interesting for so many reasons. Aside from one of the witnesses being a hot butch who fucked me every possible way, I'm genuinely interested in why somebody would purposely burn down a warehouse and get caught. What were they hiding?

I got lucky to have this as my first case. There are enough questions to keep it from being cut and dry, but there don't seem to be any surprises either. Even though it's not a high-profile case, it's meaty enough that people are either jealous I'm hearing it or laughing at me since I'm so green and they think I'll fuck it up.

When the alarm goes off, I feel like I just got to sleep. I'm sore everywhere. I stretch for several minutes and drink a bottle of water. I should have done that before I fell sleep last night. I put on my black suit with a stylish sleeveless turtleneck sweater. It's the best I can do, given that the temperature outside is in the nineties. Emery marked my neck, and I can't cover it with makeup. I'll have to set guidelines for next time. If there is a next time. I'm not a next-time kind of woman, and last night sated my appetite. At least for now. I'm curious to see if I cross paths with her again, especially since we know how to get in contact if we want.

I pour a cup of coffee and grab my bag of notes I didn't review last night. Trust-fund baby Cassidy is dragging in from somewhere, and she looks wrecked. I lock my door and stop when I pass her in the hallway.

"Are you okay?"

She nods and holds her head. "Just a little bit too much last night. Ugh."

I'm thankful she didn't hear me last night. Our bathrooms share a wall. Sometimes I hear her singing in her shower. "Take aspirin and drink cold water before you get some sleep."

"Uh, thanks."

She slips into her apartment before I hit the elevator. I can't wait to move. Soon I'll be in my new place, where hopefully my new neighbors are closer to my age. I think I'm the oldest person on this floor.

The security line is short this morning. "Good morning, Judge Weaver."

I hand the officer my bag and take off the jewelry I put on twenty minutes ago. "Good morning, Wayne." He smiles at me because I'm the only one in line who knows him by name. He hands me my things and nods as I leave.

I have forty-five minutes before I have to slip into my robe and head to the courtroom. I pull out my notes, click my pen, and stare at the pages I wrote yesterday. Emery's name is doodled in the top right corner. Not only is it unprofessional, but also high-school-girlish. I cover it using a black Sharpie and flip to the next page. Visions of last night pop into my thoughts, and I shake my head to get rid of them, as if that's even possible. My sexual encounters with Emery have pushed me to a different level. It's one thing to meet a woman in a bar when we both know exactly what's going to happen. It's a whole different thing to meet a stranger in a museum, have sex in a public place, and not even know their name. It's decadent. It's dangerous. Emery has given me the biggest sexual high of my life.

"Judge Weaver? Court's in ten minutes."

April's voice through my intercom jars me back to reality. Where did the last forty-five minutes go? I clear my throat before I answer. "Thank you." I put on my robe and twist my hair up. When I open my door, April points to her lips. Shit. I nod and retreat to my office for a tissue to remove most of my lipstick. Old habits are hard to break.

"All rise."

The rest of the day flies by. It's like a tennis match watching the prosecution cycle witnesses in and the defense take a whack at their credibility. By the end of the day, I'm exhausted. I barely remember lunch. I can't imagine what the jury's feeling. I hang up my robe and look out my office window. Emery isn't there. Not that I expect her to be, but it's worth a check. I can't tell if I want to see her again or leave the entire thing a mystery. I remove my suit jacket and sit behind my desk. I have a feeling I'll get more done here than at home.

I'm overwhelmed. I've taken a break from reviewing case notes to box up anything personal that I don't want the movers to touch. I have only three empty boxes left and too many things. I've already packed my lingerie and most of my sex toys. The dildo Emery gifted me is on top in case I need a stress reliever this coming week, which is a high probability. This case is growing bigger by the witness. The prosecution surprised me last week. Their opening remarks were lackluster at best, whereas the skillful defense dropped doubt from the opening remarks. But the prosecution presented a solid case. And Emery's testimony was hard to refute. The defense asked a few questions that did nothing to discredit it. But starting tomorrow, they would have the floor.

The intercom at my front door buzzes. "Yes?"

"Ms. Weaver, it's Downtown Delivery."

Sunday dinner is angel-hair pasta with garlic and herbs from a small Italian restaurant not far from my apartment. I could have picked it up myself, but I'm too busy packing. I rarely cook, and I do it even less now that I'm in the middle of moving. I buzz the delivery person up. I'm expecting a pimply-faced teen. Instead, the delivery person is a man in his mid-thirties, dressed in slacks and a button-down shirt. Something's off about him. He's smug and entirely too confident to be a delivery person. I step outside my apartment and pull the door partially closed behind me.

"Ms. Weaver?" he asks.

I take a step toward him to let him know I'm not easily intimidated. "Yes. Thank you." My voice is crisp and dismissive.

"Oh, hey. That smells great," Cassidy says from down the hall.

Thank God for the trust-fund baby. She's headed out somewhere, but I draw her into conversation so I'm not alone with this guy. "Have you tried Brio's pasta? It's delicious. They have the best garlic bread. Plus, their drinks are amazing. You and your friends should go there." I hate digging for conversation, but she seems excited that I'm engaging her.

"We go there for drinks all the time. Hey, you should come with us one night," she says.

It's so hard not to roll my eyes at her, so I nod. "That sounds great."

Smarmy guy smirks and hands me the bag. I watch as he turns, slides his hands in his pockets, and looks around before getting into the elevator. I'm not letting Cassidy get in the elevator with him.

I point at her wrist. "I love your bracelet. Where did you get it?"

She looks down as if she doesn't remember what she put on tonight. "Oh, my parents got this for me for my birthday. It was last month. I think this is the one they gave me." She shrugs and smiles.

"Okay, well, have a good night. I'll see you around, and maybe we can all go out next weekend."

She gives me a tiny wave and heads to the elevator. Creepy guy is gone. I lock my door and deadbolt it. I dump the food right into the trash. I don't trust anything about that exchange. I find a yogurt and an orange to eat instead. Not as satisfying, but safer.

I call Jenn. "Can you talk, or are you busy?"

"We're just hanging out by the pool. What's going on? Are you all packed?"

"Just the essentials. The movers will pack everything else Saturday." I peel the orange and pop a slice into my mouth. "The weirdest thing just happened. Some guy just delivered my dinner, and he didn't seem like a delivery guy. Well, he didn't look or act like one. He was dressed for Sunday church," I say.

"Maybe he just came from church and is simply a dude trying to make extra money on the weekends."

"Wearing designer slacks and Allen Edmonds shoes?"

"You got that close?" Jenn asks.

"No. I don't know what he was actually wearing, but I know quality when I see it. That man didn't need a ten-dollar tip. It was just weird."

I hear children splashing in the pool. She must be at Orlando's. He has two children from a previous relationship. Jenn dropped that bomb on me last week. "Do you think it has something to do with the case?"

"The one I'm trying now?" I ask.

"No, well, maybe. I meant the pharmaceutical case. But could it be the one you're hearing now? Is it controversial?"

I can't divulge anything other than what's released to the press, and she knows that. "Not really. Just a guy who's accused of burning down a warehouse."

"Oh, maybe it's the mob, and he was hired to burn down the warehouse because it housed all their incriminating files or something sinister like that," she says. Jenn has the more overactive imagination of the two of us.

"First of all, I think the mob left Kansas City in the seventies. Sure, there might be a straggler here, but I doubt it. And second, don't scare me. You know I'm all alone here."

"I'm sorry. You need more friends." She's right. Most of our friends from law school got jobs elsewhere after we graduated. "What about anybody at your old law firm?"

"No. Everybody hates me because I landed the judgeship." Most of my so-called friends either wanted a handout or a boost. I didn't like any of them enough to give them either.

"Join a MeetUp group there in town. Or do it the old-fashioned way. Go to a bar. But not for the reason we normally go to a bar. Look for friends or get a hobby."

I hear the teasing in her voice. "I definitely need more friends here, but I just don't have the time and certainly don't have time for a hobby. Maybe once this case is over."

"You'll always have cases. Find something fun to do. Well, after you move. Hey, maybe some of your new neighbors will be awesome. Doesn't your new building have a coffee shop and a library? Didn't I see that in the link you sent me? And don't worry about that creepy guy. It's probably nothing."

I take a deep breath and sit on the couch. She makes a good point. The new place has a coffee shop, a theater, a health club, and a rooftop pool. I'm bound to find new friends there. "You're probably right. Let's move on. Tell me about you and Mr. Bloom."

She laughs. "He's here with me and says hello."

"Hello, Mr. Bloom." I raise my voice so he's sure to hear me.

"Hello, Judge Judy."

I playfully gasp. "Tell him at least I gave him a young famous person. He can make me younger." We go back and forth before I end the call. Jenn doesn't have a lot of free time, so I don't want to monopolize it. It's nice to hear the happiness in her voice though.

I pack the three boxes and stack them in the corner with the rest. I don't have a lot of things. It won't take them long to move me. Most of what I have packed is clothes. I'm donating a lot of the furniture. I want a fresh start at the new place. Restoration Hardware is delivering a new living-room set and a new one for the dining room this week. The concierge will let them into my new place with specific instructions on where to put everything.

I can't relax. I'm too antsy and can think of only one solution. I open the box I just packed and pull out the dildo Emery gave me. I find the lube and head to my bed. It's still light out, but I don't pull my blinds. I get comfortable on my bed and start by running my fingers up and down my slit. I smile and think of Emery on my bathroom floor touching herself. It's refreshing to find somebody as sexually free and unguarded as she is.

I'm already wet and still sore, but that doesn't stop me. I lie on the bed and bend my knees. The lube starts off cool but warms up quickly. My clit twitches with delight as I run my fingertip up and down the smooth, tight skin that's swollen and ready. The tip of the dildo slides through my folds, and I gasp as I sink the head inside myself. I pull it out before the stretching hurts. It's takes a few times of adjusting before I can push it farther inside. I moan loudly when my pussy takes all of it. I pull it all the way out and fuck myself until I'm frustrated. It's heavy and big, and I drop it several times.

My sex machine is packed away so I improvise. Since it has a suction-cup base, I stick it to the baseboard of my bed and back into it on my hands and knees. The carpet burns my still-sensitive knees, so I grab a pillow and kneel on the soft cushion. I relax and ease the dildo inside me. This is so much easier than trying to do it to myself. I start off slowly and move my hips back and forth. I want to touch my clit so I lean over and press my forehead on the carpet to free my hand. It's hard to do everything, so I build myself up by flicking my clit, and when the need to come is no longer avoidable, I push up so I'm on my hands and knees again. I move fast and hard against the shaft. When I come, I throw my head back and moan. I slide away and roll onto my back, gasping for air. My stress is gone, and I feel relieved. It really is the perfect gift and exactly what I need.

CHAPTER SIX

I give the jury their instructions and dismiss them to deliberate. It's Thursday, and I don't know how long it will take them. It seems like an easy case. As good as the defense was, the prosecution gave very little doubt. Mr. Seamus Williams, the defendant, was not only arrested near the scene, but the crime lab found turpentine—the accelerant identified by Emery and her superior—on his pants leg. His dismal bank account had a deposit of twenty thousand dollars that same night that he wouldn't explain. He's forty-four and has already spent ten years of his life in prison. In my courtroom, he looks like a middle-school math teacher. His mug shots tell a different story—unkempt, with angry eyes. I look up when I hear a knock at my door.

"Yes?"

April peeks her head in. "Judge Weaver? The jury is ready."

"Already?" I look at my watch. It's only been one hour and forty minutes. Even our practice mock-up cases were more complicated and took longer to deliberate. "Okay. Tell them I'm on my way."

I slip into my robe and wait for the bailiff to introduce me. The verdict comes back as everyone expects—guilty. I schedule a sentencing date, dismiss the jury and the court, and exit the courtroom. People in the hallway congratulate me on my first case. I nod, sometimes smile, and head back to my office. The feeling isn't what I expect. I hope that future cases are more exciting or can be settled and not take up time for a trial. I'm surprised Judge Tulver didn't push for a resolution. There aren't any notes in the files I was given. Nobody wants to go to court because of the time and money invested in prepping for trial. I'm just hoping for a break before the next one. I wonder how much of this mound of paperwork my staff can handle.

"April, can you come in here for a moment?"

She enters my chambers carrying a pad and a pencil. I'm surprised it's not a tablet.

"What can I help you with?"

"Processing this paperwork."

April takes the entire stack. "I'll grab Samuel, and we'll sort through this. I'll bring back what you're supposed to sign. Also, I've opened up your schedule for tomorrow. Looks like a full day. And there's mail in your inbox." She nods at the full tray on the corner of my desk.

"Thank you." I really hoped tomorrow would be easy, but after pulling up the schedule, I'm wrong. I groan and fall back in my chair. This is what I wanted, so I don't complain. I sift through my mail and open a fancy envelope addressed to me. It's a cocktail party at Kauffman Center for the Performing Arts thrown by the mayor in three weeks to raise money for Harvester's, Kansas City's local food pantry. The envelope is postmarked a week ago. I need to do a better job of keeping up on my mail. The paper is thick with embossed lettering. I haven't seen or felt a tangible party invitation in years. Just before I toss it in the trash, I remember how a few days ago I whined to Jenn about not having any friends. This might be a good opportunity to branch out. Cream-of-the-crop socialites and wealthy Kansas Citians attend these fund-raisers, and I miss dressing up. It's been less than two weeks, and I already loathe the drabness of the robe. I RSVP online and mark it on my calendar. Three weeks from Saturday. I'll be in my new place then, and my stress level will be lower. At least that's the plan.

❖

My new loft is even better than I imagined. The move goes off without a hitch. It takes three hours from pickup to final drop-off. The movers deliver what I don't want to a local women's shelter. Their services are worth every penny, and I promise to give them a great review on Yelp. I'm excited to unpack and get to know this building better. I couldn't pass up the open floor plan with twenty-four-foot exposed brick walls and large wooden beams. My new place feels like me. I review the instructions left in the welcome packet and decide to investigate the building first. I put on a light-blue summer dress with thick shoulder straps, refresh my makeup, and head to the lobby to grab a cup of coffee at The Early Bird even though it's early afternoon.

"Hi. What can I get you?"

Brandon, whose name tag is sideways on his chest, is friendly and talks to me while drawing a design in the cappuccino foam for the patron who placed her order before me.

"I'll take a medium iced hibiscus." I change my mind after seeing the tea on the menu.

"Do you want me to bill your unit, or would you like to pay now?"

That's a perk I wasn't expecting. "Bill me."

He nods, and while he finishes creating a leaf design in the froth of the cappuccino, I peruse the display window that houses muffins and bagels. There isn't a lot to choose from, but this isn't a place people come to lunch.

"Can I get you anything else?" he asks.

"No, thank you." Having a coffee shop in the building is going to make my morning commute a lot faster since I won't have to stop at the nearest Starbucks. Not to mention I'm only a few blocks west of the courthouse.

I study Brandon as he prepares my tea. It looks like he extended No Shave November into summer, with a curly beard that, even though I can tell he trims it, is still unruly and pokes the beard covering he's required to wear. "Thank you." I accept the to-go cup and the bill he hands me, which I add a tip to and sign.

"You're new. Welcome to the building, Claire," he says after reviewing my receipt and filing it away.

"Thank you, Brandon. It's nice to be here." I make my way to the elevators and take it all the way to the rooftop. I remember touring it months ago before I bought the loft, but it was raining and cool that day, so I didn't stay long. When the elevator opens, I walk out onto the rooftop terrace, and everything about it is magnificent. The view is incredible. I'm surrounded by tall buildings, but I can still see the Missouri river and at least three bridges that cross it. There are other rooftops I can see that aren't nearly as nice as this one. To my immediate left is a pool that a few people are using. Directly in front of me, a staircase leads up to a bar that doesn't open until four. I turn right instead, to visit the garden. I walk down rows of tall planters made of marble and run my fingertips over different blooming flowers whose names I don't know.

"Hi."

I look up and see an older woman not far from me, planting something in smaller pots near the edge of the building. She's wearing long sleeves, even though the sun is blazing down, and a hat that looks like a beekeeper's hat minus the veil. "Hello." I take a step back. "Are there bees around?" I've never been stung and certainly don't want today to be the first time.

"No, dear. I'm just protecting myself from the sun. I'm Helen. I haven't seen you here before."

"Hi. I'm Claire. I just moved in today. I thought I'd check out the building. This garden is gorgeous."

"Thank you. It's my pride and joy. My husband and I moved here a few years ago. We're both retired."

She looks at me expectantly, as if I'm going to return personal information. I oblige. I need to make new friends, and Helen seems friendly. "You're doing a great job. I have a horrible relationship with plants. As pretty as I think they are, I don't give them the attention they need. I'm sure I could pick up a few pointers from you." She smiles at the compliment. "Are you planting herbs?"

"Yes. We use a lot of them at the bar." She points her hand trowel at the bar above us. "Anyone who wants the herbs can take them, but most people don't feel comfortable picking them from the garden, so I leave bags of them downstairs in the foyer."

I'm sure baggies of herbs laying around don't raise any flags whatsoever. "That's good to know. I'll keep my eye out for them."

"If you have time now, I can show you around the building."

"That would be very nice. Thank you," I say. I can't remember where everything is, and Helen giving me the tour sounds like a great way to start this friendship.

"Obviously, the roof is my favorite place because there's the wonderful garden, a pool, a giant chess set, and the bar."

She wiggles her eyebrows at me after the word bar. I have a feeling Helen and I will have drinks together. As we make our way to the elevator, she tells me that rum is her favorite because it goes with so many of the herbs she grows, but she's never turned down a good local IPA. We stop at the fourth floor, and Helen shows me the state-of-the-art fitness room at the end of the hall.

"I only walk on the treadmill. The rest of the equipment is too complicated for me," she says.

The room is impressive, with mirrors to accentuate the already large space. There are five treadmills, three elliptical machines, three rowing machines, free weights, and leg-lift equipment. It's accessible by keycard twenty-four seven, which fits my unpredictable schedule perfectly.

"Let me show you the best place in this building," Helen says. She takes me down to the first floor and shows me where we have a small movie theater. The marquee displays a poster of a recently released superhero movie showing at five. I stick my head in and find sixteen theater-style seats, a couch, and four end tables. It's smaller than what I remember, but the screen is floor to ceiling, and I'm sure I'll sneak down here from time to time.

"You're either very early or still here from last night." A young woman interrupts our tour. She's wearing a polo with The Early Bird logo and shorts that hit right above her knee.

"Hi, Jane. I'm just showing our new tenant around. Meet Claire." Helen turns to me and squeezes my hand. "Jane can tell you more about the theater. I'm going to drop off the herbs at the front desk. If you need anything at all, I'm in 5C."

"Thank you for making me feel so welcome, Helen."

I turn to Jane after Helen leaves. "Does The Early Bird run the theater, too?"

"No. I just got off my shift there. I clean the theater for extra cash. The building office runs it."

"Do you like working here? In this building, I mean?"

"I love it. The tenants here are awesome, and it's close enough to school and my own apartment." She's shy and adorable.

"It's good to know the people here like it. What are you going to school for?"

"I'm studying Communications. I'm thinking law school after that," she says. She puts her cleaning supplies on the table. "My sister's in law school now, and she really enjoys it."

"Here in town?"

She nods. "She just started her final year."

"Impressive. UMKC's law school is a good school. I went there," I say.

"So, you're a lawyer," she says.

The door opens, and somebody bursts into the room as if they're on a mission. I take a step back out of instinct.

"Oops. Sorry for the interruption."

Her hair is the same brown as Jane's, only it's longer. They share the same features, but hers are more mature.

"You're not interrupting. We were just talking about you," Jane says.

"Yeah? About what?" She looks me up and down and smiles. "Hi. I'm Katie."

"I'm Claire. It's nice to meet you." Her handshake is firm and confident.

"Claire went to UMKC, too. She's a lawyer," Jane says.

"Actually, I'm a judge."

I see the wheels turning and surprise register on Katie's face. "I know you. You're Judge Weaver, right?" The energy in the room changes.

I nod and smile. I even throw in a slight eyebrow lift.

She walks up to me and shakes my hand. "It's so nice to meet you. You're a legend at school. Nobody's going to believe that I met you."

I've never been fan-girled before, and I like it. "Thank you. That means a lot to me." I put my hand on my heart to emphasize my appreciation of her words. I needed the boost.

She turns to Jane. "How long are you going to be?"

Jane shrugs. "Fifteen minutes?"

Katie turns to me. "Are you busy? Do you have time to chat for the next fifteen minutes?"

When it's about me and the law, I have time. "Sure. Want to go out to the lobby?"

Katie swoops her hand in front of her. "Please. Lead the way."

She follows me to the lobby, and we find two chairs close to the theater, but far enough away for privacy.

"Tell me everything," she says.

I laugh. "Can you narrow it down for me?"

She leans forward. "You shot straight to the top. How did you do it?"

"Motivation and determination. If you stay tenacious, you'll make all your dreams come true." She wants more. I've given several interviews, and normally, I'd blow her off, but I like her youthful energy. It reminds me of my own law-school days. "I studied hard, and I took the cases nobody wanted. I went with my gut. Deep down I knew something was wrong with MedPharmo. I gave up two years of my life for that case."

"Do you regret it?"

I shake my head. "It was the best thing I've ever done. That's why I went into law. I wanted to be a voice for people who didn't have one." It's a canned answer, but it still packs a punch.

"That's amazing, and now you have your own courtroom. What do you like better? Being on the bench or in front of it?"

I tell her vaguely about my first trial. Her questions are genuine and make me feel respected. It's nice. When Jane finds us, Katie groans.

"I'm so sorry to have to cut this short. It's so nice to meet you." She reaches for my hand and holds it more than she shakes it.

"Thanks for keeping my sister company," Jane says.

"It was entirely my pleasure. You both have made my first day here fun."

"Do you mind if I get a photo with you?" Katie asks. "I won't put it on social media."

"Definitely."

Katie hands her phone to her sister. "Make it a good one."

She's slightly shorter than I am, but I'm wearing heels, and she's wearing sandals. I put my arm across her shoulders. "Is this okay?"

"Yes." Her smile is infectious, and I know the photos are going to be good.

Jane snaps a few shots and hands the phone back to Katie, who immediately looks at them and beams. "They're perfect. Thank you again, Judge Weaver."

"Call me Claire. And anytime. You know how to find me. As a matter of fact, here's my business card. Call or email me with any questions you have or if you need help with anything." I write my personal email address on the back.

"I will. Thank you."

I watch as she carefully slips my business card into her purse. They both wave to me on their way out. I think I'm going to like living here. Not only is it chock full of fantastic luxuries, but I might have just made some new friends.

CHAPTER SEVEN

Kauffman Center is less than a mile south of where I live. I take a Lyft anyway because I want a glass or two of champagne, and no way will I walk that far alone wearing three-inch heels.

Inside the entrance is a table of women checking in guests. "Welcome to Harvesters' fund-raiser. Can I please get your name?" one of them says.

They want me to wear a name tag? I look at my dress. It's somewhat conservative for me, but I'm not sure where a name tag will go. "Claire Weaver. And any suggestion on where I should wear it?"

One of the ladies walks over to me and, after trimming the tag, gently pins it where the shoulder strap and the fabric of the dress meet. She taps it in place and steps back to admire the results. "There. I think that'll work." She returns to her seat eager to help the next people in line.

I smile in thanks and enter Brandmeyer Grand Hall in search of the nearest bar. A waiter stops me and offers me champagne instead. I thank him and take a crystal flute from his tray. The schedule on the pamphlet says I have about twenty minutes before the mayor addresses us. The room is getting crowded, and I'm starting to bump into people. I work my way over to look out of the floor-to-ceiling windows to admire the setting sun. I'm not being social at all, but it's nice to be out of my robes.

"Claire. What are you doing here?" Kevin McIntosh approaches me with big smile and an attractive blonde clinging to his arm. He shakes my hand and introduces me to his wife, Daphne. She pastes on a fake smile, and her hand instantly goes limp the moment we shake. I give her hand a quick squeeze before dropping it.

"It's so nice to finally meet you. Kevin has had nothing but wonderful things to say about you and your boys," I say.

Daphne gives me a slight smile and grabs a drink from a passing waiter. "Funny. Kevin hasn't mentioned you before."

I raise my eyebrow at Kevin, who slightly shrugs. "We went to judicial training together. There were a lot of people there," I say. I want to lean closer and tell her he's not my type and that she has a better chance with me, but I choose to remain courteous and professional.

"I see you tried your first case," Kevin says, changing the subject.

"Yes. It was pretty fast and went just like they taught us."

"You're a judge?" The amount of judgment and disbelief in Daphne's voice makes me laugh out loud.

"Yes, I am. That's how I know your husband." I literally just told her we went to training together. I dismiss her by turning to face Kevin. "Do you attend a lot of fund-raisers?"

"More than my share." He chuckles at his little joke and smiles sweetly at his wife. "Daphne is very involved in the community, and I do what I can to support her and her causes. Also, my parents are here, and they always strongly encourage me to attend. You never know who's going to show up." He looks around the room. "You should meet my parents. They would love to meet the lawyer who took down Big Pharma."

"Well, I didn't take them down, but I did knock them down a drug or four." I went after MedPharmo for two drugs, but they ended up taking four off the shelf.

It can't hurt to meet Kevin's parents. They don't practice anymore, but they still know a ton of judges, lawyers, and other influential people. I can almost feel Kevin's wife's hatred for me at his suggestion. He waves them over after he spots them in the growing crowd.

"Mother, Father, meet Claire Weaver. Claire, these are my parents, Aubrey and Reginald McIntosh."

Kevin's father is dashing. It's not a word I use a lot, but for some reason he reminds me of a lord or duke from a regency historical romance. His mother is beautiful, and even though she's outwardly relaxed, I can tell she's studying me intently. The next few seconds just might determine if we become friendly or not. I already know Reginald is on the Claire train, just by his welcoming body language and slightly lecherous grin. Aubrey is a different story.

"So, you're the David who took down the giant."

Like that wasn't every headline for weeks as the story of my win traveled the globe. "Something like that, only whoever the female version is."

She pauses and tilts her head back and laughs. "Figuratively speaking, but my apologies. I know women aren't given enough kudos for what we've done in this world. Congratulations. A truly remarkable feat. And congratulations on your judgeship. I'll be keeping an eye out for you."

"It's nice to meet you both."

We spend the next few minutes discussing other big Kansas City cases. I can tell they're impressed with my knowledge. Meanwhile, Kevin's wife is gulping down her second flute of champagne. He won't have a good night. I decide to excuse myself but not before I give Aubrey my business card. I haven't passed a lot of them out, but tonight I came with a handful.

"Find me later, and I'll introduce you to the mayor," she says.

Something about her is professionally exciting, and I make a mental note to take her up on her offer. The mayor is new this term. I follow him on Twitter and Instagram, so I know a little about him.

I meet other people who pique my interest, including the marketing director for Harvesters, the group we're there to support. She's confident, fresh, and queer. My sexuality never comes up, but hers does, and she can't keep her eyes off me. I feel like she's an option if, at the end of the evening, I'm up for drinks elsewhere.

"Ladies and gentlemen, can I have your attention, please." The event organizer says a few words to quiet down the hall and introduces our mayor.

Sterling Moore jumps up on the makeshift stage as though he's fun and friendly, even though I saw him on a heated phone call just a few minutes ago. "Kansas City has always been my hometown," he says. "After I went away to college, I came home after I graduated because I knew I wanted to make a difference here. This is a place I've always believed in. Our community takes care of one another. We step up when our neighbors need help or our children need safer schools." He takes a break, as if pondering what to say next, when we all know he's memorized this speech to death. He looks over the crowd and makes eye contact with several people. "We provide shelter for the people who don't have homes, and we feed people who are less fortunate. Harvesters has been around for over forty years and has fed thousands of people in our community. So, I encourage you to donate what you can. Money, food, your time. You'll find donation stations around that accept credit cards. I'm donating ten thousand dollars tonight. Imagine if we all did that." He pauses for effect and looks over the crowd. "Imagine if every single person here donated ten thousand dollars and what that would do for our food pantries across our great city." He motions for somebody to climb on stage with a Square so he can make his donation very public. I have a feeling our new mayor already has Kansas City in his rearview mirror on his way to Washington.

I applaud, as expected, and line up to donate. I chat with an older couple in front of me in line. She compliments my skin and my dress and says I'm Marilyn Monroe with dark hair. Her husband is smiling at me, but respectfully his eyes never leave my face. I tell them to stay adorable and take a moment to regroup. I look out at the Kansas City skyline and smile at all the lights that have flickered on since night fell.

"You moved." Emery's voice startles me and excites me at the same time. The commanding smoothness sends a warm rush over me, and I stifle a shudder at the instant heat. I put my hand to my throat and turn to find her standing two feet away.

It takes me a few moments to slip into my cool self. "I did." I squelch the need to smile because she thought of me enough to visit. "I'm sorry. It didn't occur to me to tell you."

Her eyebrows jump, and she takes as step back. "Oh. I'm sorry." I reach out to stop her retreat. "No, not like that. I just wasn't sure where we stood on things." I'm not about to give her some lame excuse about not having her phone number, even though it's true, because it's the twenty-first century, and anybody can be found.

She takes a step toward me. "How have you been?" Her dark-gray suit is tailored perfectly. The white shirt underneath makes her tan pop. I'd forgotten how tall she is, even though I'm wearing three-inch heels. I wonder if she just arrived. My gaze roams her body appreciatively. I feel like I haven't seen her in ages, when it's been less than a month.

"Still adjusting to my new life. I'm surprised to see you here," I say.

She points her glass of whiskey at several suits huddled over a tall bar table. "These guys dragged me out, and I'm forever thankful they did. Remind me to buy them the next round."

"Are you leaving me already?" I fold my arms in front of me to stop myself from touching her. The need is strong.

"Definitely not. I finally found you."

Her eyes are bright and are focused solely on me. I normally run from women when they give me that look, but the exact opposite is happening. I'm not done with Emery. I explode with desire at her obvious lust and take a step back. "You need to stop looking at me like you're going to rip my dress off right here."

"Something tells me you might enjoy it."

I turn around to gaze out the window again. She moves to the side of me so that she's staring at my profile, but I don't even glance at her. "I'd love that."

"How long do you have to stick around?" she asks. I watch as she brings the glass up to her lips and swallows. A tiny bit of whiskey is left on her mouth when she pulls the glass away. I want to suck her lip, taste it, taste her.

"I have an introduction with the mayor whenever the circle around him dies down, so I don't know how long I have to be here."

"Have you been to the Kauffman Center before?" she asks.

"I have season tickets to The Kansas City Symphony."

"Have you been inside all the halls?"

I smile when I realize she's trying to get me somewhere private. "It's probably quieter in Helzberg Hall, but I think the ratio of attendees to attendants is two to one. Our chances of sneaking off without getting caught are slim."

"Since when do you shy away from a challenge?"

"Since I became a judge."

She takes a step closer. My body blossoms at her nearness. "The same judge who touched a Rubens?"

I nod.

"The same judge who," she pauses and lowers her voice, "let me fuck her in a museum?"

I nod. "And a kitchen, bathtub, and couch."

She holds up two fingers. I tilt my head, and my brows furrow as I try to figure out what that means. "Two couches."

I laugh and blush, remembering the chaise lounge at the museum, and automatically place my hand on her forearm. That simple touch sends chills over me. She notices.

"How about that walk?" Her eyes dip down to my cleavage, and I can feel my nipples harden under her gaze. I have never responded to somebody physically like this before. She leaves me breathless and hasn't even touched me.

"I'll go first." I leave her and work my way slowly around the room. Two attendants are standing in the hallway that leads to the mezzanine and the orchestra levels. I just need to get inside one of the doors without them noticing. The museum was easier to sneak around in because fewer people were standing guard. I walk around the small gift shop until I can sneak through the side door behind them. I open the first door and slip inside. Only the stage is lit. It takes a few minutes for my eyes to adjust, but I find a seat in row N and wait. I know she'll come for me.

I hear a door behind me, but I don't turn. Her fingertips on my bare shoulders make me jump a little.

"I didn't mean to scare you." Her voice is raspy.

I lean my head to the side, and she places a soft kiss on my neck.

"You smell delicious and taste even better."

I moan as her lips move to my shoulders and her fingertips graze the sensitive skin of my breasts. I've missed her touch. "We're in the open here. Do you want to find a more private place?" I ask. When I look up at her, she leans over and kisses me. It's an upside-down kiss and the sexiest one I've ever had. I slide my hand up her neck to hold her close. It's a passionate yet tender moment. When we break the kiss, I stand. She waits for me in the aisle and reaches for my hand when I get close. She's warm and strong. With my hand in hers, she points to a dark corner over by the stage.

"It's really dark, so watch your step."

She pulls me closer the farther into the shadows we walk. She stumbles over a heavy wooden chair in an alcove by an exit near the stage. It's the perfect place. She checks the door, and it's locked.

"I think we'll have privacy here."

"Come here," I say.

She walks flush against me until my back is pressed against the wall. I sigh as her body molds against mine. I'm surprised by the tenderness in her kiss. I need more, so I deepen it and slip my hands under her suit jacket to pull her even closer. Her moans make my pulse race and my body swell with need.

She sits on the chair she tripped over and pulls me onto her lap. She's warm and wearing the cologne I love. "You always smell wonderful."

"Finding you here is the highlight of my night. Of my week. Of my month. Where did you run off to?" She runs her fingertip down one cheek and up the other.

"I moved to the garment district."

"I was sad that I couldn't find you."

I didn't want to think about what her words mean. This is normally the time I walk away from women because it's easier. But I want her this night. "You have my number. You could have called me or messaged me."

"I'm not clingy," she says.

Her words don't have a bite, but they hit the mark. I run my thumb over her lip and wait until she looks at me. "I never said you were. I think we both know what this relationship is and are okay with it. We both enjoy sex without attachment. Neither one of us has time to date."

"That part's debatable, but I do really enjoy sex with you." She runs her fingers down the vee in my dress and cups a breast. My nipple hardens under her touch. My breath hitches.

"Bite it."

Without hesitation, she frees my breast and sucks as much of it into her mouth as she can. When I feel her teeth graze the delicate nipple, I dig my nails into her shoulders. My legs automatically spread. I need her between them. I slide my dress up the best I can while sitting on her lap. She enters me swiftly, and I grow limp as pleasure overtakes me. I growl my approval and bite her earlobe as she moves inside of me.

"You know exactly what I want and how I want it," I whisper.

"You're all I think about," she says right before kissing me. She sucks my bottom lip into her mouth and scrapes her teeth along the smooth surface of my skin. Her skillful fingers fuck me, alternating between slow and fast. It's hard for me to catch my breath. "Shh. I think somebody's here." She stills her hand, and we both listen. "I think they're right above us."

Their voices grow louder, but instead of stopping and sneaking out, Emery keeps fucking me. I bite my lip to keep from crying out. Their nearness only intensifies the decadence of the moment.

"Don't come," she whispers in my ear.

I stop a moan from bubbling up. "I'll try, but you're so good at…" I pause breathlessly. "Good at me." I don't know if I should be embarrassed at my candor, but it's the truth. Her face is so close that I can hear her smile in the dark.

"We need to rethink the color scheme in the living room. Red fabric with blond wood is so European. I don't think I like it. We don't want our sitting room to look like a theater."

A seat rocks back directly above us in the mezzanine section. A woman with a distinctively nasal voice sits, then stands, then sits again as though she's testing the furniture. Several voices murmur in agreement. They must be important if they're unaccompanied in the theater heavily guarded by soccer moms and retirees who take their jobs very seriously. Their presence twelve feet above us doesn't deter Emery. Her hand continues to move inside of me, faster this time, as if challenging me to stay quiet. I stop her hand and readjust so I'm straddling her. She has full access to my pussy. One hand slides up behind my neck and holds me in place. I keep my mouth closed in case I moan or make any noise. She might be quiet during her orgasms, but I'm not. I move my hips against her hand, knowing that the moment I want to come, I will. The second I hear the voices recede and an exit door close, I grab the lapels of her jacket, throw my head back, and come. I am surprisingly quiet.

"Fuck, fuck, fuck," she whispers.

"We just did." I kiss her.

She laughs. "I wonder if they heard you."

I press my fingers to her mouth. "You aren't as quiet as you think." I can barely see her, but I think she's blushing. She leans her sweaty forehead against mine.

"You're just so damn sexy that it's hard not to moan with you."

I slide off her lap, but she grabs my hand and pulls me to stand between her legs. She places a kiss on my cleavage after I straighten my dress. I drop to my knees and run my hands along her thighs. "Do I have time to return the favor?" I don't want to assume she's okay with it.

She leans forward and kisses me. "Probably not. It takes me a little longer." She helps me up and pulls me into her arms. She's strong and feels safe.

"There's always my new place later. I'm just a mile up the road." I mean it, but I'm also nervous at how willing I am to have her over. Desperate has never been a word in my vocabulary, but that's how I feel.

"Why don't you meet the mayor, and I'll ditch my friends and come over later?" She brings my hands up to her lips and kisses them. It's sweet. "Let's figure out a way to sneak out of here before we get caught." She kisses me one last time and leads me to an unlocked door. She peeks out. "Coast is clear. Why don't you go first?"

I know walking out together isn't wise. I'm a judge, and so many people know that. My discretions have to be that—discreet. "Good idea." I walk up the hallway and duck into the bathroom to check my makeup and dress. Strands of my hair have come loose, and I take a few moments to re-pin them. I touch up my lipstick and check my body for marks. Thankfully, I have none.

"Oh, there you are, Claire. I've been looking for you. Are you ready to meet Sterling?" Aubrey touches my elbow to get my attention.

"Certainly. Thank you so much for taking time out of your night to introduce us. I appreciate it." I follow her to where Mayor Moore is talking with Kevin and his bitchy wife. She rolls her eyes at me.

"Here she is. Judge Claire Weaver, the muscle who took down MedPharmo a few notches."

Mayor Moore takes my hand and smiles at me. "It's a pleasure to meet you, Judge Weaver."

"Claire, please."

"Sterling."

Although he's very charming and delightful, he feels off to me. Maybe it's because he has to be on point all night, and I'm meeting him at the end of the evening.

"Looks like we have a lot in common," he says. I look at him questioningly. "We both want justice for the people in our community. That's what I'm talking about."

I see Kevin's wife roll her eyes again, and this time I don't blame her one bit, but I play the game.

"That's why I'm still in Kansas City. I like our town. It's my home," I say.

"If you're interested in talking out some ideas, just call my office, and we can meet up," he says.

I can tell he's interested in me. He stands a little too close, and maybe that's the politician in him, but I need to tell him the feeling isn't mutual. I take a small step back. He nods as if he understands. "I'll definitely give you a call. Thank you for your time." I turn to Kevin's parents. "Thank you so much for this evening. Good to meet you both. Kevin, I'll see you at the courthouse." I nod to his wife, who has returned her attention to the now-empty glass. I can tell he needs to get her home sooner than later. Kevin's too nice for that bullshit, especially in public.

The mayor looked very cozy with you.

I smile at the text. Even though it's just a phone number on my screen, I know who it's from. I add Emery Pearson to my contacts. Now I have her number. I look around the room until our eyes meet. Her pants have a wet spot from when she fucked me on her lap.

Did you spill your drink?

Emery looks down and shrugs. She's not embarrassed. I'm not even blushing.

I'm headed out soon. Here's my address.

I order a Lyft and leave through a side door when the car arrives to avoid having to walk by her. If I do, people will surely know.

CHAPTER EIGHT

I light a few candles and wait for Emery. I take a quick shower and slip into a silky robe and loosely tie the sash.

I'll be there in five.

I'll open the wine. Or do you prefer a whiskey?

What kind of whiskey do you have?

I have a Bushmills twenty-one-year-old malt that a client gifted to me.

I love new things. See you in a few.

It's ten on a Friday night. I'm good to go for at least three more hours. I leave word with the doorman that Emery Pearson is on her way to see me. They will let her up. Ever since that creepy guy showed up with my food, I'm hesitant to just leave my door open. I wait for her to knock.

She's wearing dark jeans and a navy button-down shirt that shows off her toned arms. "You changed," I say.

"So did you."

She reaches for the sash of my robe and pulls me toward her for a kiss. I drag her inside and break the kiss, only to lock the door behind us. "We don't want another incident where a delivery person sees more of me than they should."

"We made his night for sure."

"I only want to make one person's night," I say.

"I believe you've already done that."

She picks up the bottle of whiskey and gives a low whistle. "The amber color is gorgeous. May I open this?"

"Definitely. I'll have a sip as well." Whiskey isn't my drink, but maybe I need to branch out more. Emery tasted delicious when she drank it earlier tonight. Watching her appreciate the liquor is delightful. She smells it, holds it up to the light, and looks at the bottle as though it's a work of art.

"Is there a noticeable difference between an eighteen-year-old whiskey and a twenty-one-year-old whiskey?" I ask.

"It's not your drink of choice?" She looks at my impressive selection.

"No, but people I know seem to enjoy it. Most of them are from clients." I pointed to the first bottle I received from a client after we won his case. I tell Emery a quick history behind every bottle lined up on the bar.

"As a judge, your memory must be astounding." She pours two fingers and hands it to me. It's more than I want, but I take it from her hand.

"As a lawyer, it's more impressive."

"I stand corrected," she says.

She pours herself the same amount and joins me on the couch. I'm not covering up very well, and my breasts are a few deep breaths from popping out of the robe. She notices but sips her drink as though I'm fully dressed and we're having a simple conversation about the weather.

"This is fantastic whiskey. Thank you for inviting me to your new place, which is gorgeous, by the way. All new furniture and decor. It fits you."

"Thank you. I'm sorry I didn't tell you I was moving."

She shrugs. "I get it. I know what I am to you."

That confuses me. "What do you mean?"

Her gray eyes roam my face and drop to my cleavage and exposed legs. "I'm somebody you like to have sex with. That's it."

"Sex is fantastic with you, Emery. I enjoy our chemistry and how you're able to get me to do things I've only ever dreamt of doing, but neither one of us has time for complicated relationships," I say. I take the glass from her hand and set it on the table, my meaning clear. I want to fuck. She's here to fuck me, and we both know it.

"Is anything off-limits for you? Sexually? Is there anything you don't want me to do?"

I purse my lips as though I'm seriously thinking about the question, when I already know she can do anything she wants with me. "No."

Where's the present I gave you?" She quirks her eyebrow at me, and I shiver with excitement.

"Upstairs. Come on up. I'll show you." She follows me upstairs and into my closet but doesn't touch me, which I find odd.

"Your closet is the size of one of my bedrooms."

"It's a bit much, but apparently I needed it." I look at my closet as though seeing it for the first time. My wardrobe is excessive, my shoe collection even worse. I pull open a drawer full of dildos. Emery looks over my shoulder and gives a low whistle.

"Wow. I'm officially impressed and feel somewhat inadequate." She holds up a dildo larger than the one she gifted me. "Do you use all these?"

"Since I've met you, only the one you gave me, although it's hard to use on myself. I should try it on my sex machine."

I hear her swallow loudly behind me. "You have a sex machine? I didn't think that was a real thing."

I smile at her. "Oh, it's a real thing for sure, and not just found in porn."

She finally touches me. "Maybe we can play with that sometime."

"Only if I can watch you use it." I smile so she knows I'm joking.

She laughs hard. "Um, no. I was thinking more like watching you."

"Next time. Tonight, I want you to fuck me. In a bed this time. Like normal people."

"I don't think there's anything normal about us." She grabs the dildo and excuses herself to the bathroom.

I grab my favorite lubricant and shut off the lights. I open the blinds and crawl into bed. The buildings around me illuminate the room enough to create a sexy ambiance. The silence inside the room is perforated with faint honks from cars down below. When she comes out of the bathroom, she's wearing black boxer briefs that bulge and a white sports bra. I get chills just looking at her gorgeous physique. She's perfect in shape, toned, and tan, and she's all mine for the evening. I try to think of something witty to say but fall short. I reach out and bring her down to me. She doesn't kiss me even though I want her to.

"Roll over."

"Mm. Anything you want."

She pulls off my robe while I turn over. She throws it onto the floor but keeps the sash. I breathe out. I love being tied up. Emery spreads my legs apart with her knees and lies on top of me. I feel the dildo through her boxers run along my ass and down to my pussy. The movement is so hot and I'm so ready for her to fuck me, but she takes her time. I lift my hips every time the head teases my opening. She pushes hard, and I grab the covers with my fists as I imagine her fucking me.

"What do you want, Claire?"

I don't have to be quiet here. I haven't heard my neighbors at all, not even voices unless they're in the hallway.

"I need you inside of me. Fast and hard." She feels so good on top of me. Her hands grab my wrists, and she holds me down. I wonder if she's going to tie me up, and I sigh disappointedly when I feel her weight leave me. I wiggle my ass, looking for friction, and am rewarded with a stinging spank. That's a first for us. She soothes the burn with the palm of her hand.

"Was that okay?"

I exhale sharply and search for words, but I can only nod. I smile when I feel her lips on the red mark I'm sure is there. "Definitely." I feel her weight shift on the mattress and hear the snap of the lubricant lid. My pulse jumps at the sound. "I'm so ready." I've missed this dildo. I've missed being fucked. She gently pulls my hips up. "I wish we could have done this earlier," she says.

She slides the head up and down along my slit. I push into her, but she holds my hips in place. I can't move. Only she can. I lean up so I'm on my hands and knees. Patience isn't my thing right now, and she knows it. She pushes slowly into me and waits for me to adjust to the size. The angle takes my breath away, and I concentrate hard to relax my pelvic muscles. The lube warms, and once I feel stretched out enough, I press into her to let her know I'm ready. She rubs my back. Her hands feel smooth and strong on my skin. Her touch feels intimate, and I'm surprised that I feel something besides lust. The softness of the moment fades as she sinks into me. I gasp and open my eyes. My bed overlooks my entire living space and downtown. This is now my favorite place to have sex.

"Yes, Emery." It's the first time I say her name during sex, and I don't know why. This is supposed to be no-strings-attached sex.

"Do you like this?" She is moving slowly, just the way I like it. I nod. She knows that I do. But she knows what I like more.

I moan when she pulls all the way out and yell when she pushes all the way back in. She knows my sounds by now and does it again and again. I can tell she needs to come. Her body's vibrating, and she's making noises I haven't heard before. She's always been so quiet. Tonight, she's vocal, and that intensifies my experience. I move with her, and we both climb closer and closer. My pussy is drenched, which allows Emery to get in deeper. We both come at the same time. It's glorious to hear her shout out her orgasm while I'm exploding with pleasure. She pulls out of me and falls on the bed next to me. I sink slowly onto the bed, completely sated.

"That was perfect," I say. A thin line of sweat beads along her hairline and dampens her temples. I want to wipe it away, but I am too exhausted to lift my hand.

"I never thought I'd use that again," she says.

I turn my head. "Why?" She shrugs and runs her hand through her hair. I notice a few tiny gray hairs right above her ear and run my fingers over them. "How old are you?"

She laughs hard and it shakes the bed. "How old do you think I am? And why would you ask me that right now?"

"I was just thinking that I don't know a lot about you."

"We're doing this all backward. You know, people usually date first, then have sex," she says.

"We don't want that. This arrangement works for both of us."

"Oh, this is an arrangement? And this is what I want? You know what I want?"

"You always know what I want." The comment falls flat, and I feel the tension in her grow. I've struck a nerve, and there's no way around it. It's as if she's a different person. One minute she seems to be okay with a sex-only relationship, but the next she's acting like I just broke up with her.

"What do you really want, Claire? I mean, I like fucking you, but you have to want something out of this other than sex. I mean, you have a sex machine. What do you need me for?"

She's starting to get worked up, and I have no idea where it's coming from. I've triggered something. Her stomach tenses when I touch her, so I tread lightly. "I really enjoy our relationship." I stutter over the word relationship because that implies more than I can give. "I'm just not in a place where I can offer anybody anything other than this." The corners of her mouth twitch down and finally relax.

"I'm not asking for anything," she says.

I'm sure she's lying. "I think you are." I always know when women I hook up with start getting attached. They tell me they want simple, but inevitably they start developing feelings, and I'm not that girl. I like Emery. We have a lot of fun together. "What's wrong with just being women who like to have sex together?" We lie there quietly, and even though I stroke her arm and move closer to her, I can feel her pull away. That was the wrong thing to say. She sits up slowly.

"I should go."

"Come on. Please don't go. Let's talk through this."

"There's nothing else to discuss."

I sigh. "Okay, I understand."

She slips into the bathroom and I find my robe and tie it tightly with the sash I find tangled in the sheets. I no longer feel sexy. I feel sad. When she comes out of the bathroom, she's back in her jeans and shirt and doesn't look me in the eye. She leans her shoulder against the wall and when she finally faces me, she's fierce.

"Claire, I find you fascinating and intriguing. You're smart, beautiful, we both love our careers, and our sexual appetites are the same. I'm not looking for a relationship either, but I want to get to know you better. Who you are, what you like, what your hobbies are, and just little things about you. What's wrong with that? What's wrong with us pursuing something that might be there, even if it's just a casual relationship?"

"I haven't had a relationship in a long time because work has always been my life. I just started this job and want to be really good at it. I simply don't have time to date right now." I hate that I'm repeating myself, but she's several steps ahead of where I am or want to be.

"Thanks for the whiskey. I enjoyed trying something new." She slips on her shoes without tying them and stops in front of the door. "And just so you know, I'm thirty-five."

I stare at the closed door for several long seconds, expecting Emery to come back, but she doesn't. I throw my hands up in frustration.

CHAPTER NINE

The mayor is on line one for you."
April's voice startles me. I'm busy working on Seamus Williams's sentence, reviewing the pre-sentencing investigation for what feels like the thousandth time. With a record like his, the sentence is going to lean on the heavy side. Rehabilitation isn't working for him. After a five-year stint for armed robbery, he was thrown back in for twenty-seven months for a previous arson charge and then three years for sexual assault. The most I can give him is fifteen years, and honestly, I want to do that.

"Sterling. How are you?"

"I'm great. How are you?"

We exchange pleasantries. I hate small talk, so I move my hand in a circle as if we're in person and he can see that I want him to hurry up and get to the point. However, in real life, I'm not that rude.

"Do you have time for a quick lunch today?"

I wonder if he knows I'm not in court. He has to or else he wouldn't be so cavalier about going to lunch in the middle of the week.

"Sure. Where are you thinking?"

"How about The Providence? In an hour? They have great food."

It's close but not within walking distance. Thankfully, I'm pretty sure they have valet. "Sounds great. I'll see you there."

I'm confused. What does the mayor want with me? I'm too busy to attend a lunch, but nobody turns down the mayor. I'm visiting

Jenn and Orlando this Labor Day weekend, so I'm staying late every night this week getting through motions and reviewing upcoming cases. I have meetings with two lawyers tomorrow and am at a point where I think all parties can come to an agreement and not go to trial. I take two more pages of notes before my phone alarm dings, telling me it's time to meet Sterling. I grab my suit jacket and head to the parking lot. When I approach my SUV, it seems off balance.

"What the fuck?" My front tire is flat. I quicken my step out of panic, even though what I see is true. I kick the rubber out of frustration and glance at my watch. I can't have it changed and still get to lunch on time.

"Oh, flat tire? That sucks." A lawyer I've seen around the courthouse is standing behind me. She's pretty, if a little on the thin side.

"It really does." I glance at the time again and sigh.

"Can I give you a ride somewhere, Judge?" she asks.

"No, thanks. That's sweet of you to offer."

"Everything okay here?" I turn to find Kevin idling behind me in a silver sedan.

"Yep. I just have a flat." I scowl at my misfortune. "I'll have to call the car company after lunch."

"Hop in. I'll give you a ride," Kevin says.

"I already offered. She said she's okay," the pretty lawyer says.

Kevin looks at me and sees my discomfort. "It's okay. We're going to lunch at the same place."

I smile at the lawyer. "He's right, but thank you for checking to make sure I was okay."

"Of course." She waves at Kevin and continues to her car.

I walk to Kevin's car. "Thanks for that. I didn't want to be rude, but it didn't seem appropriate either."

"Of course. I'm just glad I saw you here. Where are you headed?"

"You really don't need to give me a ride."

"It's not a problem. Get in."

"Okay. Just around the corner to The Providence, if you don't mind."

"Not at all. Let me throw this stuff in the back." He gathers a stack of files from the front seat, not seeming remotely embarrassed by the mess.

"Thanks so much." I could've asked April or Samuel to drive me and only be a few minutes late, but this way I'll get there on time. The entire drive takes four minutes. We spend the time discussing his docket.

"I'd pick you up, but I'm not going back to the courthouse today," he says.

"Trust me, this has been a lifesaver. Thanks again. I owe you a drink or a cup of coffee."

"Sounds good. I'll definitely take you up on it."

I enter the restaurant and find the mayor immediately. He's the one charming the staff and patrons. I smile when I catch his eye, and he excuses himself and greets me with a kiss that catches the air beside my cheek. I pull away before it lands. It's an awkward moment, but I don't appreciate people who assume I'm okay with them in my personal space.

"Claire, it's so good to see you again." He motions for me to sit down.

"I was surprised to hear from you. What's going on?"

"What did you think of the fundraiser? I thought it was a big hit." He nods for more iced tea. From the looks of it, he's been here a while. Two empty sugar packets are folded into tight squares, and an unused lemon wedge is soaking through a cocktail napkin.

"It was wonderful. I hope Harvesters received enough donations to make it through the holidays." We're two days into September, and it's hard to think about Thanksgiving and Christmas with sweat still trickling down my lower back every time I go outside.

"I'm told the fundraiser was a success. We raised almost twenty percent more than at last year's."

"That's wonderful, but I don't think you called me here to talk about Harvesters."

He laughs. "You're right. I like to know what kind of new judges we have in our court system. Congratulations on winning your big case."

"You did some research."

"You're tenacious and tough. I like that. You won't let anybody get away with anything."

I study him over the rim of my iced tea. He seems relaxed and his smile is charming, but he wants something from me. "I fought hard for that case, and leniency isn't really in my vocabulary. MedPharmo was a danger to society."

"That's what I want to talk to you about."

He clams up when the waiter arrives to tell us about today's lunch specials. After listening attentively, he orders the smoked salmon with a cucumber side salad. I opt for the Waldorf salad and breadsticks.

After the waiter leaves with the menus, Sterling leans back in the booth and drapes his arm across the cushion. Nobody's sitting near us. In fact, we're the only ones on this side of the restaurant. The tiny hairs on the back of my neck stand up as I survey the area.

"What's going on, Mayor?" I paste on a fake smile and lean back in the booth, too.

"I have a favor to ask."

And there it is. "I can't imagine what I can do for you unless it's to donate more money to Harvesters."

He waves that off. "Oh, I'm sure you donated plenty." I have a feeling he knows exactly how much. He takes another drink and leans forward. "I know you're going to deliver sentencing for Seamus Williams on Friday, and I just ask that you don't throw the proverbial book at him."

I hold my hands up. "I'm sure you know both parties have agreed upon a predetermined sentence."

He nods repeatedly. "I know, I know. I just want you to lean on the lighter side of the sentencing." He looks around again to ensure no one can hear us. "He's a friend of the family, and I told him I'd see what I could do. I'm only asking you to keep my request in the back of your mind."

Nobody like Seamus is a family friend to any family unless your family is dirty. Holy shit. Maybe Jenn's right, and corruption's more prevalent than I realized. "A family friend?"

He nods and tries to look sincere. "A friend from a long time ago when I wasn't the mayor or out to change the world."

"So, like a friend you hung out with growing up and you two ended up falling on different sides of the law?"

"Just like every crime movie ever filmed. One goes legit, and one tries to but gets sucked into the wrong crowd," he says.

He's lying, but I nod like I understand. "Must be rough seeing your friend behind bars for a quarter of his life."

"My mom is still friends with his mom." He shakes his head.

"I can't make any promises, but I'll consider it. With a preset amount of time already determined, it's hard to get around it." I'm not going to sentence him any differently than I decided earlier today. I'd rather not have to explain why I didn't throw the book at a repeat offender. That's the kind of shit that happens.

"Thank you. That's all I can ask." He squeezes my hand, and it takes my best effort not to pull away in disgust. Again with the personal-space invasion. Sterling is creepier than I remember.

Lunch arrives, and we change the topic to weekend plans. I don't tell him I'm leaving town because, truthfully, I don't trust him. I wonder if he's like this with all judges or just me because I'm a woman and new to the circuit. He probably thinks he can schmooze me into being one of his minions. I didn't come this far to be squashed by a politician who's using his position as a stepping-stone. Kevin had mentioned he overheard Sterling discuss running for governor next major election. Again, not a surprise.

"I have a pop-in at Children's Mercy on Saturday, but after that, I'm going to a family barbecue and watch fireworks down at Union Station," he says.

"I'll stay out of the heat and probably read things that aren't about the law, like a good thriller." In reality, I'll be with Jenn at Orlando's pool or at a bar somewhere in a totally different time zone. I leave Friday night and get back Monday afternoon. Jenn and I have even more to discuss after this surprise lunch. After ten more minutes of polite conversation, Sterling motions for the check and thanks me for lunch.

"Do you need a ride back to the courthouse?" he asks. He stands by the car that magically appears the moment we walk out of the restaurant.

"I'm good. My car's not too far away."

Surprise flashes across his face before he smiles. He must have seen me get out of Kevin's car, which explains his confusion. "Okay. Have a great weekend. Thank you again for taking time out of your busy schedule for me."

I turn and walk the other way after he gets in the car. Fuck. I still have to deal with the tire. I hit the Lyft app, and a car appears in two minutes. "I'm sorry it's not a longer drive."

The Lyft driver shrugs. "It's too hot for anyone to be out walking in the middle of the day."

I tip him heavily and call Audi's roadside assistance. They promise to send somebody within the hour. I look at my tire again but can't see a nail or screw. I head up to my office and wait until they contact me. It's too hot to wait for them, and I've already missed out on valuable time because of lunch with the mayor and his attempt to strong-arm me.

My phone rings. It's an unfamiliar number. "Hello?"

"Ms. Weaver?"

"Yes."

"This is Audi Roadside. I'm down here in the parking lot."

"Okay. I'll be there in a few minutes." I slip my shoes back on but forgo my jacket. I have a feeling I'll be out there in the heat longer than I want.

The service engineer greets me with a handshake and says, "Did you piss somebody off?"

I'm confused. "What?"

"Your tire?" He points to the flat black rubber that's barely keeping the rim from touching the asphalt. "Someone slashed it."

Panic rushes through me. "Okay, let's talk about your delivery. Never tell a woman her tire has been slashed. Maybe use words like punctured deliberately." I'm taking out my fear on him. Deep breath. "Why do you think that?"

He bends down and shines a flashlight that reveals a definite line in the tire that I didn't see earlier. "Right here. It looks like there's a two-inch cut in the sidewall. Don't worry. I have a new tire for you. It won't take long to change it."

"Thank you."

"Maybe you can check security to see if this was a single incident or if other people had damage to their cars."

"I'll do that. Thanks for the advice," I say.

He walks back to his truck and pulls out an industrial jack, then stops in front of me. "You don't have to stand out here. I'll call you when I'm done. It's too hot to wait."

I march into the courthouse and ask Wayne to take me to the security office. He waves over another officer to take his place and escorts me down the end of the hall, where I'm ushered into a room full of cameras.

"Hey, Boss. Judge Weaver needs to speak with you," Wayne says.

"What can I help you with?" His boss towers over me and crosses his arms in front of him as though I'm about to complain about something security did wrong.

"My tire was slashed in the parking lot, and I want to see if there's anything on camera." My anxiety ramps up when he directs us over to a monitor and pulls up video from this morning. He finds my space in the lot and fast-forwards through the video.

"Son of a bitch." Sure as fuck, there's a guy who sticks a blade in my tire. When he yanks it out, he pulls up on the knife for emphasis. He hides his face from the cameras, so we don't get a clear shot of him when they zoom in. I shiver. My blood feels ice cold. I shake my hands because everything feels surreal. I've never felt fear like this before.

"Look. He slashes the tire four cars down from yours, too. And in the row behind you. And another car."

"How did nobody see this happen?" Wayne asks.

I'm thankful he asked the obvious question. Under two minutes pass from the time the man enters the lot until we see him leaving.

When the cops show up, I have nothing more to add. If it were just my car, they would have treated it as a personal attack against a judge, but he also slashed a lawyer's tires, an unmarked cop car, and a delivery vehicle for the coffee shop on the first floor. They tell me it's random and take my statement before advising me to get an escort out to my car at night and maybe leave before dark.

Wayne turns to me. "If I'm still around when you leave, I'll be more than happy to walk you to your car." He stands a little taller and puffs out his chest.

"Thank you, Wayne. I'll keep that in mind. I plan to leave about the same time as everyone else for a while. Thanks for your help on this."

"Just doing my job," he says.

His boss motions for him, and he excuses himself. There's nothing left for me here, so I grab my keys and head back to my office.

"Glad you're back. Where've you been?" April asks.

I first think something must've happened besides my tire getting slashed. My second thought, which pops up right behind the first, is that it's none of her damn business. I choose the professional response. "Downstairs working on a security issue. What's going on?"

She hands me a stack of unimportant messages, and I review them as I walk to my desk. I can't wait to leave this weekend and hang out with Jenn. I need it after such a draining day. I have two days until I sentence Seamus Williams, and honestly, Sterling really threw me for a loop. I wasn't ready for the political games to begin so soon. I'm having a shitty week and it's only Wednesday. I haven't heard from Emery since the weekend, not that I really expect to. I regret being so direct with her because she gave me everything I wanted and needed sexually. Selfishly, I should've waited before dropping the ultimatum, but I don't need a messy entanglement while dealing with a career change. My life needs to slow the fuck down sooner than later.

CHAPTER TEN

Jenn pulls up right as I walk out of LAX, as if we've timed it perfectly. She hugs me tightly until a pissed-off driver behind us honks for us to move.

"Asshole," Jenn yells and pulls into traffic. She leans over and squeezes my knee. "I've missed the shit out of you. How are you? And why aren't you wearing your robe? I was so looking forward to that."

I laugh. "Besides it being weird and that it's one hundred degrees here? I'm wondering why I even bothered with packing a bag. I plan to wear nothing for the next forty-eight hours."

"I'd rather you be clothed when you meet Orlando," she says.

We plan to hang at her place in Santa Monica tonight and drink wine. Tomorrow, we'll have lunch with Orlando, then spend the afternoon and evening in Malibu at the Shutters on the Beach resort. I need sand and sun. Jenn loves chilling and pampering as much as I do. "Definitely. I love that it's still hot here and I can wear my summer dresses. I ordered a few nice ones online. You'll love them."

"When do we get to talk about the job?" she asks.

"When I'm sitting in your living room with an open bottle of wine between us."

"When do we get to talk about Emery?"

"When I'm sitting in your living room and we've finished the open bottle of wine between us."

"Oh, no! I'm sad. Why am I sad?"

"She was doing that thing where she wanted more than I could give." I hear the sadness in my voice and suck it up. "We just wanted different things."

"What would be so wrong about a relationship?"

"I don't do relationships. Can we talk about this later?" I sulk and look out at the scenery that's so different than mine, but I can't even appreciate it. "This week took so much out of me. Listen to this. I had my tire slashed Wednesday."

"What?" Jenn looks at me. "What the hell's going on?"

"Nothing. It was apparently random. The guy slashed four tires in the parking lot. There's video, but you can't see his face at all."

"Were you stuck in a dark parking lot dealing with police and waiting for a tow? That sounds scary."

"No. I had a lunch, so thankfully, I saw it in the afternoon."

"Look at you being a fancy judge, leaving in the afternoon for lunches," she says.

"Oh, so that's a weird story, too. The mayor asked me to lunch and then told me to take it easy on sentencing with my first case. Said the perp was a childhood friend of his."

"Shut up. He did not! See? The mayor is definitely corrupt. Claire, you have to be careful. I don't like this."

"Do you really think the mayor's corrupt? I mean he creeps me out, but that doesn't mean he's in the mob." I nod as if I believe my own lie.

"What sentence did you award?" Jenn pulled into her driveway and parked.

"Fifteen years. Nobody's going to tell me what to do," I say.

She high-fives me. "That's my girl."

"Now let's go inside and open a bottle, snack on fattening foods, and catch up on the rest of our lives. It sounds like we have a lot to discuss."

Even though it's only nine here, my body's on Central Time, and I'm almost ready for sleep. Jenn has a fluffy robe on my bed, and I strip down and slip into its softness. My feet are sore from walking so much in heels at work and at both airports. I wiggle my toes into the plush carpet and decide it's time to start my weekend fresh with renewed vigor. I join Jenn in the living room and sink into the couch. She hands me a glass of wine.

"Being a judge hasn't been all that great," I say.

"That's because it's new and it's more political than you thought. We learned that in law school. You were the best lawyer, and you'll be the best judge. You have a passion for truth and justice that only a few people have." Jenn clinks her glass to mine. "Now let's get to the good stuff. Tell me about Emery. How many times did you hook up?"

"Let's see. It all started at the museum." I drag out the words and smile at her.

"I'm so jealous. That's superhot. My sex life, although I'm not complaining, is so normal compared to yours."

I wave her off and continue my count. "Then we met at my place for dinner after my first day in court. And the one time at my new place. That's it. Three times." I shrug like it's no big deal, but I already miss Emery. "Oh, wait. Four. I forgot about the Kauffman Center."

"Do you seriously think you won't see her again? I find that hard to believe. It's hard to find somebody who can handle your appetite."

I sip on my wine and think back to how cold Emery was toward me when she left. "If we see one another again, it won't be for a long time. I really thought she didn't want a relationship."

Jenn leans forward as if she wants to get her point across. "Maybe she doesn't want one. Maybe it's more of a respect thing. Like a fuck acquaintance. Tell me what happened."

I curl my legs underneath me. "She said we did it backward. Most people date first and then have sex. I told her I don't date, and she just up and left." Jenn shoots me the I-don't-believe-you look. I hold my hands up. "Seriously. She said I didn't know what she wanted and for me to quit thinking I did and left."

"Can you walk away from that deliciousness? I mean, if she's available, maybe you should give me her name and number."

"Ha-ha. She's too much of a top for you."

"Still sexy as hell. Maybe I can make an exception."

I laugh. "What about Orlando Bloom?"

She waves him off as though he doesn't matter to her. I know she's lying. "Honestly, he's pretty great. I'm excited for you to meet him tomorrow. And his kids are so sweet. I don't mind spending time with them."

"What happened there?" I grab a blanket from under the coffee table and wrap it around my shoulders, even though I have a robe on. It's a comfort thing.

"There are three sides to every story, but it seems as if she was more into money than family. She cheated on him and told him she didn't want kids, so she walked. That's why he has full custody of them."

"Ouch. Good for him. How old are the kids?"

"Six and eight. Still manageable."

I never was around children. I was an only child and never babysat or hung out with friends who had younger siblings. "That sounds like a fun age."

"Their personalities are coming out. Both are very funny and love Orlando so much. They idolize him. I mean, I do, too, but for different reasons." She winks at me.

"I have to say, Orlando looks good on you. He's good for your soul."

"He's really good for my pussy."

We both laugh. I miss her. I miss having a bestie. I need to try harder. Jenn and I hung out with a few lawyers in Kansas City when we were all getting started, but their careers and relationships got in the way. It's just me and Jenn. Eventually I will have to give her up to Orlando or someone else. Her happiness is far more important than my selfishness.

"Tell me about Orlando. Have you met any famous people through him? And how does one even become a sports agent?"

Jenn reaches for her phone and pulls up an album marked Celebs. I scroll through about three dozen pictures of her with athletes I recognize but can't name.

"He played football at the University of Alabama, and then a season in the NFL before blowing out his ACL. His degree is in Communications, and he already had a bunch of contacts in the league. Nothing But Sports signed him as an agent, and he's been with them twelve years."

"Wait. So, how old is he?"

"He's thirty-four."

"So, he's younger? You cougar."

"By like a year only."

"Insta-family so you won't have to pop out any kids," I say.

"Hold up. Nobody said anything about marriage or family. I'm not ready for that kind of commitment. Baby steps. I just was introduced to his kids, and while they seem adorable and sweet, that's a massive undertaking." She leans back against the couch.

"If this all works out, maybe you can start a business together. You're familiar with entertainment law. He's an agent with a lot of connections. And if my judgeship fails, you can hire me." I put my empty wineglass on the table and reach for grapes. Dinner was a ten-dollar salad on the flight, and I'm hungry.

"You've lost weight," she says.

"My schedule's off, and I'm scared to order food from restaurants since that one creepy guy showed up."

"Why don't you just pick it up? Or have one of the admins get it? That way you still get decent food and are taking care of yourself. I worry about you."

I worry about myself for entirely different reasons. We chat for another hour before she gently shakes me awake and tells me to go to bed. I don't argue with her, even though I know our time together is short and I miss her.

Orlando greets me warmly and kisses my cheek before joining us at the table. I don't mind his kiss because I trust Jenn, so I trust him. "Claire, I've heard nothing but great things about you. Congratulations on your new position."

Orlando is, for lack of a better word, dreamy. He has full, flowy, dark hair that brushes his shoulders and is purposely messy. I bet he spends more time styling his hair than Jenn does. "Thank you. It's been challenging, to say the least."

Our conversation is smooth, and I watch how attentive they are with one another. I know they haven't said I love you yet, but it's obvious they do in the little touches and softer voices when they communicate.

It was inevitable that one of us would fall in love, but truthfully, I always knew it would be her. I haven't opened my heart up to anyone since college, and that was a tough lesson learned. I'm not going to lose my dream job to change diapers or wipe snotty noses because somebody I love wants me to. Love isn't forever. But a career can be, and it's also rewarding.

By the time Orlando leaves us so we can continue our girls' weekend, I'm internally worked up about how I won't ever sacrifice myself for love. I'm sure a part of me is jealous that Jenn has this and a career, but for how long? Will he expect her to sacrifice for him and his family?

"Are you ready to be pampered? Because I am," Jenn says.

"I'm so ready for a massage, and then I want to head to the beach to hear the waves roll in." I'm still tired from traveling, but once we pull into the hotel's driveway and she hands the keys to the valet, a burst of energy fills me at the sight of such a beautiful place. "Jenn, this beats Vegas. I always want to come here."

"Except there aren't as many people, and we can't gamble here. But yes, if you want to be treated like royalty, this is the place," she says.

A bellhop disappears inside with our luggage, and we slowly follow him, looking at the decor. It has a very Cape Cod vibe. It's a crowded weekend, but we get our room key quickly.

"We have a suite with separate bedrooms. Not that I'm expecting anything to happen here, but you'll have privacy just in case."

"You're too much. We could have just hung out at your place."

She stops me. "Absolutely not. My bestie wants the beach, my bestie gets the beach. Come on. We have massages in fifteen minutes."

❖

I'm instructed to remove my robe and lie facedown on the table. I slip under the sheet and wait for my masseuse. Low, gentle light and the smell of lavender and eucalyptus put me immediately at ease. I hear a gentle knock at the door and mumble, "Come in."

A woman about my age enters and introduces herself as Emma. She's gorgeous. Her hair is pulled up and out of her face. Soft curls spring out from the bun and rest against her neck.

"Is there anything you don't want me to touch, or are you sensitive anywhere?"

I look her in the eye. "Nothing is off-limits."

She nods, and even in the low light I see her blush. I moan the second she touches me.

"You're very tense." She adds warm massage oil to her hands and starts at my shoulders, working her way down both arms and to my lower back. I don't even try to stifle my moans. This feels too good. I'm just thankful we're in a private room.

"That feels wonderful," I say.

She lowers the sheet to right above the swell of my ass. She slides her hands beneath the sheet, continuing her massage over my ass. "Tell me if you're uncomfortable with anything I do."

"Mmm-hmm." I can't help but roll my hips slowly. This is wonderfully torturous, and I wonder how far she'll go.

Her hands move to my inner thighs. I almost pant every time her thumbs get close to my pussy. I spread my legs apart, so there is no doubt as to what I want. She excuses herself for a moment, and I think I'm going to be in trouble, but she returns with a wedged pillow.

"Put this underneath your waist."

I tuck it under me so it lifts my ass and thighs in the air. She runs her hands down my thighs and then back up again. I'm squirming for release. More oil. She spreads me and massages everywhere but where I want her to. I know she's being professional, but I feel like she's toying with me, too. She knows I want her to fuck me. I take a deep breath and wait. I'm used to waiting, but I'm not patient. We're only twenty minutes into the massage, and I'm already thinking of different ways I want her to touch me. Her fingers are long, slender, and strong. Visions of her fisting me have me biting my lip and praying for either release or for the massage to end so I can run upstairs to my room and have a proper and loud orgasm.

"You're tensing up again." Emma's voice is raspy and low.

"I'm sorry."

"Don't apologize. How can I help you relax?" she asks as her thumbs barely graze my pussy.

I moan and roll my hips again. "Please don't stop."

She finally cups my pussy and runs her fingers between my folds. I moan. The oil is warm, but her fingers are warmer. I squeeze the thick padding of the table when she slowly presses two fingers inside me. I push my hips back into her hand. God, I need this. I tamp down unfamiliar guilty feelings as she increases her speed. She runs her thumb along my clit, and I jerk with pleasure until I come quietly.

"Time to flip," she says. She gently pulls the wedge from under my stomach and holds the towel up so I can turn. She takes her time lowering the sheet and smiles smugly at me. I'm still sensitive and shaky. She stands where my head is and leans over to massage my shoulders. I pull the sheet down. My nipples are hard, and a thin sheen of sweat rests between my breasts. She stretches to massage them. I'm too weak to do anything but enjoy it. She makes appreciative noises as she rubs my body. She strokes my arms and legs until I'm completely limp. My eyes fly open when she touches my pussy again. She holds her hands still until I nod. I'm ready for another orgasm. She runs her hands continuously over my lips and my clit and, without any additional pressure, builds me up until I come a second time.

"That was incredible." I breathe deeply.

She smiles and rubs my legs until we hear the ding signaling the end of the massage.

"Thank you, Emma, for the best massage I've ever received," I say. She helps me into my robe.

"Thank you for letting me touch your beautiful body. I hope we can do this again soon. Here or somewhere else," she says.

"I'll let you know."

She winks as I leave the room. I sign off on a massive tip and have it billed to our room. I'll give Jenn a heads-up, so she doesn't question the charge. I meet her in the dressing room and raise my eyebrow at her.

"You're not going to believe what just happened," I whisper so nobody can hear me.

She shakes her head. "Shut up. I don't believe you." It's as if she already knows.

"You should."

"I really do," she said.

I sit on the bench next to her and sigh. "But I feel guilty. Why is that?"

She stops and stares at me. "Oh, my God. I know."

"What?"

"You feel guilty because of Emery."

CHAPTER ELEVEN

I never thought I would be that person. Weak and needy. I pick up my phone and text Emery before I change my mind.

What are you doing? I'd like to see you.

I regret it the moment I hit send. I wait ten minutes before I hear the ding of an answer.

Sorry. I'm busy tonight.

I groan. It's been weeks since Emery and I have spoken. That clip of an answer tells me it's not going to happen any time soon either. If at all. I don't blame her. I assumed things I shouldn't have. I turn on the television and sit on the couch as though this is a nightly routine for me, but it isn't. Winston Interior decorated my place beautifully, and it's nice to come home to a place that feels classy and still like a home.

I'm restless though. I need to be out and be around people. It's nine, and the closest bar is the Phoenix. It's only a few blocks away and one of my favorite hangout spots. I find a pair of black leggings and an oversized sweater. I know the bar will be hot, but the temperature outside is cool. I pull my hair up and leave a few tendrils down. It's a completely different look for me, but I like it. I don't look like a judge. I look like a woman who wants to be out on the town. I add a pair of black ankle boots with a small heel to complete my look. The only thing missing is makeup. I spend several minutes getting the perfect smoky look with eyeliner, eye shadow, and thick mascara. I finish with my favorite lipstick, smack my lips together, and smile. God, I miss lipstick. I miss dressing up and feeling pretty. My weekend with Jenn was weeks ago. I'm tired of wearing black robes and pulling my hair back in a severe bun almost every day. I deserve this spontaneous outing. I walk to the Phoenix, thankful this area of town is so well lit.

"It's been a while, Judge." The bouncer knows I'm into women, but he flirts with me anyway.

"Hey, Tony. It has, but I'm glad to be out tonight. Who's on stage?"

"A newbie. Hey, my break's in ten. Let me buy you a drink."

"You're married with two small children at home."

He nudges my shoulder with his. "Just an innocent drink."

He's attractive, charming, and I have a feeling messing around is a perk for him. I don't judge him. "I'll pass. Just sit anywhere?"

Tony waves his hand across the room. I choose a small table near the bar and order a glass of white wine. This is the kind of joint where the music is so loud that conversation is pointless. I can blend in and be a part of something without any effort. The music is great, and everyone in the place is having a good time. It's not packed, but people are close. There are obvious couples and some single people like me. I wave off two men who approach me and tell them I'm only here for the wine and the music. They are respectful, but I can tell by the way they keep looking at me that I'm still on their minds.

My table faces the stage and the front door. I catch some of the cool air that wafts in from new patrons or ones who leave the bar, and it's refreshing. I'm not a fan of the changing seasons, but right now the coolness feels good. I take a sip of wine and close my eyes as the music slows. I open them just in time to see Emery and a woman walk into the bar. Different emotions cross her face when she sees me. I'm in shock, but I manage to hold my expression still and slowly tilt my wineglass in her direction in acknowledgement.

She stumbles over her date, who has stopped by the door, either confused by where to go or waiting for her eyes to adjust. Emery looks flustered, and I smirk and stare at them until they're ushered to a table on the other side of the bar. I can still see them, but it's hard to detect Emery's expressions in the darkness of the room and the brightness of the stage. Their body language isn't fluid like people who are comfortable with one another. Tonight just got very interesting. I catch her looking at me far too many times, and I never look away. I'm sure people notice that my attention is on them, but I don't care. One of the guys tries to buy me a drink again, and I thank him but inform him nothing's going to happen, and I'd prefer for him to leave me alone.

When I look at Emery again, she seems tense and isn't trying to hide her disdain for the man. I can't imagine her date is happy with her total emotional involvement in me. Her date looks at me several times, and each time our eyes meet, her mouth folds into a frown. I finish my wine and order a water and wait. I barely hear the music, but I nod to its constant beat. I can't shake Emery from my thoughts. The excitement of her so close, yet so unavailable, is overwhelming. I avoid eye contact when Emery's date walks by on her way to the ladies' room. I'm ready to leave anyway. My relaxing evening has crashed and burned. There's a slight chance of something far more exciting, but I don't have a feel yet for how the night will play out. I stand, throw money on the table, and slowly make my way out of the bar. Before I cross the threshold, I look over my shoulder and find Emery in the crowd. She's staring at me. Game on. I hustle and make it back to my loft in less than ten minutes.

"Somebody may be stopping by in the next hour. Her name is Emery Pearson. Please send her up."

"Will do, Ms. Weaver." The doorman nods respectfully. I'm so happy discretion is part of his job.

I head up to my place. I could hang out at in the giant foyer with couches and chairs scattered about and wait to see if she shows up, but if she doesn't, I'd feel dumb sitting there. Being alone at a jazz bar is different than being alone in an almost-empty lounge.

I have a feeling Emery will be joining me within the hour. I leave my door ajar, flip on some 40s big-band music to keep the vibe going and pour two whiskeys. I look out at the city I love. It doesn't have the wow factor that Vegas does or the beautiful beaches with soft sand of Malibu, but it has its own charms.

"Is this for me?"

I don't turn but smile at her reflection in the large window. "I thought you were busy tonight?"

She locks the door and drapes her coat on the couch. "I was, but not anymore." She moves closer until she's beside me.

I finally look her in the eyes. "What changed your mind?" I know the answer, but I want her to say it.

"Your lips."

"Are you sure about this? I mean, we left things undecided." I cross my arms, my drink still in my hand. I want her to say the words.

"I'm sure. I don't know what was wrong with me. I'm sorry for leaving without a good explanation. I've missed you the last few weeks."

I pull her close to me and kiss her. She smells like sage and tastes like the sharp whiskey I've poured for her. "How did you get out of your date?"

"It wasn't a date."

"It looked a lot like one." I set my glass down. She puts her glass on the windowsill and pulls me to her until I'm flush against her. I put my hands on her chest and play with the buttons on her shirt. I've missed her confidence and the excitement that dances in her eyes. "Let me rephrase. How are you here right now, when less than an hour ago you were with another woman who wasn't your date?"

"Are you jealous?"

"No." I shrug.

She smiles. "No?"

I shake my head. "No, because I know you're not fucking her."

"Would you be jealous if I were?"

I gauge my reaction and find that I wouldn't be. I haven't felt jealousy or rage in years. I would feel sad at the loss. What we have can't be matched. Seeing Emery with her date only bumped my heart rate up a notch. Not because I was jealous, but because it was her. No one has ever matched my sexual appetite before now. I could care less about the woman with her. "No."

She laughs. "I totally believe you."

"You and I have something special. I know you want to put a label on it, but the only thing I want, at the moment, is for you to fuck me."

She reaches for my sweater and pulls it over my head. "Let's go upstairs. Your bed's far more comfortable than your couch."

I unbutton her shirt as she pulls me up the stairs to my bedroom. By the time we're at the bed, her shirt is off and my bra undone. Her hands are on my breasts. I'm trying desperately to take her pants off. She's warm and hard, and I'm getting wet just thinking about what she's going to do to me in the next few minutes.

"Can we play with your sex machine?"

"After you fuck me first." Nobody has ever watched me fuck myself with it. The idea of Emery watching sends chills across my body and makes my already hardened nipples ache. I need the quick relief of Emery's hands and mouth on my body, and then we can bring out the toy. I pull her onto the bed and lift my hips so she can take off my leggings. She crawls off the bed to remove her pants and boxers, and much to my surprise, she returns completely naked. She's never been fully nude with me before. "How am I wearing more than you are?"

She laughs, removes my panties, and crawls between my legs. Our pussies touch, and we both moan at the contact. She isn't smooth like I am but trimmed. The friction of her soft hair rubbing against my engorged clit makes me cry out. She licks her lips before kissing me. I find that I've miss that about her. Her tongue plunges deep into my mouth and swirls around my tongue. I scratch my nails down her back and over her ass. She grinds against me, and I lift my hips to greet her thrusts. I don't want to come this way. I break the kiss. "I want you inside me." I run my thumb over her already-swollen bottom lip. "And your mouth on my clit."

She rolls on her back and pulls me on top of her. She squeezes my breasts and pinches my nipples exactly how I like. "Turn around." She makes a twirling motion with her finger.

I turn as instructed and place my knees on either side of her head. "Like this?" I ask. I don't need an answer because she pulls my pussy onto her face. I can't reach hers with my mouth because she's so tall, but I start rubbing it with my fingers. It's hard to concentrate when she's tongue-fucking me, but I touch her enough to get her hips rolling into my hand. "Can I go inside?"

She nods, and I slip into her tight, wet, pussy. She stops licking me and moans. This isn't something she's used to, so I go slow. I don't want to scratch her. I hate myself right now for having long nails. She feels so smooth and slick. I want to taste her because she's allowing me to touch her. I've always put my own orgasm first, but tonight's special. I know Emery won't always allow me to touch her, so I pull up from her mouth and crawl down her. I lick her smooth, velvety clit. I lap up her juices and press my entire mouth over her. Her hips buck into me, and I press my hands on her thighs to slow her motions. I know how much mobility she has when she's fucking me.

Her fingers slip inside me, and I gasp with pleasure. I push up to my knees to allow her more room. She bends her knees and gives me the same courtesy. Her orgasm hits first. She's quiet. I'll have bruises from the hand that's squeezing my thigh, but I don't stop until she squirms. She pulls me back to her mouth, and I move my hips back and forth while her tongue moves side to side. I throw my head back and come loudly. I stop her from giving me another one. I want to save it for later.

"I've missed you," she says.

I crawl off her and flop down beside her. "You've missed my pussy."

"I've missed fucking you," she says. She rolls over and runs her fingertips over my breasts. "When I saw you tonight, I knew where I wanted to be."

Her confession unsettles me. I need to get out of my own head. A part of me sees Emery as a victory, but also a small part is relieved that she's here. That she's come back to me.

"It's been a while," I say.

"Maybe we should have like one night a month where we get together. You know, like a book club."

I can't help but laugh. She joins in. I like it when she laughs at her own jokes. "You mean like every third Thursday of each month? I like the way we're doing things now. Let's not complicate things with a schedule or rules." I roll so I face her. "This is okay, right?"

She brushes her fingertips over my breasts. "This is definitely okay, but can I have more?"

I raise my eyebrow at her. "More as in the sex machine?"

She nods enthusiastically. "I've never seen one before."

I give her a look.

"Okay. I mean in real life," she says.

"It's not a very big one. I figure if work gets too busy and I get too busy for even our kind of get-togethers, I'm going to invest in one that needs its own room."

"We can make the third Thursday of every month a thing."

I get up and pinch her playfully. The sex machine is in the bottom of my closet. I put on my robe and pull it out while Emery slips into the bathroom. It's set up when she returns. I take a minute to appreciate her muscular tone. "You're gorgeous."

She waves me off and blushes. "Thank you. Now let's see this contraption."

I hand her the remote and the lube. "It's all yours."

"Oh, no. I'm not doing this."

My robe falls to the floor, and I climb into bed. "I don't mean that." I spread my legs as she puts the machine between them. "Move it closer."

"This is heavy," she says. "So, what do I do?"

I scoot down so that the tip of the dildo, our dildo, is right at my slit. "Angle it down a little more."

She can barely contain her excitement as she places it where I direct her. "Now what?"

She kneels between my legs and adds lube at my direction. My pussy clenches when her fingers rub up and down my still-sensitive clit.

"You have control."

She kisses my thigh softly. "I always have control."

I press the dildo gently inside me. The size always takes my breath away. After I get comfortable with it, I nod. She breaks into the biggest smile and turns it on. It starts off slow, and as much as I want to reach down and touch myself, I hold off. Emery's delight is too much of a turn-on to come right away.

"Oh, my God," she whispers repeatedly as she watches the machine fuck me. I'm concentrating so much on her that it's difficult to relax and appreciate my own pleasure. I drop my head onto the pillow and close my eyes. Her fingertips press along the inside of my knees as she moves closer. "You're so beautiful, Claire. So open and free."

"Faster," I say.

She obliges and hits the button again. I arch my back as the dildo moves faster and deeper. Tears well in the corner of my eyes as I try to process my sexual gratification.

Because the girth of the dildo is so big, my clit is stretched and almost numb. My body twitches when I finally feel her frenzied touch on it. I almost tell her to stop because I'm going to come fast, but she's so turned on that I let her have my orgasm. It rips from my body, igniting a fire that pushes out every pore and leaves me a sweaty mess.

She turns off the machine and moves it from the bed.

"I'm going to have to change the sheets." My voice is hoarse and scratchy since I've been gasping for breath.

Emery kisses my dry mouth. "That was the most amazing thing I've ever seen."

My laugh sounds strained. "That was very exhausting."

"Thank you so much for using it and letting me watch. Wow." She reaches for my hand and interlocks her fingers with mine, which feels unfamiliar. It's personal and comfortable, but I don't pull away. "How did that feel? And should I be worried that a machine might be better?"

"It's for pleasure only—no excitement other than the orgasm it gives me. It doesn't smell like sandalwood or sage or taste like whiskey. It doesn't rip down my panties when I want to have sex. It can't read me like y—" I stumble a bit. "Like people can."

"Like me, you mean. Or are there others?"

I look at her. "Did you just ask if we're exclusive?" I push aside the hand job I got a few weeks ago out in California. "Besides, I already know you aren't." Her laughter stings a bit, and I wonder if I'm somewhat jealous after all.

I purse my lips as I think about my promiscuity. I'll have to reel in my encounters since I'm a judge now. The last thing my career needs is a scandal. I'm a single woman with a healthy sexual appetite, but I still have a reputation to uphold. Maybe I need to concentrate on a real relationship, not just a fuck buddy. The thought gives me an ache in the pit of my stomach. It's cute when other people, like Jenn and Orlando, have dinner dates and go to movies, but it's just not something I've ever wanted. At least not since college. This is why politicians are riddled with scandals. We have an image that people want to see, but we're flawed just like they are, so we fake it. At least that's how I see it, but nobody's perfect.

"I'd love to find somebody who's okay with my schedule and doesn't question me every single time I leave at a random call," she says. "That's harder to find than you think. One day I'm sure I'll settle down, but right now I'm enjoying life and my job, and I don't want a complicated relationship, but I want something."

"I feel like you're the person who wants the kids, the house, the white picket fence." I'm totally serious. Emery says she isn't looking, but she sure was upset when I said we couldn't have a relationship.

"My job has me out at all hours, and most women want somebody home or with them after work. I can't do that. Fires and investigations don't happen from eight in the morning to five at night. Most of my cases are in the evening, and once there's a fire, I'm on it for several days. I don't have normalcy, and the women I've dated don't understand. They say they do, but they really don't."

Her words have a bite to them. She's hardened her heart against any emotional connection and only wants the physical. It's safer. Uncomplicated. I understand it better than anyone, but I think Emery's fooling herself. "I get what you're saying. I mean, at some point I'm going to have to make drastic changes because of my position. Probably sooner than later." I look at the time. It's almost one thirty, and I have to get up at seven. Thank God I don't have court tomorrow.

Emery suddenly sits up. "Shit. I should go. I'm sorry I've kept you up so late."

I don't stop her. I need sleep. Tomorrow's another long day. We start a new trial Monday, and I'm going to try to get them to settle. I'll review everything about the case today and chat with the lawyers Friday. Most of the time, we can reach a settlement because trials are long, messy, and expensive. Plus, the evidence gathered usually makes for open-and-shut cases. Sometimes the defendant is adamant that they're innocent, but most of the time, when presented with evidence, they take the plea.

"It was worth the lost sleep, but I do have a big day tomorrow." I roll over, and even though I try hard to stay awake to say goodbye to her, I can't. I wake up to my shrill alarm and all evidence of Emery gone, except my deliciously sore pussy and an empty whiskey glass in the sink.

CHAPTER TWELVE

Jenn calls me to check in, and I read her the latest invitation that's crossed my desk. April has flagged it as important, and I've learned to trust her. "There's a retirement party next Saturday for a judge who's been around forever, and I'm encouraged to bring a plus one. What are you doing next weekend?"

"Oh, that sounds like fun. We don't have anything planned. I can fly out Friday and be home Sunday," she says.

"Really? Nice. I thought for sure you'd say no."

"Come on. I've been dying to see your new place and to visit my little town again."

"We prefer the word city, but okay. Town's fine, I guess," I say.

"Let's get dolled up and drink a lot. Can you book us at Skyline Salon? I miss cheap pampering."

When Jenn told me she pays over four hundred dollars for highlights, I laughed. One of the perks of living in the Midwest is the inexpensive living. "I promise to take care of you here as well as you did for me there. Except the whole special massage thing. I did pay you back for that, didn't I?" Panic flutters in my chest as I wrack my brain trying to remember.

"Yes, you did. At the airport when I dropped you off. I'll have to pass on that kind of special treatment. I don't think Orlando would approve."

"Things are going pretty well there, huh?" My mind floats back to the last conversation I had with Emery, and I brush it aside. I need to focus on Jenn and not on Emery, who hasn't contacted me since the night she left my house.

"They are. We got into a blowout the other day, and it turns out I really want this to work, but I'm fighting it so hard. Like if I give in, I'm giving up my independence or something. He told me that's not going to happen. He's not going to be the boyfriend who doesn't trust his girlfriend when she's out with friends. I ended up a sobbing mess on the couch," she says.

I decide she's got enough going on, so I keep my opinion on monogamous relationships to myself. "He's a great guy and I really like him."

"I just don't know if I'm ready for insta-family, you know?"

"Quit fighting it. You make a powerful couple." I learned a long time ago not to refer to Jenn as cute in any relationship, even if I felt it to be true. "Anyway, bring something sexy so I can show you off."

I'm interrupted by a knock and April peeking her head in before I answer.

"I'm sorry, but Mayor Moore is here to see you," she says.

I hold up my finger. "Okay. I'll confirm times with you next week." I hang up and nod at April, who's been staring at me the whole time. I stand when Sterling enters, and April shuts the door. "Sterling, what a surprise."

"It's been a while," he says.

I reach over my desk to shake his hand, finding comfort in the space between us. "What can I do for you today?"

"I wanted to tell you that I was disappointed with Seamus's sentence."

I stare at him. He wants a reaction. I don't give him one. "I'm sorry you feel that way, but he's a repeat offender, and the pre-sentence investigation showed a person unwilling to change or reform. The sentence was within the parameters set by both parties."

His smile wavers a bit. "I get that, but I thought we had an understanding. I thought we bonded over lunch the other week."

"Mayor, I did the job that I was appointed to do. As much as I appreciated and respected your input, I can't offer leniency to a violent criminal because you played football with him in grade school." Oops. That came out bitchier than I intended. I don't want to piss him off. "Thank you for your help, Sterling, but I have to do my job well. I'm sure you can appreciate that our city is safer when judges do take their responsibilities seriously."

"Of course. Of course." He rubs his hands over his face. "I just know he didn't get a fair shot at rehabilitation. I wanted to help out. I thought you could see that."

He looks defeated. Gone is the smiley, happy-go-lucky politician who walked in only a few minutes ago. "Are you in some kind of trouble, Sterling?" It dawns on me that maybe his involvement with Seamus is shady, as Jenn predicted.

He waves his hands at me and laughs but his voice is shaky. "Oh, no. Nothing like that. I just told a friend I'd try to help out in any way I could."

I lean forward and study him. "So, you were never friends with him?" How many times has this man lied to me? I still think something's off. I don't get murder vibes, but I do believe whatever he's involved in isn't good. He stares at me as if he's ready to confess something, but then sits back in the chair and takes a deep breath.

"He's a friend of a friend. I didn't know him personally, but I offered to help someone."

"A friend," I repeat. I want to throw his words back at him, but I keep quiet. Something tells me Sterling Moore is in a bad place. "I can't do anything. What's done is done. The sentencing is out of my court. Besides, I'm sure his lawyers have already appealed."

He stands. "I get it. I do. Thanks for your time."

I stand, too, but he doesn't shake my hand. He leaves without closing my door. I watch as he raps his knuckles on April's desk and winks at her as he leaves. He acts as if the last five minutes didn't happen. What the actual fuck is going on?

"What did he want?" April leans her shoulder on the door frame and hugs the stack of manilla folders to her chest.

"Nothing. Just to follow up on something we discussed a few weeks ago." She nods. It looks like she believes my lie. "Can you shut my door on the way out?" I ask.

Once my door is shut, I lean back in my chair. Something detrimental to somebody was in that warehouse, and Seamus Williams was hired to destroy it. But why would he be stupid and careless enough to get caught an hour after the fire? I can't tell anybody anything because what's there to tell? That the mayor is upset with a sentencing? That he asked me for help and I denied him?

I know favors are doled out daily. We learned that in law school. Ethics was pushed hard because it's so easy to give in to temptation. Judges are pushed harder. Fuck my life right now. I want to call Jenn back, but she's busy, and it's not fair to keep bothering her when both of our workloads are gigantic. I pick up the invitation for the party I just invited her to. She's gorgeous, smart, and will be able to hold her own talking to anyone at the party. Plus, she'll have my back and report any gossip. I email my confirmation and mark it on my calendar. I have a feeling my very near future is going to be an endless stream of holiday parties and more visits by the mayor.

"You're here." I throw my arms in the air and race toward Jenn, whose enthusiastic squeal gets the attention of the patrons in the foyer. I'm so happy to see her that my eyes well up. I didn't realize how much I needed my best friend until she's in my arms.

"Finally. I'm here. I'm sorry it's so late."

"I don't care. Just never let me go." I notice her two carry-on bags. "Tell me you're moving in and that's all your stuff."

She laughs and pulls out of my embrace. "I couldn't decide so I have two dresses, two pairs of shoes, my fluffy robe, pajamas, makeup, hair care." She nods as she lists everything in the bags. "Oh, and your Christmas present."

I step back. "Shut up. You do not. That's not for two months. Jenn, I haven't even thought about presents yet."

"Stop stressing. Come on. Show me your place. I'm so excited to finally see it."

I grab one of her bags and roll it to the elevator. "I'll come down here tomorrow and get us breakfast. This coffee shop has wonderful chocolate croissants and lattes."

"Yum. I'm hungry. The plane's snack was just junk food. Tell me you have something to eat."

I punch the sixth floor and list everything I have for her. "I went with nostalgic snacks that probably won't taste as good as they did when we were in law school. All the fruit, all the vegetables, Christopher Elbow chocolates, slices of different Andre's cakes, pretzels with cheese sauce, and Hot Tamales."

"Sounds perfect and absolutely horrible for me. Is it too late for wine?"

I hold the elevator door open as she crosses the threshold. "We have to worry about it only when we have to ask if it's too early."

"I love you. You get me," she says.

"I love you more." I unlock my door and stand back to gauge her reaction. She turns to me, her mouth open, and I beam.

"Oh, my God. It's gorgeous." She drops her bag and twirls her arms like Maria von Trapp. "This is perfect for you, Claire Bear. Absolutely high-end perfection."

"It's not too over the top?"

She grabs my shoulders. "You deserve everything. All of this. All your successes. I'm just so fucking proud of you." She pulls me into a hug, and I can't help but lean into her strength.

"Thanks. Let me give you the tour." I take her to the guest room, which is located right when you walk into the loft. The walls to her room are only eight feet tall so they don't reach the ceiling, but they give her privacy. I love the open concept. She puts her bags on the guest bed, then walks the steps up to my room.

"Your bedroom is fucking amazing. Whoever designed this loft is a mastermind. It's like they were in your head."

"I hired an interior designer to do most of the decorating. I picked out a few things, but this is mostly her work." I wait for Jenn to finish gushing about my place before we sit down to relax, and then I catch her up on my life, including the weirdness with Sterling.

"First of all, your mayor is hot."

I give her a look that says I'm not amused.

"Okay, besides that, I told you he was dirty. I knew it the minute you told me about the case. What did you find out?"

I shrugged. "Nothing. I have nothing. Honestly, I think he's in over his head. Like somebody has something on him and he's just a puppet. That explains his weird behavior and our conversation. If you find my body—"

She waves her finger inches from my face. "Don't even say it. Don't even joke about it, not a word." I see the lightly veiled anger and, for the first time, realize she's concerned for me.

I hold her hand and gently squeeze her fingers. "I'm not worried, but I need somebody in my life to know what's going on. And I need to know if I'm imagining how weird all of this is."

She rests her head on the back of the couch. "You're not. Something's off with your hottie of a mayor, but I get it. We've come a long way, and both of us need to be careful. Especially you. You live alone and have two controversial cases under your belt."

"I'll be fine. Threatening a judge isn't smart." I change the subject. "In other news, Emery's been here twice."

"Now this I can get behind. What's going on there?"

"Same. I got desperate for sex and texted her." I drop my head in my hands. "I hate that I'm so weak."

"You're a strong, passionate woman. You both want the same thing—really good sex without the complication of a relationship. If it's working, don't worry about it. Everything else will fall into place." She smirks behind her wineglass.

"What?"

"What what?"

"What's the smirk for? What do you know that I don't?" I don't love her smug look.

"Nothing really. I just think it's interesting that you've become fuck buddies and how you allegedly don't want a relationship, but you haven't talked about anyone else."

I snort. "It's not by choice. I can't do the hard-and-fast hookups anymore because people are starting to recognize me. And we know I always struggle to make friends. People don't take me seriously."

"You're cursed with a deliciously curvy body and a face that stops traffic," she says.

Heat feathers my cheeks at her compliment. I know my looks are both a blessing and a curse. I've used both to my advantage and apologize for nothing. "Oh, stop. I'm just confident."

"Oh, yeah. That, too. The important thing is that I'm here. We'll meet people at this party who'll either help you professionally or be just like us. I wonder if we'll see Macey there?"

We were a trio in law school. Macey got a job in Overland Park, and when Jenn moved, our trio fell apart. Completely my fault. During the two years I was working on the MedPharmo case, many of my colleagues moved to different cities, different firms, and I lost touch. It's been over four years since either of us has spoken to Macey. "I hope so. I miss her quiet humor."

"We should call her." Jenn reaches for her phone.

"It's eleven thirty. We're not calling anyone," I say.

"Okay. Maybe tomorrow. What time are we headed to the salon?"

"Four. The party starts at six thirty, and dinner is served at seven."

"Do you even know this judge?" Jenn asks.

"I know some of his cases. Remember when that train derailed because the engineer fell asleep and a dozen people died? That was his."

"Okay. That was like ten years ago, right?" she asks.

I nod. When we were baby lawyers. When life was both simple and overwhelming at the same time. "I never met him though. He was a hard judge. Nobody liked to be in his courtroom. Everybody going to this party is probably only going because they want to see him retire."

"Whatever you need me to do, let me know. I'm yours for the night."

I laugh at her phrasing. Jenn and I have never fooled around. I think we knew right away that we were destined to be besties, so we didn't want to ruin our friendship by having sex. That rarely ends well. "Okay. Let's go to sleep. We might have an all-nighter ahead of us, and we're going to need to rest." I hug her tightly but am reluctant to release her. I really need to start making friends who live here in town.

"Don't forget the croissants and coffee in the morning," Jenn says before closing her door. "You know how I take my coffee."

CHAPTER THIRTEEN

"You look so beautiful, Claire," Jenn says.

I walk down the stairs wearing a silver dress that shimmers in the light. I think it's too much, but the look on Jenn's face tells me I've nailed it. It's form-fitting and stops below my knee. "Am I showing too much cleavage?"

"Honey, I don't think you could hide those beauties if you tried."

"Except for the black, somber robe I wear every day," I say.

She twirls me slowly and runs her hands over my dress. "I love this dress. And they did the best job with your hair. I was nervous, but it really does look great. You look like Lauren Bacall, only hotter and with better lips."

I put my hands on my hips. "I thought I told you that you weren't supposed to look better than I do. You're truly stunning." Jenn's wearing a long, black evening gown with a slit that lands a few inches below her hip. "You've been working out, haven't you? You look toned and fit."

"Orlando and I've been cycling. And he bought us kayaks, so I'm getting both upper- and lower-body workouts."

"Mission accomplished. Yowzer."

Jenn blushes. She looks healthy and happy. "Thank you. I'm ready to mingle."

I point at her. "But definitely not single. Come on. Let's go. The town car I called is waiting." I grab a thick shawl for me and a robe coat with a giant belt for Jenn. It's fall and chilly. I don't want to leave anything in the car. We'll check our coats at the event. I grab my clutch, the invitation just in case, and link arms with Jenn. "Let's go dazzle some influential people."

"Do I need more lipstick?"

I nod.

"Crap. I should've had you do my makeup."

"You're gorgeous. I'm glad you're my eye candy."

She rests her head on my shoulder. "I have such a good feeling about tonight."

"Let's hope you're right." I know the parties Jenn attends with Orlando are celebrity saturated, and I'm afraid this will be nothing but old lawyers, old judges, and people who either paid them off or had a hand in their success over the years. I wonder if I'll know anybody tonight. I'm just thankful Jenn's with me. I've been feeling off since my last encounter with Emery. I don't know what to do with her. One minute she acts like she doesn't care that our relationship is purely sexual, but then I see the hurt in her eyes and the defeat in her body language. It's very confusing.

Thankfully, we aren't issued name tags. That would destroy my look. The room's decibel level drops a few points when Jenn and I walk in. At least around us it does. I scan the room and see most women are dressed more conservatively. Perhaps my dress is a bit much for a retirement party.

"Let's grab a drink and maybe find a table." Just as I'm ready to stake my claim to a chair, I realize we have assigned seating. I hold up a card. "Looks like we're going to have to hunt first." The venue holds one hundred and eighty people, with six people to a table. We could be searching all night.

"Excuse me, ladies? Do you need help finding your seats?"

An usher carrying an iPad stands in front of us and tilts his head as he waits for me to tell him my name.

"Claire Weaver and Jennifer Matthews."

He types in my name and ushers me closer to the stage. We're at a table with four people I don't know. The mayor, who's across the room shaking hands with everybody, is at the table beside me. The backs of our chairs almost touch. His wife is sitting at the table, alone, and even though she's smiling, she looks uncomfortable. I decide to introduce myself. "Hi. You must be Sterling's wife. I'm Claire Weaver."

"Yes, I'm Eloise Moore. It's so nice to meet you. I've heard a lot about you," she says.

I introduce Jenn to her, who automatically turns on the charm. Within a matter of minutes, we're laughing and joking with her. Eloise is poised, shy, and seems like the wrong person for Sterling. "How long have you been married?"

"Fourteen years. We dated after college and got married after he finished law school."

"You have three children, right?"

Her eyes light up. "Yes. Scout is twelve, Harper is nine, and Jeremy is seven."

"Those are great ages," Jenn says. "My boyfriend has two children who are six and eight. They're so fun."

I sit there because I have nothing to add to the conversation. I want to people-watch, but that would be rude while a conversation is happening two feet in front of me. After a few minutes of Jenn and Eloise sharing photos of the children, we finally break free after another person approaches Eloise to chat. I grab Jenn and we bolt.

"She's too sweet to be married to him," Jenn says. She hasn't even met him.

"Let's mingle wherever he isn't."

"Do you recognize anyone?"

I spot Robert Howth, one of the partners of the law firm I left. The moment I gave my notice, he pretended I didn't exist. I made that fucker a ton of money. He's standing with his wife and one of the junior lawyers of the firm. When we lock eyes, he nods and raises his glass at me. I smile and nod. I turn to Jenn. "Well, I just had an exchange with my old boss."

"Wasn't he a jerk? Because I think we should go over there and talk to him so that he's forced to play nice. How much did the law firm get?"

"Way too much," I say.

"Claire. Hello, darling."

We turn to find Kevin's parents, who greet me as if we've been friends for years. "Aubrey, Reginald. It's so good to see you both again," I say. Aubrey kisses my cheek, and Reginald respectfully shakes my hand. I wonder if they gave their son the most boring name possible to make up for how pretentious theirs are. "This is my friend, Jennifer Matthews. She's a corporate attorney out in California."

"Hello, Jennifer. It's wonderful to meet you."

"It's nice to meet you both. How do you know Claire?"

Aubrey smiles. "We met at a fund-raiser several weeks ago. She and our son, Kevin, are both judges. What brings you to Kansas City?"

Jenn flashes a dazzling smile. "I went to UMKC Law School and lived here for several years before I took a job in California. When Claire told me about Judge Williamson's retirement, I thought it would be nice to come back and see people I knew from school."

Aubrey looks around. "So far most of the attendees are closer to my age than yours, but I'm sure people are still trickling in." She grabs my arm. "Claire, have a great evening. I'll call you. Maybe we can do lunch soon."

I nod and float away with Jenn. "That was intense, right?"

"I don't know. I think they might just be better at schmoozing than we are."

"She's a wealthy retiree. I'm sure she's had a lot of practice." I look over my shoulder, and she waves at me.

"Retiree? I thought they have a construction company," Jenn says.

"Among other things, yes. But do you really think she works?"

Jenn stops me. "Oh, my God. Don't we know those guys over there by the entrance? Brad and Edward or something?"

"You're close. Edwin. Brad and Edwin. I can't remember where they ended up. Do you want to go see them?"

"That's why we're here, right?" she says.

We make our way to the front of the room to chat with our law-school alums. Brad looks different. Back then, he was fit and athletic. Now he has a softer, balding-father look. Edwin hasn't changed much. They're wearing matching wedding rings, but their body language is just as comfortable as it was in law school. It's sweet that they're still together.

"Where did you end up, Edwin?"

He stutters. Brad takes his hand, and Edwin finds his voice. "Shade & Morrow. They specialize in tax law."

"Oh, so you probably have a lot in common with Jenn. She's corporate law out in California," I say. Jenn bumps her elbow into mine, and I smile. "It looks like the mayor's waving at us. It was so nice to see you again after all this time. Good luck." I'm sure I'll never see them again unless it's at another retirement party. Brad had said his father knew the judge, and he and Edwin were his father's plus one and plus two.

"Are we really going to meet the mayor?" Jenn whispers.

Without warning, Sterling ducks into our personal circle like the three of us are besties. Jenn and I both take a step back at his intrusion. Either he's been drinking or working the room too hard. It's almost seven, and soon his circulation will be curbed by dinner being served. "Sterling, what a surprise. We just met your wife a few minutes ago. She's wonderful. And she showed us your beautiful family," I say.

He laughs nervously. "That's great. But right now, I'm more interested in knowing who this lovely woman is. I'm the envy of all the men in this place."

"And probably some of the women." I can't help myself. I like to correct people as often as possible when they assume an entire room is heterosexual.

"Touché, Claire. Good point. And true, I'm sure."

He waits to be properly introduced to Jenn.

"I'm sorry. Where are my manners? Sterling Moore, mayor of Kansas City, this is my friend Jennifer Matthews."

Jenn holds out her hand and gives him a firm handshake. "It's nice to meet you, Mayor. I've heard so many things about you." Her voice has a lilt to it, and I bite my cheek to keep from laughing as she pulls her hand away from a handshake that's gone on far too long.

"The pleasure is all mine," he says.

Somebody yells out his name, and his smile falters before he quickly excuses himself. "Ladies, I'll see you at the table."

"He's attractive, but you're right. Something's definitely shady about him," Jenn says.

We are drawn into a quick conversation when a circle of lawyers from Anister, Howth & Pullman engulf us on their way to their table. The partners might be ignoring me, but my former colleagues seem happy to have run into me.

I feel somebody's fingertips press lightly into the small of my back and turn to see Emery walk by with a woman on her arm. My mind is flooded with questions, and I don't know how to process them. Emery is here. Emery is here with another woman. What I'm feeling isn't jealousy but embarrassment. What's Jenn going to say? I paste a smile on and focus my attention back to the group that's now spilling into tables. We're standing over people. It's rude.

"Excuse us, but we need to take our seats. The party is about to start, and we still need to get drinks." I wave off the sudden barrage of offers to fetch us drinks. "Thanks, but we've got it. Have a great night." I lead Jenn away.

"What's going on? You're super tense."

"Keep smiling. Let's get to the bar. I can't believe this."

She smiles and laughs. "What's going on?"

"Emery's here."

"Wait, what? Your Emery is here? I'm not going to look, but where?"

I casually glance around the room as if I'm bored and find her four tables from ours, her back to us. I can't see her date, but she has long, brown hair and, from what I recall when they walked by, a thin, shapely body. "We're going to have to walk past them."

"Them? Who's she with?"

I sigh. "A woman. A very skinny woman with long, brown hair."

Jenn smirks. "It's probably her sister."

"She only has a brother."

Jenn puts her hands on her hips. "Look, I'm trying. Don't worry about it. I bet she's nobody, and Emery doesn't want to be here. Side note. I'm excited to see her in person."

That makes me smile. I want Jenn to see her in person, too. I hand her the old-fashioned she's ordered and take my lemon drop. "Let me drink this down a bit." Walking with a martini and not spilling it everywhere is hard.

"Liquid courage. You've got this." She clinks her steady glass against my wobbly one.

"Be careful. A bigger crime is to make me spill this tasty delight." I try hard to show I'm not nervous, but Jenn knows me too well.

"You ready? Let's do this," she says. I nod and shake my free hand down at my side. "Look at me. Chin up. Shoulders out. Smile on. You're beautiful, smart, a hell of a lawyer, and the best damn judge this city has seen since Judge Williamson."

I can't help but burst out laughing because my stress level is high and her joke hits the spot. "I love you."

She links her arm with mine and pulls me in the direction of the table. My heart races the closer we get to Emery's table. Thankfully, it's not in the aisle, but close enough that we're going to be noticed.

"Hi, Judge. Hi."

I roll my eyes and stop. Jenn and I both turn to face their table. Fuck my life right now. Sitting next to Emery, who looks stunning in her tuxedo, is the woman who offered me a ride last month when my tire was slashed. Both stand when I stop.

"It's good to see you again. I completely forgot to introduce myself to you. I'm Lily Swarnes." She reaches out, and I have no option but to shake her hand.

"It's good to see you again. Thank you again for checking on me."

"Oh, you're welcome. This is my date, Emery Pearson. Emery, this is Judge Weaver."

I look at Emery. For the first time, I can't read her expression. "Hello, Emery Pearson, date of Lily Swarnes. It's nice to meet you. This is my friend Jennifer Matthews."

"It's so nice to meet both of you."

Her eyes never leave mine. The lights flicker to let us know it's time to find our table. Jenn and I excuse ourselves, but I know Emery is watching us. I can almost feel her stare as we make our way back to the table.

Jenn grips my arm as we walk away. "Wow. Emery's more impressive in person than I thought she'd be. Such intensity. Those eyes? I can't tell if they're dreamy or steamy. And Lily? No worries there. She's way too thin. And too 'in your face' chatty. Nobody likes that. Too much energy," she says.

I don't point out that Jenn is the same size as Emery's date. For the first time, my body confidence wavers. "She's pretty though."

"You and I both can pick out any hot mess in a room. She ticks all the boxes. Don't even worry about her." She puts her hand on my knee and squeezes it. "Besides, maybe she's totally jealous of me right now. I'm with you, and I'm super-hot." She nudges me with her shoulder. "Let's toast."

"What are we toasting?"

"How every single person in this room wants to either be you, be near you, or to fuck you."

Chapter Fourteen

Dinner is painfully slow, and my senses are tripping over one another. I strain to hear her voice or catch sight of Emery out of the corner of my eye. It's frustrating. And Sterling is trying to engage our table with his, and I'm done. I lean over to Jenn. "I'm going to take a walk. Are you okay here?"

She puts her hand on my shoulder. "Take your time. I'll hold off Sterling. Find out what's going on over there." She nods in Emery's direction.

"I won't be gone long." I brush a kiss across her cheek and make my way to the front of the room. Three people stop me along the way to introduce themselves, and as much as I want to brush them off, I can't. I remain cordial and excuse myself after a few minutes of conversation. I'm dressed for attention, and I'm getting it. I can't be mad.

Emery's presence is throwing me for a loop. It never crossed my mind that she could be here. I make it to the bathroom without any more interruptions and stand in front of the mirror. I look good. My hair is still styled perfectly, my makeup isn't smudged, and my dress hugs all my curves. I hate that Lily Swarnes, or whatever her name is, shakes my confidence. Maybe because Emery was adamant about not dating weeks ago at my place, yet tonight Lily introduced Emery as her date. Is this jealousy? Or disappointment because she lied to me? I take a deep breath and head back to the ballroom.

"It's not what you think."

I get instant chills. Emery is leaning up against the wall outside the bathroom. I admire her long fingers as she casually holds her drink by the rim. The hallway is filled with tension.

"Oh. What am I thinking?"

Fuck, she looks sexy. Her bow tie is slightly crooked. I'm filled with the desire to straighten it and touch the pleats in her shirt. Her hair is mussed, and the messiness gives her a carefree look.

She sighs. "You're thinking I'm on a date."

"I've learned not to assume things with you." I walk away because I'm confused about this night, but she moves off the wall when I take a step toward the ballroom.

"The judge is her uncle. She didn't have a date and asked me."

"Okay." I nod as if I understand or believe her, but I could see how comfortable they were in each other's space. Emery is more to Lily than a date. I take another step. She blocks my progress.

"I need you to believe me," she says.

I sigh and shift my weight to one hip and cross my arms. "Emery, we aren't exclusive. We aren't dating. You don't date, and I don't date. We just have a mutual respect for our unique and demanding needs." I air-quote 'you don't date' for effect.

"Christ."

"Okay. I'm going back to my friend. I don't want her to send out a search party for me."

"Is she your date?" she asks.

"Again, I don't date."

"She's lovely, but I can't imagine she gives you what you need." Her confidence level ramps up as she challenges me.

"I can't have this discussion here. Have a good evening, Emery." I nod and walk past her. I don't get far before I feel her fingers grab my hand and pull me toward a door near us. It's locked. She tries two more doors before one is unlocked. She ushers me inside and closes the door. It's a room full of chairs for either an upcoming event or one that just ended. Judging by the straight lines of the rows, probably one that's coming up. She pulls me into an alcove for privacy.

"I really don't want this to be an issue for us," she says. She runs her fingers over my cheeks and down my neck. I think she's going to kiss me, but she doesn't. "We're free to fuck whomever we want."

She doesn't deny it, and my stomach slips a little. "Who's your date?"

I laugh a little too hard. "That's Jenn. My best friend from law school who came into town to be my plus one since I don't have time to date."

Her shoulders visibly relax. I put my hand on her lapel. "Let's not read anything into this. Let's just go about our lives." I don't mean that. I don't want her to fuck Lily and then come over to my house. For the first time, I feel used. And I hate that I know Lily from the courthouse. That's going to make my already challenging job even harder.

She presses into me and kisses me hard. I snake my arms under her tux jacket and hold her close. She always smells so good and feels so warm. We stop when we hear a door close and people whispering.

"Look, I tried everything, but I can't do anything about it."

I recognize Sterling's voice.

"Try harder. You owe us. If this thing blows up, every single person involved is going down. You get that, right?"

I don't recognize the second voice, but I know a threat when I hear it. We peek out from the dark alcove when a scuffle ensues. Emery tenses as though she's planning to get involved, but I hold her back and shake my head at her. She thinks she's going to break up a fight, but I have a feeling that whatever this is, is far more complicated.

"Get away from me. If it comes out, it comes out," Sterling yells.

"If Seamus talks, you're the first one he'll name." I hear a thump and a groan. The other guy must have hit Sterling in a soft place. "Get that bitch in line, or I will."

"My hands are tied. I can't go around threatening people. That's not how I do things. Tell him that," Sterling yells.

I look out and see Sterling hunched over. The guy who hit him has already turned his back and is walking out the door. We watch Sterling pick up a chair from the perfectly lined row and throw it. Emery pulls me back into the shadows until we hear Sterling stomp off. The door opens and closes again.

"The coast is clear. And what the hell was that about?" Emery asks. "Are you okay?"

"I'm fine, but I have to go."

She pulls me close. "We need to finish our discussion."

"I don't know what to say. I don't know what this is, but I'm not going to be the other woman for you. If you want a relationship, have it with Lily. She complicates things for us because I work with her. You understand that, right? It's a serious conflict of interest. I'm sorry, but I can't be involved in whatever this is." I touch Emery's face. I don't tell her that I hope Lily makes her happy or anything cheesy like that. I'm excusing myself from this entanglement because it's become that. An entanglement. Work and play have collided, and I can't have that. "We need to get out of here and away from whatever that was."

Emery carefully opens the door we're standing in front of and peeks out. "Okay. It's safe."

I give her hand a squeeze and walk away without looking back. I'm sure Jenn's worried about me. I order two more drinks from the bar and head back to the table. Most people are up and mingling, but I see Emery is back at the table with Lily, and they're laughing at something somebody said. She got over me pretty fast.

"Are you okay?" Jenn asks. She takes the old-fashioned from my hand and pushes my chair back for me. "You were gone a while."

I see that Sterling and Eloise aren't seated. "Where's the mayor?"

"Oh, he and his wife took off. Said something came up and they had to leave. He was very cordial and shook my hand again. I really like Eloise."

"She's nice. But listen to what just happened." I lower my voice and look around before I start my story. Jenn leans closer, knowing discretion is a must. Her smile drops when she sees I'm not happy.

"So, Emery follows me and we're having a little chat in one of the other ballrooms."

"Chat like 'hey how are you,' or chat like 'let's fuck.' Strictly need to know for context," she says.

"More like 'let's talk,' but there was a really nice kiss."

"I see that." Jenn wipes the top of my mouth, where my lipstick has evidently smudged.

"I told her that I can't have work and my personal life collide."

"Again. Collide again."

Technically, she's right. "Yes, again, but on a larger scale. Lily is a lawyer, and at some point, she or her firm will try a case in my courtroom. I can't have this much conflict of interest. She could destroy me if she finds out Emery and I hooked up prior to my first case, where Emery testified."

She rubs my arm. "I get it. And I'm sorry that has to happen."

She thinks I'm upset about that. I am, but like with every woman before Emery, I'll move on, and it won't be an issue. At least I hope that's how it plays out. "Here's the interesting part. Sterling and some guy were having a not-so-friendly chat. There were threats about a boss not being happy, and he mentioned Seamus. That's the arsonist Sterling asked me to go easy on."

"What?" Jenn's voice is laced with panic.

"Maybe it was a different Seamus." It sounds weak even as I'm saying it.

"What did Sterling say?"

"Nothing. He threw a chair."

"At the guy?"

"No, after he left, but some testosterone-induced shoving on both their parts happened. Emery almost got involved, but I held her back."

"She tried to get involved after the chair throwing?"

"No. I'm telling it all backward." I start over and tell her exactly what Sterling and the mystery man said.

"I was right this whole time. The mob, threats. You have to have somebody you can talk to. I don't like this."

"I don't want to be here anymore. Can we leave?"

Jenn finishes her drink and nods. "Let's go. We'll have more fun at your place anyway. We still have time to fit a rom-com under our belt. Can you get our coats? I need to go to the bathroom before we leave."

I head straight for the coat check. After ringing the bell three times, I walk around the corner to the coat room and find it unlocked. "Hello? Is anyone here?" Someone shoves me from behind, and I stumble inside. Then somebody trips into me. The second shove is more forceful, and I fall against the coats. I stay upright, but I don't know how. I turn and find the same man who just argued with Sterling.

"Look, you bitch. You screwed up big-time, and now you're going to pay for it." Spittle shines in the corner of his mouth. His eyes are bloodshot as though he hasn't slept in days or is drunk. His hot, sour breath reeks of cigarettes and bad hygiene, but I don't smell alcohol.

I flinch at his nearness. "I don't know you or what you're talking about." I try to keep my voice steady, even though my stomach is rolling and quivering.

He cups my face hard and moves closer to me. "Don't fuck with the power in this city." The world goes black for a fraction of a second as the back of his hand connects with my cheek.

"Motherfucker!" Even though it's filled with hatred and anger, Emery's voice comes into focus before her face does. She peels the man off me and throws him, so he stumbles into the aisle and crashes into a group of men leaving.

"Hold him. He just assaulted a woman," Emery says.

The five men walking by don't hesitate and hold him down on the floor. He struggles desperately to break free. A staffer rushes over, and Emery barks for him to call the cops.

She turns to me and winces. "Are you okay?"

Her anger frightens me, but I nod. She gently cups my face and tilts my head to see the bruise that I feel already forming across my cheekbone. "Fuck."

"Oh my, God. What happened?" Lily rushes over to us, and Emery drops her hand from my face. I am flooded with emptiness when our physical connection ends.

"That douchebag just assaulted Claire," Emery says.

"You'll be sorry," my assailant says. He smirks as if he knows something more than what's going on here.

One of the guys holding him down laughs at him. "You just assaulted a judge in a room full of lawyers and other judges. I'd say you're fucked."

"What the hell's going on?" Jenn rushes over to me and pulls me into a hug. I'm so close to crying. "Oh, baby. Did that asshole hit you?" She tilts my head, too. It must be bad because she winces as well.

My cheek is hot and swollen. "Somebody needs to take a picture before this beaut goes away." I laugh, but that makes my cheek hurt more.

The hotel manager ushers me and Jenn into a private room. I look at Emery before slipping into it. Her chest is heaving, and her face is flushed. When I shake my head, she stops where she is. We don't need any more questions. The manager hands me an ice pack after Jenn snaps a few pictures of me. I don't want to see them, and she doesn't offer.

The manager's walkie cuts into the silence. "Ms. Brown, the police are here." We all sigh with relief.

She clicks on her walkie. "We're in Ballroom C."

Thirty seconds later, two police officers walk into the room to take my statement.

"Did you recognize the man who assaulted you?" The female officer asking questions is very calm with a soothing voice.

"I've never met him prior to this evening," I say.

"Can you walk me through what happened?"

"My friend and I decided to leave the party, and while she was in the restroom, I went to get our coats. Shit, Jenn. I never got our coats."

"I'll get them after we're done," she says.

"Nobody was at the desk, so I went to the side door, which was unlocked. I opened it, and just as I was stepping into the room, he pushed me from behind. Twice. When I turned around, he hit me in the face."

Jenn squeezes my shoulders. "Bastard. I hope they throw the book at him."

We both know he'll be out within a day. I'll be sure to find out who bails him out. The officer snaps pictures of my bruise for official use. I'm too angry to be scared. Jenn grabs our coats, and an officer walks us to the town car.

"Are you sure you're okay, Judge Weaver?" he asks.

I wave him off. "I'm fine. I just need to rest and put ice on my cheek. Thank you for getting here so quickly and taking care of things." I climb into the car, grateful the trip will take only a few minutes.

"I can't believe all of this just happened. What the fuck? Like what the actual fuck? Who is that guy?" Jenn holds me, and I don't know if it's to make me feel better or for her to calm down. Probably both. She's seething.

"I would be a mess if you weren't with me this weekend. I can't imagine going home alone after that."

"The cops will probably come by in the morning and dig a little deeper. There's obviously some connection between the arson case and the mayor and your assault. They might even give you protection. I'm not going to leave you alone."

Fuck. I didn't even think about that. "You're going home tomorrow. I'll be fine. I'm sure whatever's going on ended with him."

Jenn obviously believes that about as much as I do. "I'm going home after things settle down, even if it's next week. Okay, we're here. Let's get you cleaned up and into warm pajamas."

I follow her into the building, relieved that we have security. I hand her my key for the elevator and punch the code to my floor. "Why am I so tired? It's barely ten."

"It's the adrenaline leaving your body."

I kick off my shoes and walk upstairs to take a shower. Jenn wants me to put ice on my face, but I need to clean myself first. I feel dirty. Violated. The hot water feels wonderful. I wash my makeup off, careful of my tender cheek, shampoo my hair, and scrub my skin hard. The water cools, so I turn it off and slip into lounge pants and an oversized sweatshirt. My cheek is red and slightly swollen, and I know it'll change colors by tomorrow. That really hurt. It dawns on me that I didn't tell the police officers about Sterling's confrontation with the same man earlier in the evening. Considering he mentioned Seamus's name, I definitely should have.

"You know what I forgot to tell the police?" I'm walking down the stairs towel-drying my hair when Jenn stops me.

"You have a visitor. I thought it would be okay that she's here," she says.

She moves aside. and I see Emery standing by the couch, her eyes on me. She's concerned, and a part of me wants to melt against her because I feel safe with her. Instead, I stay exactly where I am.

"How are you?" she asks.

The first thing that pops in my head is Lily. Where is she? I also hate that I'm not sexy right now. "I'm okay. Thank you again for being there for me." I've never felt so vulnerable.

Jenn hands me an ice pack and motions for me to sit on the couch. "We need to get the swelling down. God, I hate that he hit you." She turns to Emery. "How did you get there so fast?"

Emery unclenches her fists and shakes her hands. "I wasn't fast enough. I wanted to say bye before you left. I just didn't get there in time."

On instinct, I reach for Emery's hand and pull her to sit with me on the couch. Jenn sits across from us in a chair. "You got him off me, and that's important. If you hadn't been there, who knows what would have happened."

"I would have killed him," Jenn says.

"Same," Emery says.

They share a moment over me—my best friend and my no-strings-attached ex-lover. Even agitated and stressed out, Emery looks sexy. Her jacket is on the table, and her tie is missing. I wonder if it's in her pocket or her car.

"I don't know about you all, but I could use a smooth drink," I say.

Jenn jumps up and pours us whiskeys. The first sip heats my throat, and I welcome the sharpness. The second sip calms my tastebuds, and I settle into its warmth. Emery swirls her glass but doesn't take a drink. Jenn's looking at the label that I know she's not really reading. I'm the only one drinking. I take another sip.

Emery carefully hands me the ice pack. "You need to put this on your cheek to keep the swelling down."

"Thank you," I say.

Emery's tense, and Jenn's bouncing her leg. I'm the only calm one. I hold the ice pack against my cheek in one hand and my whiskey in the other. "All in all, I thought the party sucked, but the food was decent," I say.

Nervous laughter bubbles up from both, but they remain quiet.

"Okay. Let's talk about something or turn on the television or something, because I can't be alone with just my thoughts," I say.

Jenn jumps up. "I'm still upset that asshole put his hands on you. And who is he? Why you? What's going on?"

"And what were he and the mayor arguing about? Obviously, they know one another," Emery says.

"I forgot to tell the officers about that, but I'm going to have to confess we were in that room, Emery," I say.

"That's fine. Whatever it takes to lock him up."

I'm not one-hundred-percent sure I'm ready for the world to find out about a somewhat clandestine meeting in an empty room with a former witness. Especially since I wasn't her date for the evening. I sigh. Just when my career is taking off.

"Do you remember what he said? I still think it's the mob," Jenn says.

"What? What are you talking about?" Emery looks at Jenn likes she's nuts.

"I told Claire at the beginning of the trial that it could involve the mob. They burned down that warehouse to hide something, and the mayor's obviously involved," she says.

"The mob? Are they even still around?"

"Well, no. Probably not. But somebody rich and powerful had something to gain by the warehouse fire." Jenn crosses her arms and stares at us. She's still wearing her dress and heels.

"Why don't you go change clothes? You don't look comfortable," I say.

"Okay. I'll be right back, but we're not done talking about this."

When Jenn leaves, Emery turns to me. "I'm sorry about everything that happened tonight. I know I put you in a bad spot by pulling you into that room."

I put the whiskey down and touch her forearm with my free hand. "We needed to talk about some things. I'm not sorry."

"How do we leave things now?"

I smile sadly at her. "For now, we keep it as friends." I don't want to rehash that she's in a relationship with somebody who could potentially destroy my career. We had figured that out earlier, but we both need to hear it again.

"I get it. Do you mind if I stay here tonight? I can sleep on the couch. I just want to make sure you're okay."

I agree. Her presence will give me peace of mind. "That would be nice."

When Jenn returns, I tell her Emery's staying on the couch tonight.

"She can have my room. I'm sleeping with you," Jenn says.

Emery thanks her but decides to stay on the couch. I pull out a soft pillow and a blanket and put it on the couch for her.

"Thank you for everything tonight," I say.

"Good night, Claire. I hope you sleep well."

I stop on my way up to my bedroom and try to muster a smile, but my cheek is numb and my energy waning. "Good night, Emery."

CHAPTER FIFTEEN

The mayor is here to see you."

April calls me instead of popping in because my door is locked. I hear the handle jiggle a few times and a rapid knock.

"Claire, I'd like to have a word with you. Please," Sterling calls through the door.

He's the last person I want to see. Jenn begged me to take a sick day, and I promised her I would be safer at the courthouse. The place is swarming with law-enforcement officers and lawyers. After fighting with me about whether she should stay or go, she reluctantly left late last night. Emery left early Sunday after a quick breakfast and the promise to check in with me, because that's what friends do. She texted me twice during the day and once before bed. I hate the shift in our relationship.

"Claire?" The knocking continues.

When I walked in this morning wearing large sunglasses, nobody questioned me. Heavy makeup helped, but the bruise was starting to turn blue, and it's hard to cover a dark color. Wayne, the security guard who always had a smile for me every morning, wanted to say something but held his tongue. He was gentle when he handed me my briefcase, and his voice was softer as he wished me a great day. News traveled fast. April greeted me with a latte and an "oh, my God," then clamped her mouth shut and kept pulling her gaze away. At least she was trying hard not to stare.

"Now is not a good time, Sterling," I call.

"We need to talk sooner than later."

I open the door, and even though he steps forward, I don't let him in. He cringes when his eyes meet mine and he sees the bruise. "Please. We need to have a conversation."

I know this isn't a good idea, but I also know he's not going to leave my office. If I call security, it will create an even bigger scene. I'm not physically afraid of him, so I reluctantly let him in. "Hold my calls, April, and stay close." She nods.

He waits until I shut the door. "I'm so sorry you were assaulted Saturday night. I heard about it after I left. Are you okay?"

I wait for him to finish, but that's all he gives me. "I don't like bruises, and I don't like to be bullied by people you know."

He looks surprised. "What?"

"Cut the shit. Bruno Raymond, the guy who assaulted me. I know that you know him. I saw the two of you arguing before you left."

His eyes dart up and down several times as though he's wrestling with something. He sits down without asking and drops his head into his hands. "Look. I can't get into anything with you, but that was never supposed to happen."

I sit safely behind my desk. "Sterling, you shouldn't be here. You coming to my office during an ongoing investigation is sending up so many red flags. You need to leave. If you need help, we can get somebody here to help you."

"It's my problem. I'm handling it."

"Yes, but at my expense." My voice is clipped. "And I don't like that. Who is that guy to you? And why were you arguing about Seamus Williams?"

"I don't know what you're talking about."

I take a deep breath and lean back in my chair. "I think you should go. The police will handle this matter."

He stands, puts his hands on his hips, and stares at me. "I suppose you're right. Whatever happens, just remember that I never wanted for you to get hurt. I like you, Claire. I think you're going to do great things for our city."

I'm still staring at the door after he leaves. I have no idea what that was about, but I have a feeling it's just the beginning of something career-ending for him.

Daily check-in. How are you doing?

I smile when Emery's message pops up. *It's been a day, but I'm okay. How are you?*

Worried about you. Glad you're okay.

I'm staying hidden in my office, but at least I'm getting a lot of work done.

I don't tell her about Sterling's visit because I don't want to upset her. She and Jenn had a lengthy discussion about Sterling while I was sleeping. Apparently neither one is a fan.

Let me know if you need anything.

Thanks.

Maybe I can bring over dinner this week.

I'm too vulnerable for her right now. Emotions I've kept bottled up for years are at the surface, and I'm afraid I'd slip up. And sex, even though I'm desperate for it, is a bad idea. We need space.

This is a bad week for me. And it's probably not a good idea while there's an investigation.

I understand.

Then silence. I hate myself right now. She's only being kind like a friend would be, but I'm so obsessed with how the world would see our relationship that I can't accept what she's offering.

I brush all personal thoughts from my mind and focus on work, which is the only thing holding me together, but even that's threatening to shatter.

❖

They tell me to stay close to home until the investigation is over. After three weeks of only going to work and having food and groceries delivered, I'm done. The investigation has stalled, and I can't wait anymore. I need to get out. I want interaction. I haven't been to a bar in over a month, and I miss Midtown Lounge's lemon drop martinis. It's a high-end bar where you almost pay rent for a barstool, but it keeps the younger partygoers at bay. I look good since the bruise is gone. I slip into a long-sleeved black dress, my black strappy heels, and style my hair up. It's getting too long, so I make a note to have it cut next week.

Jenn isn't happy that I'm going out, so I share my location and promise to call when I'm safe at home. I know it's a little risky, but honestly, I just want to be alone and drink a delicious martini and people-watch. I'm tired of talking to people this week. I shake out the stress in my shoulders when I walk into the bar. A pianist is playing a song that sounds familiar, but I can't remember the title. For the first time in a month, I feel normal. The faces in the bar look happy and fresh. It's almost midnight and a weeknight. I expected fewer people.

"Aren't the lemon drops the best?" A beautiful woman points to the empty chair at my table. I nod, and she sits. She's wearing black pants, a flattering cream-colored cashmere sweater, and a wedding ring. Interesting.

"They are my favorite drink here," I say.

"Can I buy you another one?"

"Will your wife mind?" I don't know why I'm sabotaging a possible hookup. I can't remember my last orgasm that wasn't self-administered. Okay, I do, but I'm trying to push it from my mind.

She tilts her head and smiles. "My wife and I have an understanding."

It amazes me how lesbians find me so quickly. "How did you know?"

She points to the three different men I turned down the first fifteen minutes I was here. "So, I figured I'd try."

"You figured correctly," I say.

She flags over a waitress and smoothly orders two more drinks. "I'm Jules. Jules Perez."

"I'm Claire." I don't offer my last name. "It's nice to meet you, Jules. What brings you out tonight?"

Her dark hair falls in waves over her shoulders and down her back. "I just felt like getting out, you know?"

"I definitely know exactly what you mean." She couldn't possibly know how important tonight is to me. This is the way my life was and should be again.

"Tell me about yourself." She leans back in her chair and relaxes as though settling in for a long chat.

"Work keeps me pretty busy. This is the first time I've been out in a month," I say.

"Life's about to get crazy, with the holidays right around the corner."

She's confident, like Emery, but more relaxed. Emery was always tense, as if ready to pounce when we were together. Jules seems like the kind of person who'd shrug if I turned her down and move on to the next woman.

"Do you ever attend the Plaza Lighting?" she asks.

"I used to live on the Plaza, and I never missed it. But I moved, so now it's more of a chore to get down there. I don't know if I'm going this year." More like, if somebody is still trying to hurt me, I'll pass.

"What do you do?"

"Nothing special. Just something that keeps me busy," I say. She nods. She's not here for my background. She's here for a drink and some company.

"I get it. My family owns a restaurant. I work more than I should, so it's nice to get out and away from the pressure." She leans forward after finishing her drink and runs her fingertip along the back of my hand. I don't pull away. "Do you want to get out of here?"

"I'd like to finish this drink first." My blood flows a little faster at the look she gives me, and I like the direction my night is turning.

"Take your time," she says. She orders a water when I show that I'm not gulping down my drink.

"The mayor's flipping on the lights this year," she says. Apparently, she's going to keep talking about the lighting ceremony. It's so hard to not roll my eyes at her. Thousands of people cheering on somebody who's in the middle of an investigation surrounding his corrupt dealings. I'm surprised the press hasn't uncovered it by now. "It's usually the mayor or the hometown quarterback or somebody who's done something above average." I sound bitchy even to myself. I try again. "It's nice that it's not too cold most of the time."

"My family fixes a huge meal at the restaurant on Thanksgiving, and then we bundle up and head down with hot chocolate."

"That sounds nice." It does. I'm somewhat jealous that she has a big family and plans for the holidays. I'm going to stay in, watch the Macy's Thanksgiving Day parade, and review case notes. At least I have solid plans for Christmas. My parents are coming into town from Boston to spend a long weekend with me. My holidays are always lukewarm at best. I take the last sip of my martini and set the glass between us. My meaning is clear.

"Shall we?" she asks.

I slip on my coat and follow her out, not really knowing the plan. I frown at the soft flakes that have started to fall. No accumulation expected, but the first flakes always sadden me. That means more clothes, and I don't like to wear layers. The robe is restrictive enough.

"I was thinking I could show you our restaurant," she says.

"Okay. We can try it." I've had sex in a kitchen but never a restaurant. "I can follow you there. I'm parked across the street."

"I'm right here." She points to a black Tahoe.

I smile because that's always an option for a hookup. When was the last time I made out in a car? "Lead the way."

She waits for me to turn around and slip into traffic behind her. The restaurant is less than ten minutes away. I pull into the empty lot and park beside her. It's on the west side of downtown in an up-and-coming neighborhood that was once run-down.

"Your restaurant looks adorable," I say. This is clearly a restaurant that serves Mexican food, based on the neon sign of a cactus wearing a sombrero. It's off at the moment but no doubt is bright when plugged in. She unlocks the door and flips on the lights. "And it's very cozy inside."

She slides her hand down my arm and holds my hand as she gives me the tour. When we hit the back office, she turns and kisses me. She has gentle lips and kisses me softly. It's not what I want, so I pull her close and deepen the kiss. She moans in approval and pushes my coat off my shoulders.

"Are there cameras in here?" I ask.

"No. This is the only place without any. Look."

She points to the security system on the computer screens. She's right. I see four cameras in the dining area, one in the kitchen, one in the hall, one in the bar, but nothing in the office. I look around the room at a love seat, two chairs, and a desk covered with piles of paperwork. A honeysuckle plug-in air freshener tries to cover the smell of grease, and the result isn't pleasant.

"Okay? No cameras. Not here," she says.

"I believe you." I drape my coat over the chair and sit on the love seat. She wastes no time straddling me. I put my hands on her hips, and she cups my face before kissing me. It doesn't take long before she crawls off me and drops to the floor between my legs. Guilt washes over me, and I stop her from moving her hands up my thighs. "Give me just a minute."

"I'm going too fast, aren't I?"

I have an incredible urge to get out of there, but I don't want to be rude. I came here with every intention of having sex, but now I can't go through with it. She leans forward and kisses me. I stop myself from pulling away. The problem is me, not her. I touch her face and smile.

"I'm sorry, but I'm not ready for this. I have to go."

She looks surprised but covers her reaction. "Did I do something wrong?"

I hold her hands. "No. You did everything right. I'm sorry."

Her lips briefly touch mine. "I'm sorry, too. Come on. Let's get you out of here."

I stop her. "Thank you for understanding."

She walks me out and ensures I get into my car. "Do you know how to get out of here?"

"I do. Thank you again. I'm sorry."

"Stop apologizing. I still had fun with a beautiful woman. Have a great holiday, and come by anytime."

The trip to my loft is quick, with hardly any traffic and the lights in my favor. The tears I brush away have to be stress-related, because I don't get emotional about sex. It's to be enjoyed by both or all parties, but I've been inundated with so much change the last four months. That has to be the reason. When I'm safely inside my loft, I text Jenn.

I'm home.

Thank God. How was your first night out?

I take off my clothes and slip into pajamas. It's almost one thirty. Why do I insist on going out nights where I have to get up early the next day?

So I went back to this woman's restaurant, and something weird happened.

OMG!

Jenn FaceTimes me. "Tell me everything. Were you followed? God damn it. I knew you shouldn't have gone out."

"No. Nothing like that. I went to Midtown Lounge and this beautiful woman picked me up and we went back to her restaurant."

"Wait. You had sex in a restaurant?"

"No. I mean the intent was there, but I didn't follow through. What are you doing? Can you talk right now? It's late even for you."

"I'm at my place for once. I spend too much time at Orlando's. I feel like my own apartment is an escape." She doesn't sound upset. "How are things going? Pretty well, I guess."

"We've been talking about moving in together."

"Oh. That's exciting, right?"

She shrugs. "I guess. I just don't know. What if we fail, and I've given up my nice apartment for no reason?"

"Then you move into a different one. Orlando's perfect for you. As long as you can still get away a few times a year, then I say live where you want, and if you want to live with him, then do it. He's a really great guy."

She stares at me. I nod. She breaks into a smile.

"You're right. He's perfect. And we all seem to get along. The kids listen to me and give me space when I have to work."

"Perfect. Now let's get back to my issue," I say.

She covers her mouth and gasps. "I'm so sorry. I hijacked the conversation. Okay, you met a girl, and she took you back to her restaurant. What happened after that?"

"We were making out on her couch, and I felt super guilty, like I was doing something wrong. And she was doing everything right. It was just weird. I stopped her and got out of there," I say.

"Do you think this has to do with Emery?"

I immediately want to say no, but I can't. I ended it because I was worried that Emery's feelings were starting to show, but now I'm wondering if I ended it because of mine.

CHAPTER SIXTEEN

I review next week's docket and groan. Lily Swarnes is listed as the defense attorney for a case that's going to trial. Jury selection starts Monday. Of all the fucking luck. Lily has popped up into head far too many times since the incident, and Emery has never left. I miss sex with Emery. The texts have slowed between us. I don't know what's going on with the investigation. It feels like I'm no longer in control of my life. My phone beeps, and my pulse races when I see Emery's name on the screen.

How are you?

Speak of the devil. I crave her.

You're talking about me? she asks.

You just popped up in my thoughts.

Hopefully all good.

I send a smile emoji.

Can you talk?

Yes.

My phone immediately rings. I wait until the third one before I answer. "Hi."

"How are you?"

I've missed her voice. "I'm hanging in there. I was just thinking about the investigation and wondering if it's ever going to end."

"You know these things take forever. And if the mayor is involved and he's not the target, whatever's going on must be huge," she says.

"Wonderful way to start my career." I realize how selfish I sound. Emery is in this, too. "How are you? How's your job?"

"We've been pretty busy. You'd be surprised at how many house fires happen because people don't think to clean out their chimneys. I'm actually on my way home from a call."

"Were you texting and driving?"

"No, I was talk-to-texting and driving."

"Have you had dinner?" I don't know why I ask. It's not as if I have any food my place.

"Are you inviting me over? Because I smell like smoke, and I'm a mess right now," she says.

"I don't mind. I can order us food."

She sounds hesitant. "Is that a good idea? I mean, I don't want to overstep any boundaries you've set."

She has every right to question me. And enough time has passed that if anyone questioned us, we have public history where friendship is believable. "As friends only. I could use one right about now."

"If you don't mind me smelling like smoke, I'll pick up dinner and be there in forty-five minutes."

I jump up, excited that I'm having company and even more excited that it's Emery. I make my bed and put on leggings and a sweater. I don't look like my normal fuckable self, but the last time she saw me was the night I was assaulted. I look better. I call down to the doorman and tell him I have a guest. I open a bottle of wine and pour myself a glass and wait. She knocks, and I jump up to open the door.

"I got salads." She holds up a giant brown bag. "I figure with the holidays coming up, it might be wise to go with something healthy." I'd forgotten how sexy she is. She's not wearing her uniform, but she's in khakis, a blue sweater with identification pinned to her breast, and black boots that give her added height. "Salads are great. Thank you for thinking about me. Come on in." I step aside, and she walks into the kitchen. She smells like a campfire and her cologne. I try not to squirm with need. She stands close to look at my cheek. "No more bruise. That's great."

It's hard to look her in the eye. I'm fighting my sexual attraction, and she's walking around my kitchen grabbing plates and silverware as though she's oblivious to me, to our history. "It was sore for only a week. Work was embarrassing. Nobody wants to see a woman with a shiner. That's definitely not the kind of attention I want."

"I'm sorry it was so hard for you. And, again, I'm sorry I didn't get there sooner," she says.

I want to touch her forearm, but I don't want to give her false hope. I don't want to give it to myself either. "I'm okay, Emery. I promise." I feel so naked and vulnerable when she looks at me. It takes all my energy to stay on this side of the kitchen island. "Tell me about you. What have you been doing?"

"Work is busy. It's hard to have a life this time of year. At least the holidays are coming up. I'm excited for an extended weekend, although I'm sure I'll get calls. Thanksgiving is the time when men think they know how to deep-fry turkeys and end up burning down their fences and decks. What are you doing?" Emery sits at the table after I do and pours herself a glass of wine. She leans back in the chair and waits, for me to engage with her, I suppose.

"I only get Thursday off. I have jury selection tomorrow because a case is going to trial. Hopefully, I can mediate a settlement, but everyone seems to want to go to trial."

Emery wipes her mouth after taking a bite. "Yes. Lily said she's going to be busy this week with a trial. She's lead counselor."

I almost roll my eyes but catch myself. She'll be in my courtroom. Not that it's a secret, but I don't want to talk about it.

I wonder if Emery knows it's mine. I hate myself for asking, but I can't help it. "How is she?"

Emery blushes. A slight panic rises and sticks in my throat. I take a sip of water to suppress it as I wait for her answer.

"She's good. She's, uh, coming to Thanksgiving dinner with me. She didn't have anywhere to go. My parents make a big deal about it, and we invite a lot of people."

"Oh." I stare at Emery and realize she's serious and not just trying to make me jealous. "Oh, okay. I thought she came from a big family, since she's Judge Williamson's niece." There seemed to be plenty of family at his retirement party. She shoots me a strange look, as if she'd never thought of that. I nod at her. "That's nice of you and your family."

"What are you going to do for Thanksgiving?"

I don't want to lie, but I don't want her to pity me or, worse, invite me over. "I'm keeping it low-key this time."

She stares at me. "Thank you for not being upset."

I can feel the tiny vertical line on my forehead deepen as I try to stop myself from showing a negative reaction. "Does this mean you and Lily are dating?" I genuinely don't know how I feel about Emery and Lily possibly dating because it's never been confirmed until this moment.

"We seem to be in a place where we understand one another. Not dating, but we are getting to know one another."

She's suddenly very interested in her salad, and I put my hand on my stomach to keep it from falling. I know what she just said is not supposed to be hurtful, but it stings. "That's good then." I don't want to know anything more about their relationship. "My parents are coming into town at Christmas, so that'll be nice. Normally, I go there, but because of the new job and everything going on, I'm staying here."

"That'll be good. I mean, I go through withdrawal if I don't see my family at least every month. I have two nephews. Having an in with the fire department is super cool, and I have an image to uphold."

She pulls up a photo on her phone, the first personal thing she's shared with me. I look at the photo and instantly smile. It's Emery with two small children acting goofy. "They're adorable. Thanks for sharing. Do you take them on field trips to the fire station?"

She smiles and nods. "They love it. They get to climb on the trucks, slide down the pole, and hang out with the crew."

"What made you switch and become an investigator?"

"I like the science of it all—to fighting fires and behind why they start in the first place. It's fascinating."

I can tell she loves her job. And I know she's good at it. Her poise and knowledge on the stand was a massive turn-on. I'm going to have to change my way of thinking. "Not too many people love what they do as much as you do."

"I know you do. And as awesome as it is that you're a judge, I would have liked to see you in action in the courtroom."

I lean back in my chair and think about life before the trial that changed everything for me. "I enjoyed digging and getting to the bottom of things. I think I'm going to like being a judge more than a practicing lawyer. Not to mention all the work will be done ahead of time, so I only have to deal with what's important." I wonder what Lily's like in the courtroom. I'll find out soon enough. I refuse to allow my brain to entertain what she's like in bed. "I didn't enjoy trying cases. I enjoyed doing the research, like you, and finding out what happened. As a judge I'm literally handed only pertinent information, and most trials are done within a reasonable time frame. It's the best of both worlds." I'm not sure I love it as much as I imply. I need to find my comfort zone in my new job.

"I get it. I like the research aspect. I'm always afraid somebody might refute what I say, but so far, nobody's questioned my knowledge or skill," she says.

Normally, I would add a quick sex quip about her skill, but it might be too soon. "Your confidence is noted. You command attention in court." I'm not trying to inflate her ego, but we both know it's true. At least we still have the honesty between us.

"Thank you."

I can tell she wants to say more, but she sips her wine instead. She misses me. I can tell by her body language. The energy bouncing off her is intense. "Tell me something good about your week." Please don't say anything about Lily.

She shrugs. "I've been hanging around the fire station more, just because I miss the camaraderie. I love my job, but my boss is kind of a pain in the ass."

"Why?"

"Carl's a nice guy, but he's very controlling, and only his way is right. It's nice to hang out with the guys because they aren't perfect, and they still know how to have fun," she says.

"He's the guy who testified with you, correct?"

"Good memory. I don't think I've said his name before."

"I mean it could have been anyone. I just figure, your district and that being an important case. It just made sense. Speaking of which, have you talked to anyone about the ongoing investigation?" I ask.

"No, but I really want them to hurry the fuck up. I'm tired of looking over my shoulder. And also worrying about you."

I brush her statement off with a shrug. Oh, God. I've hit awkward small talk, and I'm drowning. I need to put space between us. "Would you like to sit in the living room?"

She thinks about it a little too hard, and I almost backpedal and retract the invitation. "Yes. That sounds nice." We move to the couch. Her impeccable wardrobe covers her from head to toe, but I see a flash of skin as she repositions herself on the couch. Same place, just a different posture.

"What do friends do at a time like this? Should we watch television or rent a movie?" I ask.

"What do you and Jenn do when you're together?" Emery runs her hand over her head several times, as if it's a relaxing thing for her. There's so much about her I don't know.

"We talk about everything. We have no secrets,"

"She knows about our past?"

I nod slowly. "She does."

Emery exhales slowly. "Okay. Tell me something about Jenn. I like her. She's fiercely protective of you."

"She's wonderful. We've been best friends for about twelve years now. I met her in law school." I pull a small blanket up and over my lap. My loft is warm, but I need another barrier between me and Emery.

"And you decided on different types of law. I mean, she's corporate law, right? And you're a pharmaceutical lawyer? Is that a thing?" she asks.

"It is, but I'm a product-liability lawyer. So, it's not just drugs. It's a bigger umbrella."

"Did you want to do that? When I hear that somebody's a lawyer, I automatically assume they're a criminal lawyer or defense attorney."

"Those are super-exciting avenues, but you can make a lot of money specializing in different things."

Emery chuckled. "I can see that by your new place. This is beautiful."

I'm quiet for a moment. "I didn't know how to tell you I'd moved. You were also the only person who'd been to that apartment. You, Jenn, and my parents."

"I liked your apartment. It was in a nice place and had charm. Or maybe you were the one who gave it charm," Emery says. She twists so that her back is against the arm of the sofa and her knee now on the cushion.

"I needed a forever place, and while The Plaza is nice, the crime rate is climbing. So far, the garment district has been nice and peaceful."

"This is a far better place, for sure. I love the windows and your bedroom up in the loft."

"Tell me about your house." I can't believe I'm making small talk and genuinely want to know her answers.

"I live in a mid-century-modern house. The backyard is very private, which is important to me. Some of my neighbors are older, and some are young families. We're a hodgepodge group."

Emery looks the type. Like she'd wrestle in the front yard with her neighbor's kids or help anyone with their groceries if she happened to be walking by.

"Why are you smiling at me?"

Busted. I shrug because my thoughts have turned cheesy. "You just seem like the perfect neighbor. Very helpful. Plus, you have EMT training and can help put out fires. I'm kind of a worthless neighbor. I won't watch your kids or your pets. No, you can't borrow a cup of sugar because I don't have any staples in my loft. And do I want to hear carolers outside my loft? No. Definitely not."

Emery looks stunned. "What? Who hates Christmas? I mean besides Ebenezer Scrooge, and even he eventually came around."

How do I explain to somebody who's had a life outside of work that the holidays have never been important in my world? "I don't hate Christmas. I enjoy the season. I just don't have a lot of family or friends. Remember, I only work."

"Okay, then. Let's talk about work. You sentenced that man to fifteen years, right?"

I snort. "An appeal was filed even before sentencing. Did I tell you about Sterling?"

"What about him? About that fight?"

I couldn't remember what Emery knew and what she didn't. "Sterling called and wanted to do lunch."

She interrupts me and rolls her eyes. "Of course, he did."

I shake my head. "Not like that. I made it perfectly clear I wasn't interested. He asked me to consider a lighter sentence for Seamus Williams." Her mouth drops open. I nod. "Yeah. He said he was a family friend and asked me to take it easy as a favor to him."

"That's bullshit. Seamus is trash. No way he's a family friend of the mayor."

"Oh, wait. This story gets better. That conversation happened before the retirement party. After I was assaulted, Sterling visited me at the courthouse. He pretended he didn't know Bruno Raymond, but I told him that I saw him and the guy arguing. I also let him know I told the police that as well. He left visibly upset. That case is covering up something big."

Emery sits forward. "Obviously, the mayor is in on whatever this is. Jenn's right. This reeks of dirty politics. But what was in the warehouse? It definitely started in the bank's storage unit."

"I could review the case files. I mean, the case was about the fire, not about the motive. Seamus kept his mouth shut. I thought for sure something would come out in the trial, but it never did." It's been a while since I got down and dirty with a case, and this one still has meat on the bones. "But if we do this, nobody can know. We don't know who to trust. That means you can't tell Lily. I can't have anybody in the courthouse knowing."

She walks over to the window and stares out at the river. "I won't tell anybody. This could be the friend thing we do together, right?" Her hands are in her pocket, pulling her pants tight across her ass. She looks delicious, but I can't think about that right now.

"I mean, we do need something to do, and this will be a way to exercise a different part of our bodies. Our brains."

"It seems rather silly. I'm positive the detectives on the case are a million steps ahead of this and have thought it through. But why not? You're right. It gives us a project together, and we get to unite our careers. And, hey, we might help take down the mob," Emery says.

"You know the mob isn't involved."

"I know, but I like Jenn's flair for the dramatic."

"The whole thing shouldn't take that long. I know this week is kind of out, but what about after Thanksgiving?" I sound desperate, and I'm not. I just happen to have extra time around the holidays.

Emery walks over to me, but she's careful to keep her distance. "What's wrong with tomorrow? Can you get the case files then? We can do a repeat of tonight. I don't have to be anywhere or do anything until Thursday. Unless I get called out, which can happen." She checks her phone, shoots off a text, and picks up her coat. "I'll swing by same time tomorrow, but tomorrow you buy dinner. Unless you want to cook."

"You just tell me Italian or Thai," I say. She smiles at me before swinging on her coat. "Have a good night. I'll see you tomorrow." I lock the door and brush off the emptiness I find inside. I'm not even horny. I have a drawer full of vibrators upstairs and a sex machine that requires me to do nothing. That's not it at all. I just miss having her desire me.

CHAPTER SEVENTEEN

I watch Lily's mannerisms and the way she carries herself around the courtroom. She's borderline high-strung and was probably the kind of child whose parents told her to settle down her entire childhood. The three or four minutes we interacted at the retirement party showed none of this energy. I like her though, even though we're complete opposites and have a history she's not aware of. She's young, eager, and not afraid to be loud in the courtroom. My mind wanders to her and Emery, and I visualize them having sex. It's only for a moment, and then my professionalism tamps it down.

"How many of you believe that large corporations put their own interests above those of their employees?" Lily asks the twelve people who are up first for jury selection. A few raise their hands, and she and her associate put their heads together and mark something down on a clipboard.

This will be most of my day. Jury selection. If I'm lucky, we'll have it done before lunch or shortly thereafter. Then we can dismiss the people who were called in to do their civic duty so they can get back to their lives. More questions are asked, more people are cycled into the courtroom, more are dismissed, and by noon, we have a jury and alternates. I dismiss the courtroom and return to my chambers.

April has a club sandwich and chips on my desk waiting for me. She alternates between salads and sandwiches each day, at my request. I'm glad today's carbohydrate day, because the afternoon is going to be as grueling as the morning was, and I'll need protein. My eyes hurt from the fluorescent light that fills the room with a bluish-white color that I can't imagine is healthy. The courtroom is twice as bad. I open my curtains for warmer sunlight and wish I hadn't. I watch Lily walk into the parking lot and climb right into Emery's car. It's hard to be certain, but I think they kiss. I move away from the window and sit down to my lunch. I don't know how to feel about that. Lily's a nice-enough person, but I can't imagine she's fulfilling Emery's needs. I take a bite of my sandwich and review my afternoon schedule. Hopefully, it'll be easy.

Samuel knocks at my door. "Judge Weaver?"

"Come in."

"I have the copies you requested."

He holds up a folder. I wave him inside. "Thanks. Just throw it in my in-box. I appreciate your help."

I return to reviewing my docket as though what he's dropping off isn't a big deal. When he leaves and closes the door, I reach for the packet and slip it into my briefcase.

I haven't heard from you in days.

Jenn's text makes me smile. She's exaggerating. We texted yesterday before Emery stopped by.

Liar. It's been less than twenty-four hours.

It's not too late to consider spending Thanksgiving with us.

Sounds so family-ish, but I have to work Friday. THE LAW NEVER STOPS.

Smiley-face emoji. *It will for me. I took it off. Think I might do some shopping with the kids on Friday.*

It's sweet that she's already doing mom things with them.

I haven't been on the job long enough to start taking vacations. Maybe next summer.

I can't believe I've been a judge for six months. I haven't been in the courtroom that long, but my time started when I was sworn in.

And you have Christmas.

My parents are coming to town for Christmas, so not much of a vacation, but it'll be nice to see them. How's Mr. Bloom?

Wonderful. How are you doing being friends with Emery?

She's coming over tonight. Just to hang out. I don't know why I don't tell Jenn that we're reviewing the case. Maybe to have some mystery still with Emery, or maybe because I don't want her to worry. I'm in good hands. Very good hands.

Oh? So, you're doing okay with that? I like her. If things can't work out in the more-than-friends scenario, then I like her for your friend. She's a good egg.

Thanks. I miss you.

Call me tonight. I miss you more.

"Hi, Judge Weaver. Thanks for your help in court today." Lily steps into the elevator and smiles as she adjusts her bag over her shoulder and pulls out her phone.

"No need to thank me. Just doing my job," I say. I look her over discreetly and pick out things about her that I think Emery admires. Her profession, her brains, her small waistline? I could probably wrap my hands around her waist. She looks good in a suit. Her ass doesn't quite lift enough in those heels, but I give her an A for effort. She also likes my shoes. Every time we've shared space, she's noticed them.

"Hey, doll. I'll be outside in one minute. See you then."

She hangs up the phone and looks at me sheepishly. "My car's in the shop. I don't want to splurge on a new one, but I might have to. Dead water pump and something else under the hood I can't remember."

"That's too bad. With the weather changing, a reliable car might be a wise investment," I say, very boringly. I've always splurged on cars. Luxury has always been important to me. Safety, too. I switch out cars every two years. The last thing I want is to be stranded in the middle of nowhere because my car died. We walk down the hallway to the parking lot. We both stall at the door, then reach for it at the same time.

"I'm sorry. Go ahead," she says.

"Thank you."

I stutter for a moment when I see Emery's car pull up near the sidewalk. I keep the smile on my face as I walk past them, even though it takes effort for the corners of my mouth to stay turned up instead of down.

"Have a good night, Judge," Lily says.

"You do the same." I make eye contact with Emery until Lily leans into my line of vision to kiss the soft spot in the corner of Emery's mouth. I turn my head and slip into my car. I'm not ready for that display, and it slightly jars me. Is she still coming over tonight? I'm going to plan as though she is. Emery has yet to let me down.

I'm home with a glass of wine in my hand within twenty minutes. Thai food sounds warm and delicious, so I place an order for Pad Thai, spicy shrimp soup, and spring rolls. It should be here in forty minutes. I change out of my suit, take a quick shower, and pull on yoga pants, a lightweight hoodie, and thick socks. My hair is damp and my makeup light. My phone rings. It's the doorman.

"Ms. Weaver? You have a visitor. Emery Pearson."

"Thank you. Please send her up."

I pour an extra glass of wine and open the door when she knocks lightly. I hand it to her and invite her inside. "I have the files."

"And I have dinner." She holds up a bag. "It was downstairs when I got here. I hope you don't mind."

"Not at all. I hope you like Thai."

"I do."

We don't talk about Lily at all. It's none of my business. "I'll fix the plates. Start looking through the case notes. We should probably look at everyone who has storage space in the warehouse. It might not be as obvious as everyone thought. Maybe it was a coincidence that Seamus started the fire in the bank unit and the target was some other unit."

Emery finds the list of renters in the warehouse and opens her laptop. "I'll start searching the names on the list."

I hand her a plate and sit on the couch next to her. "There are so many units here. This might take a while." I pause for a moment to enjoy the spicy pepper scent of her cologne before taking half the list from her. I slide down to the floor and rest my back against the couch. I'm apt to do something stupid and regrettable if I sit next to her with our knees touching from time to time.

"So far, most the of renters are individuals. There are only a few businesses. On my list at least," she says.

"Somewhere there's a list of all witnesses involved in the case so maybe a name will pop up, but I'm certain the lawyers on both sides have already reviewed this. This is 101 Law stuff right here." I finish my plate and put it on top of Emery's already clean plate. Using both hands makes the job a lot easier.

"Why do people have storage units?"

"What do you mean?"

"If it's something important, wouldn't they keep it in a safe at home?" she asks.

"Logically, yes, but having if off site and away from your family is smart, too. I'm sure you've seen plenty of stuff destroyed by fires." I have a safety-deposit box for my important documents. My bank is going to have to explode in order for any important paperwork to disappear.

"Why not use a security-deposit box?"

I swear she's in my mind sometimes. "Too traceable. Besides, they can be subpoenaed." I hand her my list. "Let's trade. Nothing jumps out on mine."

Our fingers brush when we swap lists, and I ignore the jolt that rushes over me. She doesn't seem to be affected and steadily reaches for her wineglass.

"I like this wine. Is it local?" Emery's face lights up at the hand-sketched label. She runs her finger over the burgundy and cream colors as though she can feel the twisting ribbon under her fingertips.

"It is. I went on an alcoholic shopping spree when I moved and bought a dozen local wines to try. They're all pretty good."

She nods. "Honestly, you can't fuck up a Moscato. It's basically sugared wine and the only way I like it."

"But you like your whiskey hard with a punch," I say. I regret bringing up our past because it needs to stay there. "I can pour you a whiskey if you'd like."

She puts her hand on my shoulder. "I like the wine."

My stomach flutters at her warm touch, and I stop myself from putting my hand over hers. I clear my throat. "Just make yourself at home with whatever you want." I freeze. Even though I mean what I say, I don't want her to take it any way than what I mean.

She reviews the new list of renters. I take my list and read over the names several times before they start sinking in. I sit up. One of the names is not only different but sounds entirely too familiar. S. Jeremy Harper. "Hold up. Look at this one." My red nail leaves a dent in the paper where I poke it in excitement. "No. This can't be right." I stand up in disbelief. "He couldn't be this stupid."

Emery stands when I start pacing. "What's going on?"

"Maybe I'm wrong, but I think the fire was set because of Sterling Moore."

"What do you mean? We know he's involved, but that's quite a leap." She takes the paper from me as if it will become clear to her just by holding it.

"This is a pretty clear connection."

"Will you please share?"

My pulse races as I fix the jigsaw pieces in my mind. "Okay. Sterling has three children, named Scout, Harper, and Jeremy."

"Really? Aren't those names from *To Kill a Mockingbird* or something?"

I roll my eyes. "People are forever trying to come up with names that are cool, but ultimately, names are fads. Anyway, don't you think S. Jeremy Harper is a little too obvious? How did nobody catch this?"

"How do you know Sterling's kids' names?" she asks.

"His wife told me the night I was assaulted."

She cringes. I give her a soft smile. "His wife was talking about their children with Jenn. And those names aren't easy to forget."

"We need to call the detective right now," she says and picks up her phone. She pauses before dialing his number. "Will you get into trouble for having these files?"

"No. I'm the judge on the case. We're not breaking any rules."

She nods. "And how are we going to explain us?"

Her eyes are guarded, but I know she's worried about my reputation. I touch her arm and the muscles in her forearm jump. I miss our connection. "It's fine. Our friendship is already on record from when I talked to the detective about seeing the mayor get into an argument."

She puts both hands on my shoulders and turns me to face her. "I understand that, but this could get ugly. It could be part of a much-larger issue, and we might have to testify or something. There's a difference between telling a detective about our relationship and discussing it in open court."

I relax into her semi-embrace. Her strength is exactly what I need. "Before you say no, I need you to hear me out."

"No."

"You don't even know what I'm going to say." I take a small step closer, but she doesn't move.

"Whenever somebody starts off like that, the answer is always no." She crosses her arms in front of her.

"You don't need to be involved. I can have the conversation with the detective and your name doesn't have to come up. It's not unreasonable to say I was reviewing the case file and saw the name. He doesn't need to know you were here. That way, we have less explaining."

"No. I don't like this at all. What if the detective is one of the mayor's henchmen, and he tries to hurt you?" she asks.

I sit on the couch to show I'm completely calm, even though my stomach twitches. "I can meet him in a public place, like downstairs."

She shakes her head. "I want to be near. I'll agree to this only if you let me be in the same space, and in public there's always a chance he could see me. What about up here? I can listen from upstairs."

Her idea has merit. I sure as hell am tired of being alone with men. "Okay. I can agree to that. I'd feel better if you were here."

She rubs her hands together. "Perfect. Now let's call Detective Simpson and see if he wants to talk tonight."

I roll my neck and pick up my phone. Emery nods encouragingly. I call the detective's cell phone because it's well after working hours. "Hello? Detective Simpson. It's Judge Weaver." I tell him I have something that might help in the investigation into Mayor Moore. Either he's a really good actor, or he really dislikes the mayor.

"I can be there in twenty minutes." His voice drips with hatred and desperation.

I disconnect the call and stare at Emery. "He'll be here soon. I don't think he likes the mayor."

Emery stands a little taller, and her eyes darken. I can feel the energy ramp up and radiate from her. I'm incredibly turned on. The delicious things we could do in twenty minutes. But I know she's involved with Lily, and I can't give her what she's asking for, so I take a step back and excuse myself. Hiding out in the bathroom isn't brave, but I need space from her. I'm flushed from tonight's events, and my clit is throbbing with need. I smile. When was the last time I felt a rush of desire this strong?

After several minutes, Emery lightly taps on the door. "Are you okay in there? Do you want to cancel?"

I open the door. "I'm fine. Just needed a self-pep talk." Or an orgasm, which I'll take care of after everyone leaves. She stares at me. and her gaze drops to my lips. She wants to kiss me. I wonder if she can tell I want, no, need to fuck. Judging by the way her nostrils flare and the quick rise and fall of her chest, she knows. Right before either one of us can say or act, my phone rings.

"Yes?"

"Ms. Weaver? There's a Detective Simpson here to see you."

"Thank you. Please send him up."

Emery squeezes my arm and climbs the stairs to my bedroom. She won't be visible but will be able to see and hear our conversation perfectly from the loft.

I open the door when Detective Simpson knocks. "Detective, thank you for coming over so quickly."

"Happy to, Judge Weaver. What can I do for you this evening?" he asks. He is polite and respectful, but his energy level is high like Emery's.

"Please have a seat. Can I get you a glass of water?"

"No, thank you. You said you have some information that might help the case?" His knee is bouncing fast, and I resist the urge to put my hand on it to still it. My anxiety is high, and his nervousness is feeding it. I hope it's code for "thank you for this information, now we can nail him" instead of "have you shared this with anyone" and my world goes black.

"I decided to look over the Seamus Williams's case after my assailant said his name. I wondered why Williams clammed up and didn't try to save himself." I hand him the list of the individuals and businesses who had units at The Vault, the warehouse that Seamus burned down. "I don't think the bank storage was the target."

"That case is closed, right?"

"The arson part is, but you might want to take a look at this unit."
I hand him the map of The Vault's layout. It contains five stories
of storage units, ranging in size from twenty by forty to something
smaller, like five by ten. "The bank had two twenty-by-forty units
across from one another, but look at who had the unit right next to the
bank." I point to the name on the list. "S. Jeremy Harper."

"Who is S. Jeremy Harper?"

"Maybe nobody, but Sterling Moore has three children. Scout,
Jeremy, and Harper. It could be completely coincidental, but it could
be more." I want to spew out everything Emery and I deduced, but I
want Simpson to make the connection himself. When the realization
hits, he looks up at me and nods.

"Thank you for this information." He stands.

"I'd like to be kept out of this as much as possible, but I'll do
whatever you need me to do." I can almost feel Emery hiss with
anger. She doesn't want me to put myself in any more danger, but I
have a responsibility.

"I understand. I'll keep you posted, but I'm sure something
will happen sooner rather than later. Thank you again for the
information."

"Have a good night." I lock the door behind him, look up at the
loft, and meet Emery's eyes. She doesn't appear happy. "I know, I
know, but the sooner this gets handled, the safer we'll all be."

"At least he seemed to appreciate the information. Maybe he'll
do something positive with it." She walks down the stairs until she's
directly in front of me.

I'm nervous to be this close to her. "I really need a break from
always looking over my shoulder. I went out for the first time in
forever, and it was wonderful to just have a drink."

She stiffens at my news but smiles. "Oh, that's nice. I'm sure
you hate being cooped up."

"I'm going out tomorrow because, as much as I love my new
place, I need to stare at different walls." Fuck. Why did I say that?
Now she'll want an explanation.

"It's a good thing we Scooby-Doo'ed this case." She grabs her coat. "Looks like my job here is done."

"As a friend, you are more than welcome to stay and watch a movie."

She pauses as though reconsidering her decision but slips into her coat instead. "Thanks, but I should go and run some errands. Be careful, Claire. Promise me that, okay?"

I want to smooth the worry lines off her face with my fingertips, but I fold my arms and nod instead. "I promise. You, too."

"Have fun tomorrow night, and Happy Thanksgiving," she says right before she closes the door.

I say "Happy Thanksgiving," but she's already gone.

CHAPTER EIGHTEEN

D o I need to leave?"

"I'm so sorry, but yes. I'm working on a case, and we just had a breakthrough. My coworker is on her way up."

Ashleigh, a date I found on Tinder, kisses me swiftly and grabs her keys and phone from the counter. I'm hoping she'll beat Emery, but the knock at the door tells me I'm about to have an awkward moment. "I'll call you later. Have a good night," she says.

I open the door to find a flushed Emery. She takes a step back as Ashleigh excuses herself. I'd normally find her look of surprise comical, but guilt slips into my brain, and I offer no introduction or excuse. "Be careful," I say to Ashleigh's back. She waves. "Emery. What's going on?" I invite her in.

"Have you heard?"

"Heard what?" I follow Emery into the living room, where she stops short, and I almost bump into her. I follow her stare where I see the empty wineglasses Ashleigh and I left behind. She tenses, and I want to explain, but I remind myself I have nothing to explain. I'm not dating Emery. I don't owe her anything.

"Uh, I didn't mean to interrupt."

It's no use pretending they aren't there. "Don't worry about it." I grab them and put them in the kitchen. That gives us both a few moments to settle down. "So, what's going on?" She crosses to the window. Her back is to me as she stares out at the city. I wait because I know she's working through the shock of catching me in the middle of a date, even though we have no obligation to one another. I know the sting. I've already felt it with her whether I want to admit it or not.

"They took the mayor into custody."

She turns and folds her arms across her chest. Her cheeks are flushed with what I presume is anger, and her gray eyes are almost black. I've seen her like this only once before, when she dragged that man off me.

"What! When? Why? I mean, how do you know?" I take a step toward her, as if being closer will make her talk faster. She steps back.

"My boss is friends with the captain, and the FBI just picked him up. The name you gave Simpson led him to a shell corporation the mayor was using to launder bribes. It unraveled from there."

Who's going to flip the Plaza Lights on if the mayor's in jail? My priorities clearly need work. "Wow. Just wow. I wonder what they found? Who was bribing him? I bet he squealed." Sterling was so dejected when he was in my office last. It wouldn't surprise me if it was a relief for him to finally tell the truth, whatever that is.

"I just hope everything comes out, and you can go about your life safely and not have to worry every time you go out," she says.

"I'm not going to lie. I love my loft, but I love my freedom more." I'm tired of standing. "Hey, can I get you anything? Do you want a drink?"

"No, thank you. I should go. I'm sorry I ruined your night."

I put my hand on her arm. "You didn't ruin anything. I'm glad you came over to tell me. This is important, and I appreciate it."

She nods and steps away from me. She doesn't look at me, and even though I want her to tell me why, I also don't want to know the truth. We both had to make decisions based on what we need, and Emery and I are at different stages in our lives.

Emery opens the door and turns back to me. "She's seems too young for you."

My anger flares, surprising me, and I snort. "Oh, like Lily isn't?"

"She's young, but not that young."

I change my approach and shrug. "Works for me. Plus, she's not looking for anything more than just what it is. A hookup."

"I guess if it works for you. I've decided a relationship is the way to go. I'm getting too old for games. Plus, having one is a lot more meaningful than just random sex."

"Oh? I was random sex to you?" Even through my anger, I hear the irony in my question.

Emery leans in so she's only a few inches from my face. "You know exactly what it was. Call me when you're ready to grow up and finally admit we have something."

I watch her walk down the hallway to the elevators, unable to come up with the words that matter. Tonight is too much. I need to vent. I shoot Jenn a text.

Can you talk?

She FaceTimes me immediately. "What's going on? Ooh. Look at you. You're gorgeous!"

I muster a small smile. "I need to tell you about my night." I watch as she stops doing whatever she's doing and gives me her total attention.

"I'm all yours."

"I don't even know what's the most important thing to cover. So much has happened." Do I start with Sterling, my date, or Emery's surprise visit?

"Let's get the boring stuff out of the way."

"They arrested Sterling tonight," I say.

"That's the boring stuff? Holy shit. What happened?"

I launch into the story about what Emery and I discovered and how we shared it with the detective on the case. "It sounds like he was accepting bribes. I really want to know who was bribing him. And what they were bribing him for."

She points out the obvious. "Well, you are a judge. You could probably make a few calls."

I laugh nervously. "I wouldn't even know who to call. My list of contacts is weaker than I thought it would be by now."

"What about that one guy's parents or even Judge Martinez?"

She's talking about Aubrey and Reginald McIntosh. "That's not a bad idea, but I wouldn't know how to approach them. What do I say? Hey, it's Claire. We met twice. What's going on with Sterling? I don't feel comfortable with it."

"How about googling it?"

"For sure it'll be on Twitter. This is going to be a huge story once it blows up."

"Nothing yet," Jenn says after a few seconds of silence.

"I guess we'll just have to wait until morning."

"If that was the boring part, what was the exciting part?"

I sit down on the couch and sigh. "I met a woman through Tinder. She's pretty, smart, and totally into me. Mid-twenties. I invited her out, and we had dinner tonight and drinks at my place."

"So far, I'm okay. Young is different for you, but I see nothing wrong with a solid decade age gap. How's her stamina?"

"Here's the weird part. Here's where I need your help. We started making out, and the doorman called because Emery was downstairs insisting on seeing me."

"Did they run into each other? Oh, man. That must've been awkward."

I fall back on the couch. "It was horrible, but their run-in wasn't the worst part."

I nod. "The worst part was when Emery kind of yelled at me."

"I can't imagine Emery yelling."

"It was more of a stern talking to."

Jenn smiles and raises her eyebrows. "Sounds hot."

"You're not helping."

"I'm sorry. I'm all ears."

I'm afraid to tell Jenn my feelings. I'm afraid to admit that Emery got inside me. "She told me to call her once I figure out that we have something more than just sex."

Jenn busts out laughing. "Oh, my God. That's too hilarious."

I purse my lips and swallow the immediate "fuck you" response on the tip of my tongue. Jenn isn't the problem. I am. I groan. "How did it happen? How did she get inside me? I was so careful."

Jenn struggles for composure. "Look, Claire Bear. It's a natural progression. It was bound to happen. Emery is a wonderful woman who has pleased you more than just sexually, and you don't know how to process your feelings. How do you feel?"

I want to lie and tell her I feel nothing, because that's been my MO for years, but I can't. "I don't know. I like Emery. She obviously satisfies me sexually, and we have a lot in common."

"Then what's the problem?"

"I'm afraid. I like my life the way it is. I've been through so many changes this year. I don't think I can handle another monumental shift in my life." Finally, the truth comes out. I want to cry, but I manage a weak smile instead.

"Remember the advice you gave me when I was doubting getting into a relationship with Orlando? Look at us now. You encouraged me to accept it, and we're happy as fuck. All because of you. Now my advice is to just let go. Drop your 'sex-only' rule and admit that Emery has gotten inside your heart. It might be great."

"Or it might be the worst decision ever." You learn about playing devil's advocate in law school, and I apply it to my daily life. It's safer to be guarded. I've gotten this far, but at what price? "Jenn, what do I do?"

"She left it up to you, so figure out what you're willing to give and call her if you can try to make a relationship work." Her voice softens. "I think you should give it a try. Emery is the perfect person to help you navigate a relationship. She understands you. And she'll be patient. Trust her."

I take a deep breath. "I'll give it some thought. I mean, she's with Lily now. I don't want to destroy their relationship for a test run."

"Oh, please. Lily's just a toy for Emery. Their relationship isn't substantial. If she were serious about Lily, she wouldn't have pushed you to admit that the two of you have something."

Chapter Nineteen

I really should take the stairs. It's healthier for my body and for my head. Lily quickly walks toward the elevator, waving her phone. I barely keep my groan inside.

"Hold the elevator, please. Did you see? They arrested the mayor," she says.

I have to hold the door for her because now we're having a conversation, even though it's one-sided, and it would be rude for me to not at least try to be cordial. I wave a copy of *The Kansas City Star* that Wayne slipped me. "I'm going to read it as soon as I get to my office."

"This is unbelievable. Blackmail, secret dealings, bribes. And members of two prominent Kansas City families were taken into custody yesterday," Lily says.

So much for the juicy read. Lily's puking out all the details, and my mind is racing with questions. "Sounds like a lot went down." As exciting as this news is, I'm dying to know about her day yesterday with Emery's family. "Say, how was your Thanksgiving?" For a moment, I don't think she's going to answer because she's so engrossed in the story.

"What? Oh, Thanksgiving. It was fine. How about you?" Her lackadaisical answer gives me hope that maybe Jenn's right, and Emery and Lily aren't serious. She's hardly paying attention to me. Her features are pinched in alarm as she scans the article on her phone.

"Mine was low-key." I bolt as soon as the doors open. "Have a nice day." I don't wait to walk with her, and she's so engrossed in the article she doesn't seem to care.

April is a different story. She jumps up and hands me my coffee, even though my hands are full. "Have you seen the news?"

"Somebody said something to me in the elevator. I'm about to dig into it now, so don't ruin it for me." I tip my coffee cup in a silent thank you and plop down in my chair. My work emails can wait. I read the front page of the paper while my computer boots up. Sterling Moore was arrested for bribery, money laundering, criminal conspiracy, and extortion.

Holy shit! Aubrey and Reginald McIntosh were also arrested for criminal conspiracy, extortion, and a ton of other offenses. I recognize some of the names of other people listed, but I don't know any of them. Sterling used to work for the McIntoshes and wrote bids illegally obtained through bribes to a city-council member who directed the contracts. That was how the McIntoshes' fledgling construction company was so successful.

The McIntoshes and their crooked city-council member helped Sterling get elected in exchange for his silence. Seamus is listed at the end of the article for setting the fire that burned down a warehouse with paperwork Sterling was secretly storing as leverage, just like Emery and I thought. Seamus was nothing more than a thug hired to burn evidence. When he realized how much time he would serve, he sent Bruno Raymond to threaten Sterling. I guess that's why Sterling put the squeeze on me.

Thankfully, the paper doesn't say anything about the judge Bruno assaulted. Too many people already know I'm involved. I wouldn't be able to handle it if my name were printed in connection with this story.

I look at the clock. It's too early to call Jenn, so I copy the link to the article and text her. Wow. What a bizarre start to my day. Black Friday just took on a whole new meaning in my world.

Court starts in fifteen minutes, where I will once again run into Lily. I hope today goes quickly and smoothly. I can't stare at her all day while I'm deciding whether I want Emery for myself, if the offer is still on the table. That will make court, elevator rides, and social gatherings extremely awkward. I don't want to be guilty of breaking up any couple. That's never been my thing.

April peeks her head in my office. "Can we please talk about the mayor?"

I shake my head. "I don't have any more information than you do. Besides, I have to get ready for court." I'll hear soon enough from reliable sources. I slip into my robe and remember to wipe off my lipstick before I leave my office.

The morning is tense because nobody wants to be here. Most people want to be shopping, recovering from food comas, or spending time with their families. Even my mind is reeling from the breaking news. I'm sure Jenn has read everything and will probably fill me in on specifics. News travels fast, especially about a public figure.

As expected, Lily shows up with her client and enters a not-guilty plea. I study her closely to find out what Emery likes about her. She's attractive, thin, and young. No older than thirty. We have the same color hair, but hers is longer. I consider myself graceful, but she's not. She walks too fast. The clip-clip-clip of her heels in my courtroom reminds me of a highly energetic poodle prancing around. I stifle my smirk at the image. When she leaves my courtroom, I sigh with relief and continue going down the docket until we break for lunch.

"Samuel, can I see you in my office, please?" I ask as I pass through my outer office.

He follows me into my office. "Yes, Judge?" He's particularly pale today, making the dark circles under his eyes seem more pronounced. He's fantastic at research but lacks confidence for a courtroom.

"See if you can find me a copy of Sterling Moore's arrest warrant. And Samuel? Please be discreet." I say. He nods, tight-lipped and leaves my office looking determined. I pick up my phone to find two texts from my parents and eight from Jenn.

I answer Jenn's right away.

I've asked my clerk to grab the arrest warrant. I'll let you know if I learn anything more.

Well, I was wrong about one thing. It wasn't the mob, just really greedy rich people. I still can't believe it. So that means you're good. If they hurt you now, it would only make them more guilty. You're in the clear. She follows it up with touchdown emojis and smiley faces.

Hopefully. I really want my life back.

Any decision on Emery yet?

Nope.

More emojis, but they aren't the nice ones. *Don't let Lily win. She's not worth such a wonderfully passionate person. Come on. Roll into the holidays with a beautiful butch on your arm.*

Ha-ha. I'll keep you posted.

I put down the phone and check my emails and thumb through the mail. The Christmas party invites are starting to stack up, but honestly, I'm too depressed to confirm. What happens if I run into Emery? Or Lily? Or both? I could always invite my Tinder date, Ashleigh. Crap. I never texted her after I kicked her out. I groan and drop my heads into my hands. Every part of my life is crap. Being a judge was supposed to be this amazing opportunity, and the only people I've made connections with are now behind bars. Not technically. I'm sure the McIntoshes and the mayor all made bail. I wish Samuel would hurry up.

"I got it." Samuel bursts into my office without knocking. I raise my eyebrow, and a flush creeps past the white collar of his shirt as he realizes his mistake.

"I'm so sorry. I didn't mean to just barge in," he says. I make him sweat for a few moments before I nod. "What did you find out?" It takes all my self-restraint not to snatch the folder out of his hand.

"Here you go." He extends the folder.

I thank him for his discretion. When he shuts the door, I flip open the folder and read Sterling's arrest warrant. It's more detailed than the news article, but I don't gain any more knowledge. I sit back in my chair and allow myself to feel. Eloise Moore and the children must be struggling with the news. Maybe his wife knew of his wrongdoings, and maybe she didn't. Everybody in this new world of mine has revealed themselves to be corrupt or selfish. The only constant has been Emery.

Drinking wine alone isn't a sign of loneliness, right? But stalking somebody on social media is. I scroll through Emery's sporadic online presence and wonder what she's doing this weekend. I haven't seen any photos of her and Lily anywhere, so that gives me hope. Most of her feed is just photos of her with the firefighters she works with. That adorable smirk and those gray eyes are cracking the walls inside me. I close out social media on my tablet.

I should be sleeping because this has been the week from hell, but I can't settle down. I'm restless. Fuck this. I need to expel energy. I put on wool pants and a sweater, touch up my makeup, and grab my coat. Even though the weather's questionable, I walk down to The Phoenix.

"Judge. Where have you been?"

I smile at the familiarity of the small jazz bar and Tony. I feel free tonight. "Working hard, Tony."

"Let me buy you that drink," he says.

"Save it for the other girls."

The place is packed, and the only seat is at the bar. Tony points to it and leans closer because the music is so loud. "There's an empty spot just for you."

I nod and weave my way through the crowd. This is what I need. Attention without having to have a conversation. I order a glass of chardonnay and get as comfortable as I can on a barstool. The band plays here frequently, and I've seen them two or three times before. The first thirty minutes are fun. Music, people-watching, and a second glass of wine. Loneliness doesn't hit until after the band breaks for intermission. I realize everyone is chatting around me, and I'm not included. I'm smackdab into the middle of conversations happening around me, without me, and I feel empty. I wave for my bill and head home feeling sadder than when I left.

The cold whips inside my coat and chills me to the bone. While the music was good and a glass of wine is always appreciated, tonight was a dud, or maybe it's me. I draw a hot bath and make some mint tea. Once I'm naked and submerged, I take a deep breath and let the tears fall. Maybe it's stress, maybe it's loneliness, or maybe it's because I've turned into the person I always wanted to be, and I don't like her anymore.

There's always a rush once December starts. A steady flow of criminals who steal during the holidays because they find more money in pockets, businesses, or red metal tins, as bell ringers lean into the paths of pedestrians and ask for donations. People are friendlier and wish others happy holidays, but stress pinches their features, and I wonder what problems they have.

"More invitations. Do you need me to RSVP to any of them?" April hands me a stack of about six.

"No, thank you. I'll figure something out." I'm not going to any of the social gatherings because people will only seek me out to gossip about the mayor and the city council and the McIntoshes. I know how this world works. I'm just thankful I didn't get sucked down their hole of favors and bribes. I'm glad I threw the book at Seamus Williams. I can't imagine the problems I would have now had I not given him the maximum sentence.

April buzzes me.

"Yes?"

"There's a Lily Swarnes here to see you," she says.

My heart drops, then leaps into my throat. She knows about my history with Emery. Why else would she be here at my office? I take a deep breath. "Please send her in." I stand, ready for any confrontation that's about to take place.

"Judge Weaver, how are you?" Lily sits after shaking my hand.

"I'm well. How are you, Lily?"

"I'm okay. Just trying to get some shopping done before everything gets bananas."

"I try to do most of mine online. I never know what nights I have to work late and don't want to scramble last minute," I say. Why is she here? She's relaxed, almost comfortable in front of me. Might as well cut to the chase. "What can I do for you today?"

"This might sound completely inappropriate, but I don't want it to get in the way of our professionalism." She waves her forefinger back and forth between us.

"Okay." I sit straighter and rest my hands on my desk. My stomach clenches hard and quivers as I wait for whatever ugliness is about happen.

"I recently started dating Katie Farrell. I understand you're a mentor of sorts to her. I didn't want you to feel blindsided if you saw us at a social function or around the courthouse."

I tilt my head at her and blink. Does this mean Lily and Emery aren't dating anymore? "That's wonderful. Katie is a great girl." Katie, the law student whom I met my first day at my new place, has the bones to be a good lawyer. With my recommendation, she applied for a judicial internship that starts in January. Samuel's moving to a position at the Johnson County Courthouse after the first of the year, so that frees up a desk. She'll learn so much more with hands-on training. I'm looking forward to working with her. I get why Lily is concerned.

"Oh, she is." She smiles at some private thought. "Are you sure it won't be awkward for you?"

"Of course not."

She makes a big production of being relieved. "That makes me so happy. I invited her to several of the holiday parties and I didn't want you to feel like I was stealing away someone you've been grooming."

"I appreciate the heads-up, but that's what these events are for. We're supposed to make connections with professionally like-minded people." My second revelation almost feels bigger than the first. Everyone I've met since becoming a judge may have been corrupt, but I'm not. I can help people like Katie and Lily make names for themselves.

"Exactly! I knew you'd understand, but she refused to go to any of the parties until I cleared it with you."

"That sounds serious."

Lily smiles, and I get a glimpse of what attracted Emery to her. "It is. When it's right, it's right, you know?"

"I do. Thanks for stopping by."

She stands and shakes my hand again. "Thanks, Judge. See you in court."

I watch her walk away and hammer down the emotions that are brimming inside me. I feel a little ridiculous that Lily Swarnes helped me see what I was missing. I look at my calendar to ensure I can get away and pick up my phone.

Meet me tomorrow. Same time, same place.

I can't wear the dress. It's sixty degrees colder now. I opt for a long-sleeve taupe sweater dress and high black boots. I pile my hair on top my head in a messy bun and apply light makeup and thick lipstick. I order a car and grab my winter coat to wait for my ride downstairs. I'm beyond nervous. I slide into the town car when it arrives.

"How are you doing this afternoon, Ms. Weaver?"

I've had this driver before. He's professional and courteous. "I'm doing well. How are you?" I normally don't make small talk with the drivers, but today it doesn't bother me.

"Getting ready for the holidays."

"I love how festive Kansas City is during the season." I mean it. Kansas City is cozy, festive, and generous with holiday cheer. It's hard not to be in a good mood when you see a simple thing like a group of people wearing Santa hats walk by or the twinkle of lights on Christmas trees.

"I do as well. My children are down at Crown Center skating right now," he says.

"I don't enjoy the cold that much, but the skaters are always fun to watch." Jenn and I used to eat dinner and drink wine across from the rink while chatting about the upcoming holidays and whose experiences were going to be the worst. She won the last two years, but I had a steady run of seven years straight.

The car pulls into the lot. "Do you need a return trip?" he asks.

I don't know what to say. I don't know if I will be only a few minutes or hours. "I don't think so. I'll be sure to call the service if I do. Thank you for asking."

He nods at me in the rearview mirror and pulls up to the side entrance. "Have a nice time."

I take a moment to straighten my dress before I climb the stairs. I'm early, but only ten minutes. What if she's here? What if she doesn't show up at all?

"Good afternoon." The attendant watches as I slip a fifty into the donation box. She thanks me with a smile, and I walk to the room that changed my life. I'm the only one in the Italian Baroque room, so I get comfortable on the bench and wait.

I don't hear her approach, and her voice startles me.

"They say he killed a man."

I turn to look at her. Unguarded gray eyes gaze at me with longing and hope. I freeze because I don't know how to navigate my feelings as my heart twists and turns.

"I wish I could remember what I said," I remark.

She sits next to me. "I'm pretty sure I was blabbing on and on trying to impress you with what little knowledge I have about art. How are you?"

It's so hard to not lean into her strength at a time when I feel extremely vulnerable. "I'm okay. Scared, nervous, but okay."

"Don't be. It's me. You know me."

Her energy is exciting. I take a deep breath. "Do you want to look at some art?"

"Is this our first date?" she asks but doesn't wait for my answer. "If not, can it be?" She bites her bottom lip as she waits for me to make the call.

"It's a perfect first date."

She holds out her hand. "Shall we?"

I melt the moment I feel her skin against mine. Her fingers are warm, and she pulls me close.

"Let me hold your coat. Do you think we should check them?"

I shake my head. "I don't mind holding it." Aside from the last coat-check experience that I'd rather forget, I need something to squeeze as I process what's happening. This date has the potential for so much more. "I believe you said your favorite wing was the Impressionist hall."

"That was before I saw the early American rural-settlement displays." She winks at me. "I highly recommend it, but we'll do that another day."

I notice she isn't packing, and even though I need a fantastic night of her sexual prowess, it's a fresh start between us. I can wait. I know we'll have plenty of time for sex. "There's a photography exhibit if you're interested." She's so damn charming and cute.

"That sounds amazing." I like how she links our fingers together and rubs her thumb along my forefinger as we casually stroll through the museum as though we've been a couple for a long time. I feel her strength and excitement in the gentle way she holds my hand. "When I was in high school, I loved photography. I used to go on road trips with my best friend, and we'd take photos of the countryside or cityscapes. It was fun."

"Ah, a little morsel of info about Claire Bear's past," she says. My jaw drops open. "What? How do you know about my nickname?"

"First of all, it's adorable, and I hope I can call you that from time to time. Jenn and I had a chat the weekend she came into town."

She stiffens after she says the words. I place my palm on her bicep. "I'm fine, and it's not going to happen again."

"No, it won't."

Her voice has conviction, and I smile at her fierceness. "Let the past be the past. I don't think I'll have any issues with Sterling or the McIntoshes."

"Does this happen with judges? I mean, are threats a thing?"

"Sometimes. Maybe not to this extent, but there are threats." I stop again and face her. "I promise I'll always be careful. Lesson learned, trust me. Most of the time being a judge is very boring."

She touches my face gently. "Then why do you do it?"

"For the prestige and the sexy robe," I say.

"You joke, but I completely believe you. Besides, you look very beautiful today."

I want to be shy, but she empowers me. I see the hunger in her eyes and lick my lips. I miss the way she tastes and how she sometimes scrapes her teeth along my bottom lip. "I wanted to wear my red dress, but it's a little cold."

"I'm glad you didn't, because it would be too much to resist." She kisses my temple. "But thank you for wanting to. It's my favorite dress. Although the one you wore at the retirement party made my knees weak, too."

I'm overwhelmed with a desire to please Emery—to look good for her, to give her what she wants. And only her. I see the looks that people give me. As much as I like attention, I want it only from Emery. "I have a few things that you might like more."

She shakes her head. "Never. That dress is the start of everything perfect in my life."

Heat spreads across my cheeks, down my neck, and settles between my thighs. My heart races at the possibilities with this woman.

She looks at her watch. "It's almost time to eat. Would you like to have dinner?"

Food is the furthest thing from my mind, but a nice glass of wine to settle my nerves sounds lovely. "I'd love to. What do you like besides Thai?" It occurs to me that I know so very little about Emery's likes and dislikes outside the bedroom.

"We can do something simple like Chaz," she says.

"I haven't been there in ages. That sounds perfect." I roll my eyes at my cheesy response. All the emotions I've hidden from myself and others push to the surface. I get mushy over things like how she ensures I enter the room first or how she slows her step so I'm not struggling to keep up.

"Did you drive here?" she asks.

"No. I had a car service drop me off."

"Perfect. I can drive us." She helps me with my coat, and in the elevator down to the parking structure under the museum, she kisses me the way I want to be kissed. My back is pressed against the wall, and even though it's uncomfortable, I've never wanted anything more than her lips on mine. Her tongue delves into my mouth and dances with mine in a rhythm we know so well. It's intimate, and I moan at how much I need her, how much I've missed her.

"Let's go back to my place." I'm already breathless, and my heart flutters.

Chapter Twenty

A re you sure? I mean, it's our first date."
I bunch up her sweater in my fist and pull her to me
so my lips barely brush hers. "We can always wait until after..."
I pause and pretend to count. "The third date. That's always the
number, right? I don't date so I don't know, but I think I read that in
a romance book somewhere."

She nips my bottom lip until I moan. "You don't read romance.
You read suspense and crime books."

"Do you remember everything about me?" I whisper against
her mouth.

"I've never stopped thinking about you. I remember every
word from your lips." She pauses and rubs her lips with her thumb.
"I remember every curve of your body, every sound you make
when we have sex, and how you give yourself to pleasure more
than anyone I've ever known." She kisses me again and again until
I forget we're still in the garage at the museum and are not alone.

"Let's go." I break from her and climb into the car.

She briskly walks to the driver side, gets behind the wheel, and
pulls smoothly into traffic.

"It's going to snow tonight," I say.

She nods but doesn't respond. I put my hand above her knee
and smile when the muscles jump under my fingers. I run my hand
softly up and down her thigh, stroking her until she moans and stops
my hand.

"I can't concentrate with you touching me." She licks her lips and glances at me a few times during traffic stops. "And it's not fair that I can't touch you."

"Who says you can't touch me?" I challenge her by sliding my seat all the way back and uncrossing my legs. At the next traffic signal, I pull up my dress until it's only a few inches from revealing my smooth pussy.

"Fuck," she says.

"I can't wait." We're only about five minutes from my loft. I place her hand on my thigh. She runs her hand up my skirt but stops about three inches below where I want her. Her strong fingertips dig into my thigh muscle. She seems determined to tease me. It takes my breath away. "We're almost to my place."

She stops and takes a deep breath. "You're right. Plus, this is our first date. Weren't we going to dinner?"

"I can order delivery from the bedroom," I say.

Emery pulls into the garage, and the attendant allows her to pull up into a visitor's spot. I push my dress down just in time before he sees more of me than I'm comfortable with. "That was close."

"You would have made his night." She wraps my coat around me, pulling me close to her by the lapels. "But tonight is mine."

"And mine."

"Our night. Come on. Let's get upstairs before I drag you into a dark corner of the garage."

She kisses me hard again in the elevator, and the rush of the reality of her here with me floods my senses. I hear only her moans, smell her cologne, taste her warmth, and feel her excitement. I crave her. I'm desperate to feel her skin against mine. By the time we get to my floor, I'm soaked with anticipation. I can't decide what I want to happen first.

"Hurry up and unlock your door," she whispers before tugging my earlobe between her teeth. The shock of soft pain jolts me all over, and I press my hand against the door to steady myself.

"I can't concentrate when you do that to me."

She takes the keys from my hand and unlocks the door. The moment we're inside, she picks me up and wraps my legs around her waist. My coat drops to the floor. She presses my back to the wall. The pressure of her belt against my pussy is wonderful, and I grind against her for friction.

"I love that you're so strong." No lover has ever picked me up, and this is the third time she's done it. I'm rewarded with several hip thrusts in a row and almost come on the spot. My guttural moan stops her.

"Let's go upstairs," she says.

I slide down and follow her upstairs. She takes off her sweater and unbuttons her shirt. By the time we're upstairs, she's kicked off her shoes, and her belt is on the chair. I pull my dress over my head and stand naked in front her, wearing only tall, black, leather boots. She sits on the bed and stops me from taking them off.

"Oh, I love this look." She eyes me appreciatively and pulls me close so I'm standing between her legs.

"They're more practical than sexy." Secretly I love that the look turns her on. I stand proudly in front of her and run my hands over my body. She leans back on her elbows to give me room and smiles. I let down my hair, shake it loose, and lean forward so my breasts are inches from her face. "I've missed you. And your mouth. And how you know how to fuck me the way I want. The way I need you to."

Her eyes darken. "Does tonight mean we're exclusive? I'm yours and you're mine?"

She waits for my answer. I look over her deliciously hard body, but when my eyes meet hers, I'm taken aback by what I see and how it makes me feel. I see love, and a feeling of joy bursts inside. I'm not ready to deal with the emotions head-on. I thought it would be more of a gradual thing, but the excitement of the moment and how I embrace it shocks me.

"I have no desire to see other people. I only want you." I don't want to crash and burn before this relationship even takes off the ground. "This is new for me. You're going to have to give me allowances if I say the wrong thing. But I know I want you, Emery. I've missed you. I've missed us. Nobody can do what you do to me." That's as good as she's going to get today.

"I'll take anything you give me, Claire."

She's too solemn, so I kiss her. Baby steps, I think. She pulls me onto the bed and flips me so I'm on my back and she's between my legs. I push the shirt off her shoulders and look down at her boxers. "Take these off. Take everything off."

It takes her ten seconds to strip. She returns to me. "Better?"

I smirk as an idea forms. "Almost." I roll her over and slide down her body, running my tongue in a straight path to the junction of her thighs. She doesn't stop me. She's wet and ready. I run my fingers up and down her hot slit, eager to fuck her but going slow because I know she needs to get used to me. I press my tongue flat against her clit and gradually apply pressure until she gasps with pleasure. That's her threshold. I lick slowly, and she squirms and moans under my mouth. I pull away. "Is this okay?" I slowly trace the entrance to her pussy, and she moans her approval. I cut my nails earlier, so tonight I'm not worried about hurting her. I just want to feel her come against my hand and my mouth.

"I should be the one doing this to you." She runs her hands through my hair, but she doesn't stop me.

"Oh, you'll be busy with me the rest of the night." I add a finger and wait for her to adjust to me. She's unbelievably tight. I move my fingers slowly but speed up my tongue on her clit. When she jerks, I slow down. It takes a bit to find a good rhythm, and when she starts rolling her hips, I know she's climbing. I keep my momentum going, and when she comes, a wave of confidence washes over me. I climb up her and kiss her.

"You smell like sex." She plays with my hair while she relaxes.

"I smell like you, and it's wonderful. Thank you."

"I think I could get used to that," she says.

"Well, as my exclusive girlfriend, you're entitled to all of me, including my mouth and fingers," I say. That wasn't too corny.

I'm surprised when she gets up and excuses herself. I smirk when she heads to my closet first, then slips into the bathroom with our dildo and her boxers. I sit on the edge of the bed and cross my legs. I love these boots even more. I slowly uncross my legs and spread them when she returns wearing the marvelous dildo that weighs down the front of her boxers.

"I've missed you."

"Just me or me and my cock?" she asks.

I run my fingertip between my breasts, down my stomach, and rub my clit. "Both. I can miss both, right?"

She drops to her knees and kisses my thighs. "I missed you, your pussy, the way you taste, how much you loved being fucked, and your love and passion for sex."

I frown a bit when she unzips my boots and pulls them off. I wanted them on, but it's colder up here, and sex under the covers sounds delicious and warm. And intimate. I scoot away from her, and she chases me across the bed and flips me onto my back. She's smiling, and it's the most beautiful, unguarded look I've seen on her face. I kiss my forefinger and press it against her lips.

"Where are you going?" she asks.

"Under the blanket. You were gone so long I got cold."

She dips her head and softly brushes her lips across mine. Her knees push mine apart, and she sinks down. Her cock is resting right along my slit, and every time she moves or I move, tiny bursts of pleasure jolt my body.

"Let me warm you up," she says.

She holds my hands above my head and tells me to hold the slats. "Don't let go."

"I won't." I mean it. She's going to reward me only for good behavior.

"Now close your eyes," she whispers.

I feel her pull the covers over us, and my heart flutters with anticipation. Her legs are warm and strong against mine, and I lift my hips in anticipation of her cock sinking into me. I bite my bottom lip as I remember how big it is and how it will stretch me, almost painfully, but will also give me breathtaking pleasure. I hear the snap of the lube cap and peek through slitted eyes to watch her liberally apply the lube. I swallow hard. She looks at me. "Are you peeking?"

"No." I lie. I go limp when she presses the head between the folds of my pussy. I lift my hips, but she holds them down.

"Patience. I've been waiting for this moment forever."

"So have I. Why are you making me wait?" My breaths are quick, and I sound like I'm panting. I hiss out a breath and relax. She doesn't stretch me with her fingers first, and feeling the head push into me is shocking, but only for a moment. When the rest of the shaft glides in, I shout with abandon.

"Fuck!" I reach for her because I'm tumbling with nothing to hold onto, and I'm afraid of completely losing myself.

She gently lies on top of me. "Open your eyes, love."

My brain stumbles over the world love, but I open my eyes. She smiles and starts moving. My mouth falls open, and I moan with every slight thrust. Heat spreads from my pussy to every inch of me as she slowly fucks me. She bends her knees slightly and quickens her pace. I moan loudly in her ear and dig my short nails into her back. The first two orgasms happen back-to-back as she pumps in and out. She pulls out, and I reach for her instinctively. "No, I'm not done."

"I'm not either."

She keeps eye contact with me as she pushes in and pulls all the way out. My eyes flutter shut even though she asks me to open them. I can't. I open them when orgasm number three arrives and shakes me to my core. I'm never going to survive tonight. She rests on her haunches for a moment to catch her breath. I run my hands on her thighs. We're both sweaty and sticky, and I haven't been this happy in forever. I laugh.

She laughs because I do. "What are we laughing about?"

"This is perfect. Us, I mean. Why have I fought this for so long?" I pull her to me for a long, deep kiss. Even though we're both moaning, she pulls away.

"Roll over."

I widen my eyes in surprise and I do as I'm instructed. She is flush on top of me, and I wiggle my ass as she spreads me apart with her knees to get to my pussy.

"Tell me if this hurts," she whispers and gently pushes inside.

I exhale. "It feels wonderful."

She pulls me up so that I'm on my hands and knees, and even though she's deep, the pleasure absorbs the pain, and I come again. I'm shaking with lack of energy and too many orgasms to count. She finally comes, and I smile at how, for the first time, she's loud. She bends down and kisses my back. We both sink down on the mattress. Her orgasm is still working itself around her, and she shivers every few seconds, I assume from pleasure. I turn and pull her close to me. Emery in my arms feels nice.

After five minutes of just holding one another and softly touching, I speak first. "We're going to need dinner and water if you're staying the night."

"I'm staying?"

I can't tell if she's playing or not. "That's what girlfriends do, right? Stay the night. Fix breakfast in bed, give massages, spoil each other."

She slides her hand behind my neck and pulls me to her for a kiss. "That's exactly what girlfriends do. You know I'll do anything for you, right?"

I cover her hand with mine and nod. This is probably the most intimate moment we've ever had, and I'm a few seconds away from crying. Accepting a relationship is a big step, but it's worth it to have this wonderful woman in my life.

Chapter Twenty-one

I send Jenn the first selfie of me and Emery. I have several cute ones, but I don't want to be that person who clogs her friends' text threads with sickeningly sweet kissy photos. I managed to wait three whole weeks before giving in. Jenn calls right away.

"I'm so excited you and Emery are officially dating."

"I know, I know. It's about time, right?"

"Are you going to spend Christmas together? I know your parents are coming to town, but will they meet her?"

She's asking too many questions, and I can't keep up, so I laugh. "Wait, wait. You've already shipped us. Baby steps on meeting the family."

"What did you get her for Christmas?"

"I found a nice antique watch for her collection. I found one online I think she'll love." It was pricey but worth it. "What did you get Orlando?" Jenn doesn't know that Orlando called me a few days ago and asked if I thought Jenn would marry him. I played it cool, but inside I was squealing with delight. My relationship with Emery is softening every part of me, and I'm emotional about everything, it seems. I told him yes and even gave him advice on the cut and size of the diamond. He's going to propose Christmas Eve after the kids go to bed.

"I got O a sound system for his car. Sounds lame, but what do you get a guy who has everything? He buys anything he wants."

"Listen to yourself. You're just as difficult," I say. Jenn gave me a painting from a local artist when she visited me a few months ago. I sent her a case of wine she loves. I'm going to have to make my gifts more kid-friendly if she marries him. I sent the family fun things from Kansas City, including books, board games, and some local candy.

"What do you think Emery's going to get you?"

I'm not used to gifts. I'm uncomfortable receiving them unless they're from Jenn. "I don't know." We haven't really talked about it, but she did ask for an evening before my parents visit. They're flying in on Christmas Eve and leaving two days later. They want to see my place and get caught up. I'm sure they'll want to know about the job and if I like it. I still haven't fully embraced it, but I'm getting more comfortable with my responsibility. "Maybe sex toys."

She laughs. "Sounds romantic."

I'm embarrassed to tell her how romantic Emery and I are. We're doing all the things I used to roll my eyes at when I saw how cutesy people were with each other. "I really don't know." As much as I love toys and lingerie, I hope she goes with something more personal. "What about O? What do you think he's going to get you?" I try hard to keep the excitement out of my voice.

"I don't know. Maybe a trip somewhere? I mentioned wanting to go to Fiji, so maybe he'll surprise me with one."

I'm thankful we aren't on FaceTime, or she'd realize that I know something and try to pump me for information. Certain things I don't mind giving up, but I haven't even told Emery about Orlando's gift. It's not that I don't trust her. I just don't want her to let anything slip. "Good luck. I'll give you a call on Christmas. I need to go. We're going to decorate Emery's tree."

"It's a week before Christmas. Why did she wait so long?"

"Because we've been too busy fucking. Her nephews finally pushed her to get it done." Every time we get together, we end up naked. I'm headed there right after work. I told her to get started without me in case we needed together time.

"I'm forever jealous of you. Go. Have fun, be safe, and I'll call you for Christmas."

"I love you. You be safe, too." I disconnect the call and look at the clock. I have only a few minutes before I can leave. I'm not a clock watcher, but since agreeing to a relationship with Emery, I'm counting down the days, hours, and minutes until I see her again. And I'm checking my phone for messages on breaks. I feel better knowing she's doing the same. We agreed to keep our relationship away from the courthouse for obvious reasons. At five, I turn off my computer and walk out of the office. "Have a good night," I say to April on my way out. This is the first time I'm leaving before her. The look on her face is priceless.

"You too, Judge."

I need to get my clerks something for the holidays, even though I know nothing about them. Generic gifts are easy, but I want to try a little harder. A happy clerk is a helpful clerk. I send Emery a quick text and tell her I'm going home to change clothes first. She tells me she has a surprise for dinner. I promise to be there sooner than later.

❖

She greets me at the door and kisses me hard. "I've missed you."

I love the feel of her arms around my waist as she pulls me close. "I missed you more." Really? Did I just say that?

"You look beautiful." She closes the door and leads me to the fireplace to warm my hands. "I didn't get far with the decorations. What do you think of my nephews coming over tonight to help?"

She looks so hopeful I can't say no. "I guess that would be all right." If Jenn can do it, so can I. Besides, we can always send them home if they get to be too much. She kisses me.

"Thank you so much. They're super sweet and well-behaved."

I smile through the anxiety building in my stomach. "I'm sure they are. I'm not worried."

I dig through the boxes of decorations while she calls her brother. I would have tossed a lot of the homemade decorations I pull out but find it endearing that Emery has them for whatever reason. I should get a tree next year. Right now, I have a few decorations up, but no tree. A wreath's on the door, and Emery insisted on putting lighted garland strands up the staircase. They give the place a nice holiday feel.

"Okay. They'll be here in ten minutes. I'm going to order pizza for them, but I'll order something else for us." She walks over to me. "Are you sure you're okay with this?"

The old me would simply walk out if I didn't want to be a part of something, but I'm really trying with Emery, and she knows that it's a struggle sometime. "Surprisingly, I am. I'm not going to lie. I had a moment of panic, but I'm okay meeting your nephews. If it was your entire family, I'd freak out."

She kisses me until I'm soft in her arms. "You're going to meet my brother tonight because he can't just drop off the kids. He'll want to meet the woman who tamed his older sister, but only him."

"How do I look?"

Emery exhales and touches her heart. "More beautiful every day, and I don't know how that's possible because you were perfect yesterday."

I playfully push her away. "Suck-up."

She pulls me back to her and waits until I relax against her. "It's true. I'm in deep." She shrugs as though it's a casual statement, but it means everything.

I don't know how to process what she's telling me, or if I'm even taking it the right way. I flash her a small smile and alleviate the heaviness of the moment with sexual humor, my one and only defense. "Not yet."

She throws her head back and laughs. "Maybe not at this moment, but soon. What can I get you to eat?"

I lift an eyebrow at her.

"What would you like for dinner besides me?"

"We can eat pizza with the kids. I don't mind." I can't remember the last time I had pizza. Not that I'm on a health kick, but I'm trying to not gain holiday weight. My clothes fit me perfectly, and Emery likes me the way I am right now—curvy and flexible.

"Great. What would you like?"

"Buffalo chicken. Or chicken Alfredo," I say.

"Placing the order now."

She types the choices into her phone, and the moment she hits the order button, the door bursts open, startling me. I place my hand on my heart in alarm. Two dark-haired, bright-eyed boys barrel into the house, screaming for Emery.

"Boys." She growls and crouches to their level. They attack her from both sides and squeal when she scoops them up and drops them on the couch, roaring like a monster or a dinosaur. Her playfulness makes me smile.

"I'm so sorry they didn't knock. Hi. I'm Brock, Emery's brother. You must be Claire. It's so good to meet you." He's handsome, with a chiseled jaw and the same steel-gray eyes as Emery. His hair is shorter than Emery's but just as thick.

"Hi, Brock. It's nice to meet you, too. Emery's talked so much about you."

"Boys, come here and meet Aunt Emery's girlfriend."

They scurry over to me, dropping their coats in the process, and stand at attention in front of Brock.

"Hi. What's your name?" The taller boy, Connor, thrusts out his hand for a shake.

He's adorable and looks so much like Emery that I want to squeeze him. I take his little hand in mine and give it a firm shake.

"I'm Claire. It's nice to meet you. You must be Connor."

"How did you know that?" He tilts his head at me, totally perplexed at how I could possibly already know his name.

His little brother takes a step closer and holds out his hand, too. "I'm Chandler."

I detect a slight lisp and fall in love with him immediately. "Hi, Chandler. It's nice to meet you, too. I know your names because your aunt told me them before you came over. Did you know we're eating pizza for dinner tonight?" Both boys whoop with delight. Who have I become? Even Emery lifts an eyebrow at me.

"Okay. I'll get them at seven forty-five. It's a school night." Brock gives me a quick wave and pats Emery on the cheek. She abruptly swats his hand away.

"Get out of here." She closes the door before I can hear what he whispers to her. She blushes. I'll ask her about it later. "Okay. Who wants to decorate the tree?"

More cheers and laughter from the boys. I sit on the couch and watch them. Emery is so good at giving both of them attention, and the love between all of them is obvious. I wonder if Jenn felt this way in the beginning with Orlando and his children.

"Why don't you ask Claire if she wants to join us?" Emery pokes Chandler in the stomach, and he giggles and walks over to me.

"Do you want to help us?"

He holds out his tiny hand so trustingly, and I make a weirdly emotional sound and quickly clear my throat.

"Definitely." I take his hand as though it's a precious gift. He leads me to Emery, and I sit with them on the floor as they sort through ornaments and lights.

"Do you remember when we made these?" Emery holds up a snowflake made of yarn and popsicle sticks. The boys nod enthusiastically and dig in the box looking for more. "We made these this summer at camp."

"You went to camp with them?"

"Art with Aunts." She shrugs. "It was only for an afternoon." She winks at me, so I don't know if she's telling the truth.

"It's great that you're so involved with them."

When the doorbell rings, the boys jump up and cheer. Who knew kids were this excited about pizza?

"One cheese pizza, one pepperoni, and one chicken Alfredo."

At Emery's nod, the pizza-delivery person hands the small pizzas to the boys.

"Go put the pizzas on the table and show Claire where the plates are." She pays for them, while I follow them into the kitchen. "And wash your hands before you eat."

We all wash our hands and sit down to eat. I'm surprised when the boys pray with Emery, and I wait until they're done to fill plates. "Who wants cheese?"

Both boys raise their hands. I dole out slices of gooey cheese pizza. I should've never worn a cashmere sweater to eat pizza or hang with kids.

"Aunt Emery, do you love her?"

Chandler giggles at Connor's question. I freeze and stare at my pizza, afraid to look at her but curious about the answer. Emery knows I'm a flight risk, but so far, I've handled everything with grace. Our eyes meet across the table. She smiles at me but answers Connor.

"I do love Claire. I think she's smart, beautiful, and very loving. Do you know what she does for a living?"

"Does she work with you?" Connor asks.

"No. Better. She's a judge, which means she puts bad people in jail so they can't hurt anybody anymore or steal anything anymore. She's very powerful, and I'm thankful she's looking out for all of us."

"Wow."

Connor looks at me with amazement etched on his tiny, perfect face. Emery makes me sound better than I am, but she's not wrong. The two boys sitting on either side of me are the reasons I got into law. I wanted to stand up for people who didn't have a voice or whose voices weren't heard. I was thinking adults at the time, but now I'm doing it for anyone who needs to be heard. I get why Emery is so fierce about them. Thirty minutes into this new relationship, and I would throw the book at anyone who hurt them.

"It's a pretty important job," I say, completely bypassing Emery's confession. We'll talk about that later.

After ten more minutes of pizza, Emery rounds them up to wash hands again and start stringing the lights. It's already seven, and we both know that once the boys leave, very little decorating will get done. I sit on the couch and watch them wrap the tree with colored lights, heavy on the bottom half, and hang both handmade ornaments and shatterproof decorative balls. Twenty minutes in, Chandler makes his way over to me and curls up on my lap. "Are you tired?" I ask.

He nods and leans his head against me. That can't be comfortable, so I adjust him so that he's more in the crook of my arm. It's hard to believe this little boy will one day be as tall as his dad, or even taller. I watch his little fingers play with my bracelet and my ring. When the doorbell rings, he sinks lower into me.

"Daddy's here," Emery says.

"Hey, boys. Grab your coats and say good-bye," Brock says.

Brock commands attention like Emery does. It must be a family trait. He smiles at us on the couch, and Chandler reluctantly crawls off me to put on his coat. Emery hands him the rest of the cheese pizza.

"It was nice meeting you, Claire," Brock says. He turns to the boys. "Tell Aunt Emery and Claire bye."

Both boys hug me first and then race over to Emery, who picks them both up and kisses them until they struggle to get down. "Thanks for your help tonight with the tree."

I stand when Emery shuts the door and it's just the two of us. "The tree looks pretty sad."

Emery surveys their work and points to it. "I think it looks great. We can add another strand of lights on top here, maybe a few ornaments up high, and it'll be perfect."

"They kept looking under it for presents," I say.

"Yeah. I learned a long time ago not to put any presents under it until Christmas Eve. Last year I had to rewrap several that weren't even theirs." She pulls out the last strand of lights. "Will you help me so we can even it out?"

"Definitely." I'll have to work around the elephant in the room until she's done with decorations, but a discussion is in order. It takes us only about twenty minutes of quiet concentration before we finish. Emery stacks the empty boxes and slides them into another room.

"This tree could have been decorated weeks ago if only we'd taken thirty minutes to do it," she says. She pulls me into her arms and rests her head on the top of mine. "I think it looks better."

"It actually does."

"What did you think of the boys?"

"Your brother is handsome and strong," I say, teasing her. Her mouth drops open, and she playfully tickles me. I laugh and push her away. She pulls me back to her. "I'm talking about the boys. It was okay that they were here, right?" I kiss her softly. "They're adorable, and I might be in love with them already."

"Speaking of love," she says. She turns me so that I'm facing her and wraps my arms around her waist before she reaches up to cup my face. "I hope I didn't shock you earlier with what I said."

"What did you say?" I cock my head and furrow my brow as if I'm straining to recall words that we both know I heard perfectly clear.

"I said I love you. Well, I didn't say the words, but it's true. I know you aren't ready to hear them yet, but the holidays always get me so emotional. I know we're taking things slow, but the boys asked, and I don't lie to them."

I mull over her words and find that I love being loved. Emery completes me emotionally and sexually. What I feel for her is love on a level I never knew existed, but I don't know how to tell her without completely losing it. I move my hands from around her waist and lock my fingers behind her neck. "You know this has been a difficult six months for me for so many reasons."

"You don't have to say anything," she says.

I put my fingertip up to her lips. "The judge is speaking. That means you aren't allowed to interrupt."

"Or I'll be in contempt?" She tilts her head playfully and smirks as though she'd just said the cleverest thing.

I roll my eyes. "I can put you jail."

"Will you handcuff me?"

"Would you let me?"

She laughs. "Yes."

"I'll file that away for later. What I'm trying to say is that it was a nice thing to hear." My voice grows softer as I search for the confidence to say what needs to be said. "I know I'm not easy and not good at this yet, but I love you, and I want this relationship to work." I look down because I'm too emotional and don't want to cry.

She tilts my chin up. "You love me?"

I nod and bite my bottom lip. She's never seen me cry before, and I really want to be strong at this moment. "I do."

Her kiss is tender and full of emotion. I deepen it because words are one way to express emotions, but I'm used to physically expressing myself, and kissing is one of my new favorite ways.

"I love you, too. And I'll try not to say it all the time because I know that gets annoying, but know that you have my heart." She places my hand over her heart and holds it there with hers.

"Lock the door. We don't want anybody busting in right now." I pull her down for a kiss that I hope conveys my message.

"Yes, Judge Weaver."

"Oh, I like it when you call me Judge Weaver." I get a flash of us role-playing a courtroom scene. "I find the defendant guilty of breaking and entering, theft, and the crime of being too damn sexy. How do you plead?"

That sexy smile of hers flashes across her face. "Guilty to being too damn sexy, but the other charges? Breaking and entering? Theft? Not guilty, your Honor."

I run my nails over her short hair. "I'm throwing the book at you."

"What did I break, enter, and steal?"

She pulls me closer and runs her fingertip over my lips as she waits for my answer. She wants to kiss me. She always wants to kiss me. It's funny how I used to not like it because it led to emotions I didn't want to feel, and now I kiss her as often as I can. I brush my lips over hers before I answer.

"My heart."

Epilogue

"We're going to miss our plane."

Emery's nerves are wearing on me. "Then we'll catch the next one. It's fine. The wedding isn't until tomorrow night. Even if we have to drive there, we'll still make it on time. We're good." That's not entirely true. If we drove really fast and didn't stop, then maybe, but probably not. "Wait. Are you afraid of flying?"

"No. I just hate being late," she says.

I flip her wrist over to check the time. "The plane doesn't take off for three hours. We're thirty minutes from the airport, and we're TSA prechecked. It's a direct flight, and we have carry-on luggage. I'm almost ready. The car isn't even here yet." I kiss her until I feel the tension leave her. "And I love you."

She nods. "I'm sorry. I don't know what's wrong with me."

I zip my luggage and pat it. "There. I'm done. We can go downstairs and wait for the car." I pull up the app on my phone. "The driver is seven minutes away. Let's go."

Forty-seven minutes later we're sitting side by side waiting for an airplane that isn't even at the gate yet. I don't say anything. I pull out my tablet and scroll through the news.

"I'm sorry." She takes my hand and squeezes my fingers.

I lean over so that others can't hear us. "You should trust me more."

"I really should. You travel all the time. Maybe that's it. I don't travel enough."

That makes me pause. "Maybe we should go somewhere tropical. You have a passport, right?"

"Yes, and I've never used it."

My jaw drops open. "Never? You've never left the country?"

"Nope, but let's definitely plan it. Where's your favorite place in the world?"

"Maybe we should find a new one together." Again, the sap drips from me. This woman has changed me for the better. Even Jenn notices a softness to me. She mentioned it once and never again, but I see it in the way she looks at me. Sometimes I give her an eye roll to let her know that deep down, it's still me, but I notice the change in myself, too.

My phone rings, and Emery reaches over me to grab it. "Let me answer your phone."

I shoo her hand away. Her sister-in-law Amanda and I have been steadily building a nice friendship over the last several months on the basis of wine and antiques. "Hi. How's it going?"

"Did you make it to the airport on time?" Amanda asks.

"With a zillion minutes to spare." I turn to Emery so she can hear. "I don't know why Emery was so worried."

Amanda laughs. "I'll just tell you that nervousness runs in the family. Brock doesn't like to be late to anything."

"No. We're here, early, and waiting for the plane. We're going to make it there tonight."

"That's great. Emery will be able to relax, and you'll get to see Jenn again," she says.

Amanda's a genuinely nice person. I already know Jenn's going to love her, and I can't wait for them to meet. "This is going to be an amazing wedding. I'll take lots of pictures. And we'll be at the beach. How could it be better?"

"Best weekend ever. Have a great time," she says.

I disconnect the call to find a text message from Jenn.

How's it going? Are you on the plane yet?

Jenn needs me for encouragement. I'm spending Jenn's last night as a bachelorette with her. We have the Presidential Suite and a ton of wine and snacks.

Not yet, but we should land about seven and be at the hotel by eight. Which means I will walk into the suite and expect a glass of wine at exactly 8:08.

It's going to take you eight minutes to check in? I read the panic in her text and try to reassure her and calm her at the same time until I can do it in person.

A lot of people will be in line. There's an amazing wedding tomorrow on the beach with roughly two hundred guests.

I'll check you in. Just come up to the suite, and we'll give Emery a key.

Perfect. She's excited for tomorrow. We've been talking about a vacation longer than just a weekend away somewhere.

"They're boarding." Emery leans over and kisses my cheek. "Tell her I say hello and we'll see her in a bit."

On our way! See you soon. I send a heart and a kiss emoji and turn off my phone.

We aren't in line long, and Emery and I are on our first drink before the plane is airborne. She sleeps the whole way while I review notes on an upcoming case. Work has been tough for her. June is notorious for pre-Fourth of July firework accidents that lead to bigger fires. I'm glad she's able to get the weekend off to spend it with me at Jenn and Orlando's wedding. I'm in the wedding party, and my dress is already there so in case of a luggage mishap, so I don't have to worry about it getting lost.

"Sweetheart, we're almost there." I gently shake Emery awake. She licks her lips and reaches for her water. "Really? Did I sleep the whole time?"

I nod. "You've had a rough week and needed it."

"I'm good now. Thanks for letting me sleep." She cracks her neck and stretches her long legs out. Business class is a definite with Emery and her legs that seem to go on forever. "Let's help your best friend relax before the biggest day of her life."

Emery's been around during the half a dozen times Jenn doubted her decision to marry Orlando. When she told us last Christmas Eve that he'd proposed, she was giddy and excited. I never told her that he called me for my advice. That was his story to tell.

"Oh, my God. You're here!"

Jenn's hug turns into something more emotional, and I end up holding her while her tears fall. "I'm here now, sweetie. I'm here."

Emery's wide eyes speak volumes. She's not sure how to get involved or if she should. I smile weakly at her. I mouth "I don't know." I point to the desk where I see two key cards and a piece of paper, hoping that's for us. She rubs Jenn's back for a moment and leaves with the keys and our luggage to a suite on the same floor.

"I don't know why I'm crying." She pulls back and laughs. "I mean, I want to marry him. I love him so much."

I wipe her tears and kiss her cheek. "I guess it's time to settle down, and we've fought it so long. You have every right to be emotional. He's wonderful, and his kids already love you so much. I couldn't be happier for you."

"We'll still have our Vegas trips," she says.

"I'm not even thinking that far. Hell, the next time we go, we'll probably have to take Emery and Orlando, and that's fine." I mean it. I have so much fun with Emery, and she satisfies me so totally on every level that the thought of hooking up with a stranger seems so foreign to me, even though that was my life six months ago. I lead her to the couch and open a bottle of champagne. "Look, I'm here to witness love in action from my best friend."

"I don't ever want to lose you to a marriage," she says.

"I won't let Orlando or the kids push me out of your life. If you're worried about that, don't. I'm not letting you go for something as insignificant as marriage." I wink, and she smiles.

She takes a deep breath and exhales loudly. "Okay, okay. I think I'm ready to do this. Should we take a bottle and head down to the beach for a quiet minute? The sun has mostly set, but it's still somewhat light out."

"I want to do whatever you want to do." I'm wearing linen pants that I can roll up and sandals I can kick off. I'd like to change my clothes, but that would take too long. "Grab your shoes. I'll grab the bottle. Let's go down there and cheer on the night."

Some people are on the beach when we finally hit the sand, but most of the crowd are either eating at the restaurant or hanging in the bar. I saw Orlando in there with about twenty guys cheering and laughing when we walked past. I grab a towel from the hotel's cabana on the beach and spread it out for us. I top off our glasses and toast my best friend.

"We're not saying good-bye to the last thirty-five years of your life, but we are welcoming a new chapter," I say. I think the toast is good, but she scowls at me.

"It's a marriage, not death. You make it sound like I'm dying."

I laugh. "You're right. It's a good thing I'm not in charge of a speech tomorrow." We toast to love and sip our champagne as the last bold colors of the day bleed into the dark blue of night. The waves instantly calm me. "I could get used to this."

"Buy a beach house here, and come and work for my company." The excitement in her voice tells me she means it.

"I could never ask Emery to move. She's so close to her family. They're wonderful people. Plus, I'm a judge."

"I know. We're just going to have to commute for the rest of our lives." Jenn rests her head on my shoulder.

"At least until we retire. Then I think I'll have more pull."

"Stop. You know Emery would do anything for you. If you wanted to up and suddenly move to South Africa, she totally would," she says.

"True, but I wouldn't ask her to. That's not fair."

"You're so sappy."

We both laugh. I tap my glass against hers. "Truer words have never been spoken."

When Jenn and Orlando exchange vows, I can't help but cry. It's beautiful to witness love so pure and honest. I refuse to look at Emery, but I bet she's crying, too. Hell, most in attendance are sniffling. Since it's a beach wedding, we're all barefoot. The bridesmaids' dresses are flowy and hit right at the knee. Jenn's dress has more length, but they're all the same style. I love this dress because of the way Emery reacted when she saw me in it. I'm nervous about how revealing it is and how everyone else in the wedding is a smaller size, but the appreciation on Emery's face gives me confidence. Everyone applauding brings me back to the present, where my best friend is now officially married. She hugs the bridal party and walks hand-in-hand with Orlando down the aisle to the several party tents, where the guests will start the reception while the wedding party has their picture taken a thousand times.

During one of the photos of just us she whispers, "I did it."

"You sure did. And I'm so happy for you."

"We need to hurry up with the wedding stuff so we can let loose, drink more champagne, and eat cake."

"I'm ready."

"Okay. We have one more photo to take. I'm going to need the bridesmaids to line up with the groomsmen behind them," the photographer says.

Orlando's buff quarterback friend is my groomsman, and he walks me to where I'm supposed to be and stands five feet behind me. Jenn is about ten feet in front of us and turns her back to us with her bouquet as though she's going to throw it.

"Perfect. I need everyone to smile and look at Jenn," the photographer says.

I hate the bouquet throwing at any wedding. It's a tradition that I wish would go away. I'm surprised Jenn has agreed to do it. She bends her arm as if she's going to throw it and the photographer snaps away. I have patience for about two more minutes of this.

"Okay, now this time, throw it," he says.

Instead, Jenn turns and walks to me and hands me the bouquet. I'm confused.

"What?" I ask.

"Turn around, Claire Bear."

I turn to find Emery on one knee behind me holding a velvet box with a beautiful diamond ring. I'm stunned and still confused.

"Claire Weaver, we've been through so much together over the last year and I know that it hasn't been easy, but I love you and I love us. You took a chance with me, and I can't imagine spending the rest of my life without you. Will you marry me?"

I explode with so many different emotions. Fear of the ultimate commitment, but also fear of losing her. Excitement at finding my perfect person in this world, and love. Love because I finally opened my heart to somebody who deserves all of it. I have no doubt when I answer her. I don't even care that I'm crying or that hundreds of people are witnessing this special event.

"Yes, Emery Pearson. I would love to marry you."

About the Author

Award-winning author Kris Bryant was born in Tacoma, WA, but has lived all over the world and now considers Kansas City her home. She spends a lot of her time binge-watching really bad TV shows, reading when she gets a moment, raising money for animal shelters, and spending time with her family and her famous dog, Molly.

Her first novel, *Jolt*, was a Lambda Literary Finalist. *Forget Me Not* was selected by the American Library Association's 2018 Over the Rainbow book list and was a Golden Crown Finalist for Contemporary Romance. *Against All Odds* was a 2019 Golden Crown Finalist for Romantic Blend. *Breakthrough* won a 2019 Golden Crown Award for Contemporary Romance. *Listen* won a 2020 Golden Crown Award for Contemporary Romance.

Kris can be reached at krisbryantbooks@gmail.com, or www.krisbryant.net, @krisbryant14.

Books Available from Bold Strokes Books

A Turn of Fate by Ronica Black. Will Nev and Kinsley finally face their painful past and relent to their powerful, forbidden attraction? Or will facing their past be too much to fight through? (978-1-63555-930-9)

Desires After Dark by MJ Williamz. When her human lover falls deathly ill, Alex, a vampire, must decide which is worse, letting her go or condemning her to everlasting life. (978-1-63555-940-8)

Her Consigliere by Carsen Taite. FBI agent Royal Scott swore an oath to uphold the law, and criminal defense attorney Siobhan Collins pledged her loyalty to the only family she's ever known, but will their love be stronger than the bonds they've vowed to others, or will their competing allegiances tear them apart? (978-1-63555-924-8)

In Our Words: Queer Stories from Black, Indigenous, and People of Color Writers. Stories Selected by Anne Shade and Edited by Victoria Villaseñor. Comprising both the renowned and emerging voices of Black, Indigenous, and People of Color authors, this thoughtfully curated collection of short stories explores the intersection of racial and queer identity. (978-1-63555-936-1)

Measure of Devotion by CF Frizzell. Disguised as her late twin brother, Catherine Samson enters the Civil War to defend the Constitution as a Union soldier, never expecting her life to be altered by a Gettysburg farmer's daughter. (978-1-63555-951-4)

Not Guilty by Brit Ryder. Claire Weaver and Emery Pearson's day jobs clash, even as their desire for each other burns, and a discreet sex-only arrangement is the only option. (978-1-63555-896-8)

Opposites Attract: Butch/Femme Romances by Meghan O'Brien, Aurora Rey, Angie Williams. Sometimes opposites really do attract. Fall in love with these butch/femme romance novellas. (978-1-63555-784-8)

Swift Vengeance by Jean Copeland, Jackie D, Erin Zak. A journalist becomes the subject of her own investigation when sudden strange, violent visions summon her to a summer retreat and into the arms of a killer's possible next victim. (978-1-63555-880-7)

Under Her Influence by Amanda Radley. On their path to #truelove, will Beth and Jemma discover that reality is even better than illusion? (978-1-63555-963-7)

Wasteland by Kristin Keppler & Allisa Bahney. Danielle Clark is fighting against the National Armed Forces and finds peace as a scavenger, until the NAF general's daughter, Katelyn Turner, shows up on her doorstep and brings the fight right back to her. (978-1-63555-935-4)

When in Doubt by VK Powell. Police officer Jeri Wylder thinks she committed a crime in the line of duty but can't remember, until details emerge pointing to a cover-up by those close to her. (978-1-63555-955-2)

A Woman to Treasure by Ali Vali. An ancient scroll isn't the only treasure Levi Montbard finds as she starts her hunt for the truth—all she has to do is prove to Yasmine Hassani that there's more to her than an adventurous soul. (978-1-63555-890-6)

Before. After. Always. by Morgan Lee Miller. Still reeling from her tragic past, Eliza Walsh has sworn off taking risks, until Blake Navarro turns her world right-side up, making her question if falling in love again is worth it. (978-1-63555-845-6)

Bet the Farm by Fiona Riley. Lauren Calloway's luxury real estate sale of the century comes to a screeching halt when dairy farm heiress, and one-night stand, Thea Boudreaux calls her bluff. (978-1-63555-731-2)

Cowgirl by Nance Sparks. The last thing Aren expects is to fall for Carol. Sharing her home is one thing, but sharing her heart means sharing the demons in her past and risking everything to keep Carol safe. (978-1-63555-877-7)

Give In to Me by Elle Spencer. Gabriela Talbot never expected to sleep with her favorite author—certainly not after the scathing review she'd given Whitney Ainsworth's latest book. (978-1-63555-910-1)

Hidden Dreams by Shelley Thrasher. A lethal virus and its resulting vision send Texan Barbara Allan and her lovely guide, Dara, on a journey up Cambodia's Mekong River in search of Barbara's mother's mystifying past. (978-1-63555-856-2)

In the Spotlight by Lesley Davis. For actresses Cole Calder and Eris Whyte, their chance at love runs out fast when a fan's adoration turns to obsession. (978-1-63555-926-2)

Origins by Jen Jensen. Jamis Bachman is pulled into a dangerous mystery that becomes personal when she learns the truth of her origins as a ghost hunter. (978-1-63555-837-1)

Pursuit: A Victorian Entertainment by Felice Picano. An intelligent, handsome, ruthlessly ambitious young man who rose from the slums to become the right-hand man of the Lord Exchequer of England will stop at nothing as he pursues his Lord's vanished wife across Continental Europe. (978-1-63555-870-8)

Unrivaled by Radclyffe. Zoey Cohen will never accept second place in matters of the heart, even when her rival is a career, and Declan Black has nothing left to give of herself or her heart. (978-1-63679-013-8)

A Fae Tale by Genevieve McCluer. Dovana comes to terms with her changing feelings for her lifelong best friend and fae, Roze. (978-1-63555-918-7)

Accidental Desperados by Lee Lynch. Life is clobbering Berry, Jaudon, and their long romance. The arrival of directionless baby dyke MJ doesn't help. Can they find their passion again—and keep it? (978-1-63555-482-3)

Always Believe by Aimée. Greyson Walsden is pursuing ordination as an Anglican priest. Angela Arlingham doesn't believe in God. Do they follow their vocation or their hearts? (978-1-63555-912-5)

Best of the Wrong Reasons by Sander Santiago. For Fin Ness and Orion Starr, it takes a funeral to remind them that love is worth living for. (978-1-63555-867-8)

Courage by Jesse J. Thoma. No matter how often Natasha Parsons and Tommy Finch clash on the job, an undeniable attraction simmers just beneath the surface. Can they find the courage to change so love has room to grow? (978-1-63555-802-9)

I Am Chris by R Kent. There's one saving grace to losing everything and moving away. Nobody knows her as Chrissy Taylor. Now Chris can live who he truly is. (978-1-63555-904-0)

The Princess and the Odium by Sam Ledel. Jastyn and Princess Aurelia return to Venostes and join their families in a battle against the dark force to take back their homeland for a chance at a better tomorrow. (978-1-63555-894-4)

The Queen Has a Cold by Jane Kolven. What happens when the heir to the throne isn't a prince or a princess? (978-1-63555-878-4)

The Secret Poet by Georgia Beers. Agreeing to help her brother woo Zoe Blake seemed like a good idea to Morgan Thompson at first...until she realizes she's actually wooing Zoe for herself... (978-1-63555-858-6)

You Again by Aurora Rey. For high school sweethearts Kate Cormier and Sutton Guidry, the second chance might be the only one that matters. (978-1-63555-791-6)

Coming to Life on South High by Lee Patton. Twenty-one-year-old gay virgin Gabe Rafferty's first adult decade unfolds as an unpredictable journey into sex, love, and livelihood. (978-1-63555-906-4)

Love's Falling Star by B.D. Grayson. For country music megastar Lochlan Paige, can love conquer her fear of losing the one thing she's worked so hard to protect? (978-1-63555-873-9)

Love's Truth by C.A. Popovich. Can Lynette and Barb make love work when unhealed wounds of betrayed trust and a secret could change everything? (978-1-63555-755-8)

Next Exit Home by Dena Blake. Home may be where the heart is, but for Harper Sims and Addison Foster, is the journey back worth the pain? (978-1-63555-727-5)

Not Broken by Lyn Hemphill. Falling in love is hard enough—even more so for Rose who's carrying her ex's baby. (978-1-63555-869-2)

The Noble and the Nightingale by Barbara Ann Wright. Two women on opposite sides of empires at war risk all for a chance at love. (978-1-63555-812-8)

What a Tangled Web by Melissa Brayden. Clementine Monroe has the chance to buy the café she's managed for years, but Madison LeGrange swoops in and buys it first. Now Clementine is forced to work for the enemy and ignore her former crush. (978-1-63555-749-7)

A Far Better Thing by JD Wilburn. When needs of her family and wants of her heart clash, Cass Halliburton is faced with the ultimate sacrifice. (978-1-63555-834-0)

Body Language by Renee Roman. When Mika offers to provide Jen erotic tutoring, will sex drive them into a deeper relationship or tear them apart? (978-1-63555-800-5)

Carrie and Hope by Joy Argento. For Carrie and Hope loss brings them together but secrets and fear may tear them apart. (978-1-63555-827-2)

Death's Prelude by David S. Pederson. In this prequel to the Detective Heath Barrington Mystery series, Heath discovers that first love changes you forever and drives you to become the person you're destined to be. (978-1-63555-786-2)

Ice Queen by Gun Brooke. School counselor Aislin Kennedy wants to help standoffish CEO Susanna Durr and her troubled teenage daughter become closer—even if it means risking her own heart in the process. (978-1-63555-721-3)

Masquerade by Anne Shade. In 1925 Harlem, New York, a notorious gangster sets her sights on seducing Celine, and new lovers Dinah and Celine are forced to risk their hearts, and lives, for love. (978-1-63555-831-9)

Royal Family by Jenny Frame. Loss has defined both Clay's and Katya's lives, but guarding their hearts may prove to be the biggest heartbreak of all. (978-1-63555-745-9)

Share the Moon by Toni Logan. Three best friends, an inherited vineyard and a resident ghost come together for fun, romance and a touch of magic. (978-1-63555-844-9)

Spirit of the Law by Carsen Taite. Attorney Owen Lassiter will do almost anything to put a murderer behind bars, but can she get past her reluctance to rely on unconventional help from the alluring Summer Byrne and keep from falling in love in the process? (978-1-63555-766-4)

The Devil Incarnate by Ali Vali. Cain Casey has so much to live for, but enemies who lurk in the shadows threaten to unravel it all. (978-1-63555-534-9)

BOLDSTROKESBOOKS.COM

Looking for your next great read?

Visit BOLDSTROKESBOOKS.COM
to browse our entire catalog of paperbacks, ebooks,
and audiobooks.

Want the first word on what's new?
Visit our website for event info,
author interviews, and blogs.

Subscribe to our free newsletter for sneak peeks,
new releases, plus first notice of promos
and daily bargains.

SIGN UP AT
BOLDSTROKESBOOKS.COM/signup

Bold Strokes Books
Quality and Diversity in LGBTQ Literature

*Bold Strokes Books is an award-winning publisher
committed to quality and diversity in LGBTQ fiction.*